OTHER TIMES, OTHER WORLDS

Selected by John D. MacDonald and Martin Harry Greenberg, with an introduction by Mr. Greenberg

Fawcett Books
by John D. MacDonald:

All These Condemned
April Evil
Area of Suspicion
Ballroom of the Skies
The Beach Girls
Border Town Girl
The Brass Cupcake
A Bullet for Cinderella
Cancel All Our Vows
Clemmie
Condominium
Contrary Pleasure
The Crossroads
Cry Hard, Cry Fast
The Damned
Dead Low Tide
Deadly Welcome
Death Trap
The Deceivers
The Drowner
The Empty Trap
The End of the Night
End of the Tiger and
 Other Stories
The Executioners

A Flash of Green
The Girl, the Gold
 Watch & Everything
The House Guests
Judge Me Not
A Key to the Suite
The Last One Left
A Man of Affairs
Murder for the Bride
Murder in the Wind
The Neon Jungle
On the Run
One Monday We Killed
 Them All
The Only Girl in the Game
Other Times, Other Worlds
Please Write for Details
The Price of Murder
S*E*V*E*N
Slam the Big Door
Soft Touch
Where Is Janice Gantry?
Wine of the Dreamers
You Live Once

The Travis McGee Series

The Deep Blue Good-by
Nightmare in Pink
A Purple Place for Dying
The Quick Red Fox
A Deadly Shade of Gold
Bright Orange for the
 Shroud
Darker Than Amber
One Fearful Yellow Eye

Pale Gray for Guilt
The Girl in the
 Plain Brown Wrapper
Dress Her in Indigo
The Long Lavender Look
A Tan and Sandy Silence
The Scarlet Ruse
The Turquoise Lament
The Dreadful Lemon Sky

JOHN D. MacDONALD

Other Times,
Other Worlds

FAWCETT GOLD MEDAL • NEW YORK

Contents

Other Times, Other Worlds

Former science fiction writers who became famous in other fields of literature constitute an interesting and rather select group. John Jakes, Michael Shaara, Kurt Vonnegut, Jr. (who is not an ex-science fiction writer since he never stopped writing it), and John D. MacDonald are among the best-selling authors in the United States. MacDonald is one of the most celebrated authors in the English language and one of the top four or five mystery writers in America. Not a bad group. Their attitudes toward science fiction range from respect to alienation.

All of them suffered from relative neglect as science fiction writers (although Vonnegut did better than most) as have several dozen other fine authors who have not achieved fame. They were neglected for a variety of reasons, not the least of which was the fact that they published in paperback at a time when softcover books did not enjoy the status they are beginning to receive now—indeed, it was almost impossible to get a major review unless one published in hardcover (outside of the specialty magazines and a very few newspaper columns). Even in hardcover it was difficult to get proper attention if what you wrote was, or was marketed as, sf.

John D. MacDonald published fifty science fiction short stories and novelettes and three novels, and was gone but not quite forgotten. He was reprinted frequently in the fifties and sixties, and still receives attention from anthologists and bibliographers. He wrote science fiction for two reasons—because he liked the freedom it gave him and because it was a large market when he first became a professional writer.

Becoming a writer was certainly not his destiny. John Dann MacDonald was born on July 24, 1916, in Sharon, Pennsylvania, the only son of a corporation executive who moved the family to Utica, New York, when John was twelve. Planning on a career in the business world, he enrolled in the Wharton School of Finance at the University of Pennsylvania, stayed less than two years, and transferred to the University of Syracuse, from which he graduated with a B.S. degree. He then went on to get an M.B.A. from the Harvard Business School. While attending Syracuse he met and married Dorothy Prentiss, and they have been married for more than forty years. They have one son, Maynard, who now lives in New Zealand.

The outbreak of World War II precluded any possibility of his practicing his newly acquired business skills immediately, and John was commissioned as a Lieutenant in the United States Army in June, 1940. Posted to Asia, he served in China, Burma, and India, and in true pulp hero fashion, joined the Office of Strategic Services, the predecessor to the Central Intelligence Agency. He left the service as a Lieutenant Colonel in early 1946.

Although he did not know it at the time, his wartime separation from his wife was to prove pivotal to his future career for, one day late in the war, he sent her a short story instead of his usual letter. Dorothy MacDonald liked it, put it into manuscript form, and sent it to *Story Magazine*, the leading market for short fiction. The magazine purchased his story for twenty-five dollars.

This initial success proved decisive and MacDonald decided to try to make writing his life work. The method he chose tells us a great deal about his dedication and his energy. With sufficient funds to cover four months' living expenses, he set out and wrote at an incredible pace, producing eight hundred thousand words. Writing for a wide variety of magazines, he kept more than thirty stories in the mail constantly, not giving up on a story until it had been rejected by at least ten markets. In the process he accumulated almost a thousand rejection slips after five months of effort. During this period, MacDonald worked fourteen hours a day, seven days a week, literally learning his craft and gaining the experience of a decade as he went along, which was important for a man who made no serious attempt to write until he was thirty.

Not all his stories were rejected, and he began to sell at a steady clip to a bewildering variety of the soon-to-die pulp magazines—adventure stories, mysteries, westerns, sports stories (at which he excelled), and science fiction and fantasy. In all, he published more than six hundred stories, the great bulk of them between the late forties and the midfifties. His first full-length book, *The Brass Cupcake,* appeared in 1950, and he has since published more than sixty-five novels and one autobiographical nonfiction book, *The House Guests* (1965), a very funny and moving account of the MacDonalds' life with, and relationship to, their pets.

MacDonald was so prolific that the use of pseudonyms was mandatory, and he frequently employed the house names "Scott O'Hara," "Henry Rieser," "John Wade Farrell," and "John Lane" for this purpose. "Peter Reed" was employed occasionally in *Super Science Stories.* Concurrent with his pulp appearances, he sold steadily to higher-paying "slick" markets like *Collier's* and *Esquire.* Indeed, his output has been so prodigious that an entire journal, *The John D. MacDonald Bibliophile,* edited by Len and June Moffatt of Downey, California (who prepared the bibliography for this book), is devoted to his work.

In a writing career that has spanned more than thirty years, spent in New York, Mexico, Texas, and Florida, John D. MacDonald has sold between seventy and eighty million books. He still maintains a rigorous writing schedule, normally working on at least three books simultaneously and revising constantly. In the mystery field he is best known for his novels featuring Travis McGee, one of the more memorable private detectives in the genre, who operates out of a houseboat in Florida. The seventeenth Travis McGee book, *The Empty Copper Sea,* published by J. B. Lippincott Co. in 1978, will be published in paperback by CBS-Fawcett in 1979.

Many of his books are outstanding, especially the highly praised *A Flash of Green* and *The Executioners.* The latter novel provided the basis for the film *Cape Fear,* the story of a lawyer (Gregory Peck), whose family is endangered by a vengeful ex-convict (Robert Mitchum in one of his best roles). It is one of the best stories of revenge and terror ever brought to the screen. His Florida-based novel, *The Last One Left* was nominated for an Edgar (the mystery field's equivalent of the Nebula Award) by the Mystery Writers of America in 1968, and he has won several awards, including the Benjamin Franklin Award for the best American short story in 1955 and the Grand Prix de Litterature Policiere of France in 1964.

In science fiction he is best known for three novels: *Wine of the Dreamers* (Greenberg, 1951), an excellent manipulation story of a near-future Earth under the control of alien telepaths; *Ballroom of the Skies* (Greenberg, 1952), a "test" story, a category very popular with writers in the fifties, in which various crises on Earth are staged by aliens as a way of selecting natural leaders; and *The Girl, the Gold Watch, and Everything* (Fawcett, 1962), a wild, hilarious, sexy (for its time), and very well-done tale of one man's possession of near absolute power and its consequences.

However, his short science fiction was even better, if less well known. All his fiction, both sf and mystery, is characterized by strong portrayals of social and psychological types, and the strengths and weaknesses that typify the human condition. John D. MacDonald has not written science fiction and fantasy for many years, but he has left us with a number of memorable stories, at least three of which ("Spectator Sport," "A Child is Crying," and "Game for Blondes") are minor classics. His best work enriched the genre—one hopes that he will pass this way again.

—Martin Harry Greenberg

This is a famous story, even if its fame is rather restricted. "The Mechanical Answer" is the first story in the first anthology ever published on the theme of artificial intelligence (the other), Martin Greenberg's **The Robot and the Man** (1953).

It is also (outside the work of Isaac Asimov) one of the most optimistic stories ever written about the implications of artificial intelligence.

THE MECHANICAL ANSWER

Astounding Science Fiction
May, 1948

JANE KAYDEN, the traces of dried tears on her pretty face, said, in a hopeless tone for the hundredth time, "But why does it have to be you, Joe?"

Joseph Kayden, Director of Automatic 81, paced back and forth through the room of their apartment that they called the Main Lounge. After they were married, when permission was given for Jane to live on the premises at Automatic 81, she had designed the apartment. Automatic 81 was in the Mesilla Valley, eighteen miles from Albuquerque.

The two opposite walls of the Main Lounge were of clear glass. One wall looked out across the valley. The other looked out across the vast production floor of Automatic 81, where the humming machine tools fabricated the portable tele sets. Automatic 81 was a nearly average government facility, with all unloading and sorting of incoming raw materials, all intraplant transportation of semifabricated and completed parts, all assembly and all inspection, all packing and labeling accomplished by the prehensile steel fingers of automatic equipment. Joe Kayden, lean and moody, was the director and only employee.

On the end wall was the warning panel. With any breakdown, a buzzer and flashing lights indicated the department and the specific piece of equipment. That portion of operations dependent on the breakdown stopped automatically until the production break was repaired. Kayden was responsible for the complete operation and maintenance. Each month his production quota figures were radioed from Washington and he adjusted his production to fit the quota.

He stopped by her chair and looked down at her, his bleak look softening. "Honey, I can't say no. The government spent eight years and a lot of money filling my thick head with electronics, quantum mechanics and what all. I'm their boy and when they say jump, Joe jumps."

"I know all that, Joe. I know that you can't quit. But why do they have to pick you? They've got what they call their high-level people, the theorists and all. People all wound up in the philosophy of mathematics. You're one of the workers. Why does it have to be you?"

He held his hands out in a helpless gesture. "I don't know. But I can make a guess. They've been appropriated two hundred million a year for the past four years on the project and they aren't getting anywhere. So I guess that some congressman has told them to bring in one of the practical boys from the Department of Civilian Production. They picked me."

"Out of over two hundred men they picked you? Why, Joe? Why?"

"Because I've never missed a quota. Because I've cut

the warning board down to less lights than any other outfit. Because I rigged up a new standby system and because I shifted more maintenance over to automatic equipment than anybody else. They just stuck the two hundred and something cards in the sorter and sorted for the guy with the most practical imagination and the best ratio of accomplishment. My card dropped out. So they called me up and said, 'Come on down here to Poughkeepsie, Joseph, and take over the Thinking Machine.' "

Out of the midst of her distress, she looked at him proudly and said, "You have done a good job, Joe."

He kicked a small stool closer to her chair, sat on it and took her hand. "Here is the big trouble, Jane. They don't know it and I don't think you do either. But by myself I couldn't have done these things. You're the guy who has . . . what do they say? . . . given me pause to think. You don't know a thing about production or about electronics, honey, but you've got a terrific quotient of horse sense. You've made me see things about this place I'd never have seen by myself. The board is small now because you did so much griping about how much of my time answering the board took. Remember all the times you've started a sentence with, 'Why don't you—?' "

"Yes, but—"

"You've brought the simple outlook of a child to this problem and all I've ever done is take your direct ideas and put them into shape. They don't want me, they want us."

She brightened visibly. "Then why can't—"

"No. They won't do it. They've surrounded the whole project with a batch of phony secrecy. Back in the days when it was called a Project to Develop a Selective Mechanical, Numerical, Semantic and Psychic Integrator and Calculator, we could have both gone on the job. But then, after the press got hold of it and labeled it the Thinking Machine and stated that in the field of warfare it would give better, quicker answers than any General Staff, the War Department made it Top Secret and that's the way it stands. For you it would be no soap."

The quick tears came again. "Joe, I'll be so lonesome!"

"So will I," he said quietly.

"And I'll be afraid, Joe, darling. Remember when you met Toby Wanderer in El Paso? Remember what he said?"

Kayden nodded. He remembered. Toby had just been fired from the Thinking Machine Project. Not fired, really, but retired with a pension for life. Poor Toby. Toby had got a bit tight and talked more than he should have. He talked about the tremendous strain of the Project, of the strange mental breakdown of the men who worked on it. Something about a machine to duplicate the processes of the human mind. When Toby had cracked the first time, they had given him shock treatments and put him back to work. Finally the interval between the necessary shock treatments grew too small and Toby was given his pension. Toby had cursed the Project with cold fury and said that it was impossible—that the most they'd ever accomplish was a machine which could duplicate the mental processes of a four-year-old child, emotionally unstable, with a limited I.Q. for its years.

Unfortunately Joseph Kayden had told Jane the entire story, never believing for a moment that he would be selected to join the Project, that political expediency would result in his being placed in charge. It was obvious to him that his appointment had been made out of desperation.

"Will you be able to write me?" Jane asked.

"Probably. With censorship. And out of the goodness of their heart they give me two days chaperoned leave every two months."

It was time to leave. The shuttle aircraft was due. Joe packed moodily while Jane wept some more. The shuttle would bring the new man for Automatic 81. He'd live outside until Jane could find a place to move their possessions to.

At last he was packed and they stood, his arms tight around her, her fair hair brushing his cheek. He whispered, "I'll probably make a blob of it, honey, and they'll boot me out quickly. To keep yourself busy, why don't you brush up on your neurology and psychiatry?"

When he kissed her, her lips tasted of salt. His last look at her was from fifteen hundred feet. She was a forlorn figure, standing out on the patio, waving listlessly.

HE WAS a pale man, almost luminous in his pallor, and he announced himself as Roger Wald, Kayden's Executive Assistant. Wald flapped his pale hands and Kayden though that he looked as though his face was of moonstone dust, held together with luminous putty.

"How long have you been on the job here, Wald?"

"Oh, over two years. I've been the assistant to some very great men and—"

Kayden grinned. "Yeah. And now you're the assistant to a guy with grease under his fingernails. Buck up, Roger. I brush my teeth and everything."

Wald flapped his gray hands some more. "Oh, I didn't mean to imply that—"

"Skip it, Roger. You just keep telling me the score and we'll get along fine. Is this my room?" Wald had led him into a small plaster cubicle containing one single bed, a chair, a bureau and a glass ash tray.

"Yes, it is. I admit it's a bit bleak, Mr. Kayden—"

"Call me Joe, please."

"Yes sir. The room is bleak. They all are. Dr. Mundreath who was in charge three years ago felt that there should be no distractions, you know."

"No, I don't know. Let me check this. I'm in charge?"

"Oh, yes sir."

"Then your first job, Roger, is to get me a suite of rooms. I want luxury on a Sybarite scale. I want rooms with music, tele sets, wine lists and everything but beautiful hostesses. Got it?"

"Yes, sir."

"Now show me the production setup, the labs and all."

The Project was housed in a series of long, one-story buildings surrounded by a high electrified wall. Interception rocket stations were set up in profusion in the surrounding countryside, the scanners revolving perpetually.

One building housed the best approach to a Thinking

Machine that had been devised. The guard let them through the door and Kayden stopped dead. The main room was five hundred feet long and about eighty feet wide. All along the walls stood independent units of the machine. Each unit was plastered with switchboard panels, plug sockets and lamp indicators. Between the interstices of the panels showed an array of electronic tubes, circuit elements, relays.

Kayden looked at a small vehicle rolling smoothly across the floor. A uniformed girl sat in it and guided it. He recognized it as a massive variation of a master programming unit. The girl wheeled it up to one of the independent units against the wall, consulted a chart and plugged in the programming unit. The indicator lamps glowed and the girl took the tape that was ejected from the wall unit. She glanced at it, unplugged and wheeled away toward a far part of the room. He could see at least a dozen other master programming units.

"What are they after?" he asked Wald.

"Test problem. With each improvement in the basic equipment, we run the same test problems through."

"What's the problem they're working on now?"

Roger Wald beckoned to one of the girls on the vehicles. She stopped beside them, smiled prettily.

"Mr. Kayden, Miss Finch. Miss Finch, what is the test problem?"

"Chemical exchange separation method, Mr. Wald."

The girl drove away on the silent wheels. Wald said: "We just feed the machine all the factors of a problem—i.e., to devise a simple way of preparing carbon-13 compounds. We know the answer, of course. Other test questions concern other fields—rules of harmonics, heat radiation and so forth."

They walked into the room and, as Kayden looked more closely at the independent units, he began to see the point of approach to the problem. He said, "Give me a short statement of the reasons for failure."

Roger Wald bit his lip. "My training . . . I'd better get Dr. Zander for you. He's in charge of testing and analysis of results. We'll go to his office."

Zander was a man constructed of overlapping pink spheres. His face was covered with a constant dew of perspiration. He had the build, the complexion and the blue eyes to go with what should have been an amiable disposition. But his small mouth was an upside down U of sourness, his eyes were smothered bits of blue glass and his voice was a nasal whine. He looked at Kayden with what could have been contempt. Kayden sat and Wald stood on the opposite side of Zander's paper-littered desk.

"So! You're the new director," Zander said.

"Right. Glad to know you, Dr. Zander. I've heard about you. Suppose you give me a brief on the present difficulties."

"You want it in layman's language?"

Kayden smiled with his lips alone. "I think I can struggle through the big words with you, Doc."

Zander frowned and put his fat fingertips together, stared at Kayden through the puffy arch. "History first. By 1953 the Electronic Mechanical and Numerical Integrator and Calculator was carried to a point of development where it could solve any problem given to it in the mathematical field, provided the automatic sequencing was fed to it on a paper tape or punch cards. Iconoscopes were set up to act as accumulators to expand the memory factor, and calculations were put on the binary obviating the use of digits two through nine.

"With the first appropriation to develop a Thinking Machine, as it is called by the layman, our problem was to switch from mathematics to semantics. In other words, instead of absolute figures, we had to change over to the fuzzy values of words and phrases. Instead of asking for the cube root to ten thousand places of minus two, we had to ask it what happens when a cat is shot through the head and have it answer that the cat dies. As simple as that.

"To make the changeover, we had to select a language for it. We selected English and took out all variations which add little or nothing to connotation. We gave each sound a numerical value, and combined the numerical values into words. Then, into the expanded memory factor, we fed thousands of truisms. Naturally, with number sound valuation, each truism became a formula . . . an equation. Assume that we had fed into the memory factor the phrase, 'Roses are red'. The machine tucks it away as a numerical formula. Then we ask the machine, 'What color are roses?' It translates the question into an open-ended formula, digs into the memory chamber and says back to us, 'Roses are red.'

"Now we can ask a question based on any truism or proven statement that we have fed the machine, and we get the answer. We get it either written or spoken, though I personally consider the vocal attachments to be more toys than anything practical. The voice makes an impression on distinguished visitors, particularly when we permit the visitor to ask his own question. It is embarrassing when the question concerns a statement not previously fed to the memory factor. One congressman asked when his mother would die. The machine gave him a detailed definition of the word mother and a physiological explanation of the meaning of death—what happens when death occurs.

"The next step was to teach the machine basic differentiations. We selected a quality—such as calorie content. Then we stored in the memory factor a complete list of caloric ratings of food. Now, if you ask it the calorie rating of a given food, it will answer, or if you ask it which of two foods has the highest rating, it will select the proper answer. We have fed the machine eighty thousand differentiation lists covering eighty thousand different methods of grading myriad items.

"In addition," he continued, "we have read to it philosophical concepts, records of phenomena, all types of data and information. At the present time we have a super-abundance of response. Should you feed it just one word, such as 'steel' or 'indigestion' the machine will give you several volumes of data."

Kayden nodded. "All you've done, in other words, is build yourself an automatic library."

Zander's eyes widened and narrowed quickly. "You are perceptive, Mr. Kayden. In effect, that is what we have. As yet we have no indication of the least creative impulse in the equipment, or how to initiate it. We have had hopes. At one time, in answering an astronomy question the machine faltered and then wrote, 'The moon is ardium.' We were excited and we speculated about new elements, until we discovered that it was merely a partial short in the wiring that had escaped the specialized equipment we have built for the sole purpose of diagnostics and repair."

"And what is the current program?"

"We are feeding the machine more data each day. Each day we expand the memory factor. Our present theory is that eventually, under the pure mass of data given it, the machine itself will break down. Psychoneurosis on a mechanical plane if you will. The place and manner of the breakdown may in itself stimulate us to provide it with some form of intellectual selectivity." He smiled woodenly. "We would all be very happy if the last words of the machine were, 'The hell with it!' "

"But you keep giving it these problems."

"Quite right. The problems are our control. So long as the machine merely repeats back to man what man has fed into it, it will be a failure. So far, that is all that it does. The problems are our continual check to see if by any chance the machine has struck on any creative method."

"If the creative method isn't built into it, how do you expect it to acquire it?"

Zander's smile was broader. "That, my young friend, was the problem which stopped your predecessor. And now it is your problem. If you want to come with me, I'll show you the mechanics of the machine."

Kayden rubbed his forehead with the back of his hand. "No thanks. I'll look at the woods from a distance and climb the individual trees later. I want some time to think about it."

Zander stood up, smirked. "What are your orders, sir?"

Joseph Kayden looked at him in irritation. "Follow existing orders until they're countermanded."

Zander sighed, smiled in a superior fashion and picking up some papers from his desk began to work.

Outside Roger Wald said, "He . . . he's a bit peculiar, Mr. . . . I mean . . . Joe."

"O. K. I'm going to wander around. You get me fixed up with something to live in besides that shoebox with running water." Wald hurried off.

KAYDEN wandered around. He talked to watchmen, electricians, lab assistants, cooks, janitors. At six he was back in his room with his mind full of figures. Nearly nine hundred people lived and worked within the Project Area. Since its inception, the Project had used up over nine hundred millions. There was little chance of a complete cancellation of the Project, as no politician would be willing to take the chance of saying to the people that all that had gone before was a dead loss.

He sat on his bed and stared out the window at the low, pale buildings. Someone had told him that he had an office, but he was too discouraged to even find it. Probably a secretary or two went with the office. "What are your orders, Mr. Kayden? What are you going to do next, Mr. Kayden?"

Roger Wald came at six, eager and breathless. "Your place is ready, Mr. Kayden. I ordered a complete pre-fab, entirely equipped. The crew has offloaded it at the north end of the area." Wald had one of the little cars used within the Project area waiting and he helped Joseph Kayden with his luggage.

The pre-fab was small, but luxurious. Kayden felt better as soon as he walked in. He said, "All I need now is Jane."

"Jane?" Wald asked politely.

"My wife."

"Oh, of course. Too bad she isn't permitted."

"I'd like to take a run down to New York and get stinking," Kayden said wistfully.

Wald flapped his pale hands. "That isn't allowed either."

Wald had dinner brought to the pre-fab and they ate together. After dinner he sat in front of the synthetic fire, after shooing Wald away, and began smoking jittery cigarettes.

"Jail," he muttered. "Prison! What am I accused of, judge? Joe Kayden, head of the Automatic Mechanical Library of Nonessential Information. I'd like to kick Zander's fat head. What do they expect me to do? Hide inside the machine and give the right answers?"

He walked nervously back and forth through the rooms, kicking petulantly at the furniture, scowling at the rugs. Jane might have a plan. Any plan. The whole thing seems wrong. The wrong slant. The wrong angle. A machine that thinks. What is thinking? Got to get basic about it. Very basic. They're too loaded up with tubes and connections. Need Jane around.

Slowly he felt the pressure of responsibility settling over him. Kayden, the fall guy. The stooge. When would he see Jane? Two months. And then it wouldn't be like being with her. Chaperoned!

He left the pre-fab and started to walk. The area was brilliantly floodlighted. After sixty steps a guard stopped him and sent him home. He told the guard that he was in charge of the place, but the guard rested a hand lightly on the deadly air gun and said that no exceptions were made and that the guard detail answered to the War Department, not to the Head of Project.

TWO WEEKS later and twelve pounds lighter, Joe Kayden sat at his big desk in the executive offices and wrote his fifth letter to Jane. It was the third time he had written the same letter. The first two versions had been returned because of matters touched on which concerned the Project. Jane's letters to him carried so little real news that he suspected that she was having the same trouble, but, of course, would not be permitted to say so in a letter.

She was living in El Paso, where she had found an apartment, and she missed him and she was looking forward to seeing him in New York when he got his first leave.

He puzzled over his letter, trying to find some acceptable way of telling her that he was getting no place on the Project. He watched the shaking of his own hands as he lit another cigarette. He wondered how long he would last—whether it would be better to fake a mental upset as soon as possible. But the thought of the shock treatments scared him. There might be a subsequent personality change which would alienate Jane.

At last he wrote, "I'm very, very happy here, and things are going very, very well. I'm as happy as I told you I'd be when we parted."

The next morning he had her answer. "Darling, I'm so glad that you're happy," she wrote. And then she ignored the entire matter. She babbled away about how she felt that her letters were probably "engramatical," about how she had played tennis and that the girl she met kept putting "lobes" over her head, about how she was enjoying the "frontal" apartment, about a new three-di movie she had seen about a "Woman of Syn," about how she had been looking over some of her old school "thesis."

He felt a quick wave of pity. Jane was trying so hard to be gay in her letters, but he could see that she was going to pieces. Her spelling was usually perfect. He shoved her letter into the top drawer of the desk, and sat, brooding, cursing the fate that had stuck him into the Project.

After lunch he re-read her letter. Its absurdity struck him again. Surely Jane knew how to spell "sin." Jane had a fine neurological education and had had two years of advanced psychiatric nursing.

As he read the letter he took a pencil and circled the obvious errors in spelling. Wald came in and said, "What are you doing?"

"Oh, the wife wrote me and I think she's going to pieces. Look at the mistakes."

Wald picked the letter up and glanced at the circled words. He frowned. "Joe, does she know any neurology?"

"Why, yes! Why?"

"Look at this. Engram. Know what this is? A lasting trace left in an organism by psychic experience. And look at this! Frontal. And over here is lobe. Add syn to thesis and you have synthesis. Hey, this is a code, Mr. Kayden!"

Joe snatched the letter. "What?"

"I'll have to report this to security, Joe."

Kayden glanced up at him. There was no trace of expression on Roger Wald's gray face. "You will?"

"Certainly. I'm going to write a detailed report. I certainly hope I won't forget to send it over to them. Would you like me to get you a good text on neurology?"

Kayden saw the flicker in the gray eyes. He grinned. "You're O.K., Roger. Yes. Get me a text."

AT three in the morning, Kayden finished the book and tossed it aside, turned out his light. But he couldn't sleep. Jane had been the first one to make sense. She had guided him to the heart of the problem. A mechanical approach to thinking. When he did fall asleep, it was to dream of her.

DR. ZANDER stood up behind his desk and said firmly: "It is unthinkable, Mr. Kayden! An absurdity!"

"You just work here, Doc. I know what I want."

"You want to run a kindergarten, yes?"

"Possibly. I said to turn off the juice to all your gimmicks. Now listen to what I have to say. What are the two processes in the human mind that we're trying to duplicate? We're trying to build engrams, habitual pathways through the mind. Also, we're trying to create a process of synthesis. Do you agree?"

Zander sat down and said, sullenly: "If you say so, Mr. Kayden."

Kayden suddenly leaned across the desk and fluttered a paper out of the line of Zander's vision. Zander turned his head quickly.

"You see what you did? When you saw motion out of the corner of your eye, your nerves told the muscles of your neck to turn your head. You didn't think about it. That's an engram, a habitual pattern a mile wide. It would take conscious and hard thought to keep you from turning your head. Does an infant? No. The engram is developed. Listen to me—and stop acting so sullen and superior.

"Take synthesis. In cases of anxiety neurosis, the patient can make no decisions. He thinks of all possible eventualities and they frighten him. Some psychopaths think of no related fact except the one they have in their mind at the moment. In the first place, there is too much synthesis. In the second place there is too little.

"Combine those two factors. Suppose you had a machine into which you built, through varying strengths of electrical current across a field, varying factors of resistance, the faculty of being able to find a path of least resistance depending on the circuit where the electrical impulse started. If your chemists could devise some sort of molecular memory factor, you would have a continually decreasing resistance across this hypothetical field for certain standard questions. In other words, engrams! Don't you see? Habitual thought patterns! Any new item would have to find its own way across, but the old ones would have an established channel."

Zander looked faintly interested. He said: "I think I see what you mean, but—"

"Now add the quality of synthesis. I can think of one way to do it. Use a shifting ratio. Each fact stored in the machine's memory is given a ratio number. Through a sliding value scale, you can alter the ratio numbers in the same way that they affect the problem at hand. For example, the machine may know something about rabbits. If the question you ask the machine, the task you set for it, concerns the orbit of Uranus, then rabbits would get a ratio number of zero. If you're talking about waltzing mice, rabbits might have a distant bearing and get a very small ratio number. If you're talking about lettuce, rabbits might have a high ratio number. You people should be able to figure out some method of making the ratio numbers plus and minus. Then, in effect, the machine could add up the pro side, the con side, and arrive at a decision. The decision arrived at would set up the beginning of an habitual pattern across this field I was talking about, thus eliminating some of the processes when a related question is asked. Tell me this, Zander: Do you know what I'm talking about?"

Zander examined his pink, dimpled knuckles. "In a way, I do. It is . . . is very new, yes? Hard to adjust oneself."

"Natürlich, my friend. But if your technicians can work it out, it would be beautiful. Just imagine. With any question asked of it, the machine would be able to call on all the vast stored knowledge of the ages, go through the weighing motions, and come up with an unemotional answer. That would be creative thought, because the new is always born from the old. We even had the wrong slant on creativeness. There isn't any such thing. It's all a question of engrams and synthesis."

Zander said, "So for this . . . for this dream of yours, you want everything we are doing scrapped? You want us to start from scratch with nothing but our developments in memory storage facility?"

"I want you to do just that."

"You have my verbal resignation. I'll confirm it."

Kayden leaned back in his chair and smiled at the ceiling. He said softly, "Citizens of North America. Today Dr. Artur Zander resigned from the Thinking Machine Project. Joseph Kayden, in charge of the Project, has announced that, with success in sight, Dr. Zander resigned because of petty jealousy, because he didn't wish to take orders from a man with fewer degrees than he has. Dr. Zander attempted to refute this statement, but in view of the record of failure of the Project during the time that Dr. Zander—"

"Wait, Mr. Kayden. I have been thinking, and possibly there is more in what you suggest than I at first realized and I would—"

Kayden grinned at him. "Doc, I don't want to force you. I want you to work for me because you want to work for me. How about it? I'll let you resign and I won't say one little word. Of course, it'll be tough for me trying to bumble along with men who don't have your background."

For the first time, Zander gave him an almost human smile. "I stay."

Eleven weeks later Wald stood in Kayden's office saying, "Joe, why don't you go down on the floor. They should be running the first test. They were hooking up when I went by."

"Why should I?" Kayden snarled. "If it works, a grateful government raises my pay and keeps me on the stinking job of managing the monster. If it doesn't work, I'm stuck here until it does. Heads you win; tails I lose. Why don't you go down?"

Kayden sat alone as dusk gradually misted the office, hazing the sharp edges of the furniture, obscuring the picture of Jane on his desk.

The door opened and Dr. Zander walked in. He didn't say a word. He stood in front of the desk. Kayden switched on the light and saw to his surprise that tears were running down Zander's cheeks.

"So it didn't work," he said dully.

In a monotone, Zander said: "The first question asked was: 'What hath God wrought?' The answer was vocal. After a few seconds it said: 'There is no adequate definition of God except that He must exist in the spirits of men, in their hearts and minds. Man, this day, has completed a machine, a device, which, in its mechanical wisdom, will help Man to clarify and explain his environment. But the machine will never supplant the mind of Man. The machine exists because of Man. It is an extension of the inquisitive spirit of Man. Thus, in one sense, it can be said that God, as the spirit of Man, has builded for His use a device to probe the infinite.' "

Kayden couldn't speak. He licked his dry lips.

"Some of them screamed and ran from the room. Some of them thought that it was a trick of some sort. To the rest of us the Machine is already a personality. And yet nothing that it said was emotional. It was factual. The question was asked. It dipped into its store of knowledge and came up with the simplest and most direct answer. The thing knew that it had been built. It knew that it existed. Its existence is a fact. Its own recognition of that fact is something that I hadn't anticipated."

Kayden suddenly saw how shaken Zander was. He

came around the desk and took the older man's arm. He said gently: "Sit down, Artur. Let me get you a drink."

Zander drained the glass in three quick gulps, set it on the corner of the desk and grinned up at Kayden. All of the man's pretense was gone. He was humble. "You did it," he said simply.

It brought back the sense of loss. "I didn't do it," Joseph said bitterly, "my wife did it. My wife that isn't considered acceptable to come into this place."

"You miss her, don't you?" Zander said, his voice soft.

Kayden jumped up. "Now we've got to demonstrate this thing. I'll get hold of our bevy of angels and we'll give it a coming-out party. Make it for tomorrow afternoon, or the day after. You fix up a list of questions, Dr. Zander, and I'll have Roger fix up the surroundings. Can we move the mike and the amplifier around? Good! We'll wire it for the main assembly hall, Building K. And by the way, get the voice of the monster as deep as you can and slow it down a little. I want it to sound like one of the major prophets."

AT five o'clock the assembly hall was filled. The President of the United States of North America was present, as were two score of congressmen, a hundred scientists, dozens of minor officials. After Security had cleared the questions to be asked, the President was given permission to invite Ming, Dictator of the Federated States of Asia, as well as Follette, Ruler of Europe, and Captain Anderson, King of the States of Africa. South America was not represented.

Kayden sat with Roger Wald in the front row. At the appointed time, Dr. Zander walked out from the wings, turned and faced the men who sat in the audience—the men who ruled the world. A switch was turned on and a very faint hum permeated the air. All eyes were turned toward the immense amplifier that filled half the stage.

Zander faced the amplifier and said, into a small microphone: "What hath God wrought?"

In a slow voice of thunder the amplifier gave the answer that Kayden had heard in his office. He turned in his seat and looked at the faces of the men, saw there both fear and uncertainty—and a strange pride, as though each of them had had a hand in the making of the voice that spoke slowly to them.

"When will Man reach the stars?" Zander asked.

After a short silence, the Voice said: "It is possible now. All the necessary problems have been or can be solved with present methods. When sufficient money is given to research and development, space travel will become immediately possible."

The next few questions concerned problems that the physicists had not yet solved. The machine answered two clearly and, on the third, said: "The synthesis of all available data does not provide sufficient basis for an answer as yet. But there is validity in the assumption that the solution will be found by experimentation with the fluorine atom."

Kayden glanced at the list in his hand and saw that Zander had asked the last question. To his surprise he heard Zander say, "The development of the Thinking Machine has been a process surrounded with secrecy because of its possible use in warfare. Will the machine help in the event of a war between nations?"

During the long pause before the question was answered, a man jumped up and yelled, "Turn it off!" He was ignored. The representatives of the nations sat, tense and expectant.

The deep voice said: "The Thinking Machine will help in warfare only in so far as it is possible to utilize some of the scientific advances made possible by the Thinking Machine. However, this is not a valid assumption. Warfare should now become avoidable. All of the factors in any dispute can be given to the Machine and an unemotional fair answer can be rendered. The Machine should not be a secret. It should be duplicated a score of times and made available to all nations. Thus can disputes be avoided. The effort to enforce secrecy is barren effort. Secrecy in the case of the Machine accomplishes nothing."

Zander turned and walked from the stage. The humming stopped suddenly. The assembly hall was silent. The rulers of nations looked at each other and in their eyes was a new promise of trust, of acceptance.

. ROGER WALD was whistling as he came into Kayden's office. "The bans are lifted today," he said happily. "Come and go as you please. O fine and happy day! When does Jane arrive?"

"At four."

"Good. You'll get cocktails at your place at four thirty. I'll have them sent over."

Wald turned to go. "Wait a minute, Roger," Kayden said. "I know I owe Zander for the fact that the security measures are done with, but what on earth ever got into him to ask that question?"

"Didn't he ever tell you? He must be shy. He and I were working late on the setup, and just for the hell of it, he asked that question. You see, he and I had been talking about you and your busted home life. We liked the answer so well that he decided to use the question in front of all the folks."

Wald left the office. Joseph Kayden glanced at his watch. Two fifteen. Just one hundred and five more minutes. He walked into the silent, empty assembly hall and turned on the amplifier. He grinned and said into the mike: "Does she still love me?"

There was a few seconds of silence. Then the Machine boomed, with what was almost irritability: "Does who still love whom? The question must be specific."

Forget that the setting of this story is impossible.
Relax and enjoy a tale by a man who had the nerve to
suggest in 1948 (and in John Campbell's
Astounding, of all places) that space flight could
be boring, and who had the skill to build a wealth
of fascinating detail into fifty-eight hundred words.

DANCE OF A NEW WORLD

Astounding Science Fiction
September, 1948

SHANE Brent sat in the air-conditioned personnel office of the Solaray Plantations near Allada, Venus, and stared sleepily at the brown, powerful man across the table from him. Shane was an angular blond man, dressed in the pale-gray uniform of Space Control. On his left lapel was the interlocked C.A. of Central Assignment and on the right lapel was the small gold question mark of Investigation Section. Shane Brent had the faculty of complete relaxation, almost an animal stillness.

His hair was a cropped golden cap and his eyes a quiet gray. Below the edge of the gray shorts the hair, tight curled on his brown legs, had been burned white by the sun.

The man on the other side of the table was stocky, sullen and powerful. His face was livid with the seamed burns of space radiation before the days of adequate pilot protection. His name was Hiram Lee.

The conversation had lasted more than an hour and as yet Shane Brent was no closer to a solution. He had been carefully trained in all the arts of persuasion, of mental and emotional appeals. Hiram Lee had resisted them all.

Shane Brent said: "Lee, the whole thing is ridiculous. You're thirty-eight now. At least seven years of piloting ahead of you."

Lee snorted. "Piloting! Tell your boss that I'm unadjusted or something."

"Let's review the case again. You, at the age of eighteen, were the first third-generation space pilot in history. Your grandfather was John Lee who was an army pilot and who ran out of soup on the second swing around the Moon. As a memorial they left the little silver ship in orbit."

Lee's expression softened for the first time. "That's the way he would have wanted it."

"And your father, David Lee, was kicked off the spaceways for getting tight and balancing the old *Los Angeles* of the Donnovan Lines on its tail fifty feet in the air for ten minutes."

"And he won his bet of fifty bucks, junior. Don't forget that."

"And that brings us down to you, Hiram Lee. You made eighty-three trips with Space Combo in the VME triangle. Your education cost Central Assignment a lot of time and money. There aren't enough trained pilots who can stand the responsibility."

"The monotony, you mean." Lee stood up suddenly, his fists on his slim waist. "I told you before and I'll tell you again. When I started, it was a fine racket. You took off on manual controls and got your corrections en route from Central Astro. You made the corrections manually. You ripped off in those rusty buckets and the acceleration nearly tore your guts out. When I started we had a mean time of one five nine days from Earth to Venus. The trip was rugged. As a pilot you were somebody.

"Then some bright gent had to invent the Tapeworm. Central Astro plots your entire trip and sends the tape over. You co-ordinate the Tapeworm with takeoff time and feed in the tape. You've got a stand-by Tapeworm with a duplicate tape and you've got an escape tape which you feed in if anything goes too far off.

"The pilot sits there like a stuffed doll and the tape does everything. You don't even have to worry about meteorites. The Pusher obliques the little ones off and the Change-Scanner gives you an automatic course correction around the big one. It just got too dull, Brent. I'm not a guy who wants to play up to the rich passengers and tickle the babies under the chin and say kitcheekoo. I took three years of rocking chair circuits and then I quit. And I won't go back."

"What makes the job you've got so attractive, Lee? You're just a foreman and nursemaid to a bunch of Harids working in your herb patches."

Lee smiled tightly. "I keep 'em working and I tell 'em what to do and I try to keep them happy. You know the final psycho report on them. Their culture is much like the culture of ants on Earth—with one exception. They have a high degree of emotional instability. Did you ever see a Harid run berserk? A bunch of them are picking away and all of a sudden one will stop and start swaying his head from side to side. The others light out for far places. The one who has gone over the edge starts clicking those teeth of his. He lets out a scream that would split your head wide open and comes at you with his arms all coiled to strike. Bullets won't stop them. You haven't got time to mess with a powerpack and turn a ray on him. All you need is a knife. You just step inside the arms, slice his head clean off and get out of the way fast. See this scar? I didn't move fast enough six months ago."

Shane looked puzzled. "Then danger is an integral part of your pattern of living. Are you trying to tell me there's no danger in space?"

"It's a different kind, Brent. Once every few years a ship gets it. The people on it don't even know what happened. I like a little danger all the time."

"Would you consent to an alteration of glandular secretions to take away this yen for danger?"

"And start kissing babies again? Not a chance! Every Saturday I draw my pay and I hit all the joints along the Allada Strip. You meet some interesting people. All Sunday I have a head and a half. On Monday I'm out in the weeds again with my crew of Harids."

"Central Assignment isn't going to like my report on this."

Lee chuckled. "I sure weep for you pretty boys in gray. Tell them to mark my file closed and tell them where to file it for me, will you?"

Shane Brent stood up slowly, looking more than ever like a big sleepy animal. "Suppose, Lee, that you could take a route on one of the old ships? Manual controls, magnetic shoes, creaking plates—all the fixings."

Lee stared down at the table top for a few seconds. He said softly: "Nothing in this world would keep me out of space, brother. Nothing!"

Shane Brent asked: "And what if you had control of a modern job and had orders to take it so far that Central Astro couldn't give you a tape?"

Lee grinned. "That'd be O. K., too. I hate those smug characters sitting there in their ivory tower and supplying little strips of plastic to do the job that good pilots should be doing."

Shane Brent looked rueful. "Well, I guess you've licked me, Hiram. This will be the first time I've ever had to report back a complete failure."

"Do them good back there," Lee said, grinning. He stared curiously at Brent. "You know, Brent, you don't look like a guy who'd get much of a bang out of all this investigation junk. Why don't you take a break? I'll get you a gang of Harids. These Solaray people are O. K. to work for. Stick around. On Saturday we'll hit the Strip. There's a little gal dancing at Brownie's. A Seattle gal.

Blond. She won't even give me the right time, but you just might manage to—"

Brent grinned. "I better think that one over. Sorry to have taken so much of your time, Lee. See you around."

SHANE BRENT stood at the window and watched Hiram Lee walk off in the direction of the drying sheds. Already the thick heat had put a sheen of perspiration across the broad muscular shoulders of Lee. He walked with the carefree swing of an independent man of strength and courage. Shane Brent sighed, walked out into the heat and headed for the Solaray Communications Building.

He showed his credentials to the pretty clerk and said: "I'll need a private screen and a closed circuit and the usual guarantee of secrecy. It will be a charge to Central Assignment."

He went into the small room she had indicated, and opened the switch under the dead screen. A muted hum filled the room.

"Central Assignment," he said.

Thirty seconds later a clear feminine voice said: "Central Assignment."

"Brent calling. Give me Allison, please."

Allison's face suddenly filled the screen. He was a white-haired man with a florid face and an air of nervousness and vitality.

"Hello, Shane," he said quietly. "Closed circuit?"

"Of course, Frank. I've got a report on Hiram Lee."

"Good! Let's have it. I've got the recorder on."

"Here goes. Memorandum to F. A. Allison. From Shane Brent. Subject: Personnel for Project 81—Pilot Investigation. Case of Hiram Lee. Hiram Lee has been carefully investigated and it is recommended that permission be given the undersigned to approach Lee with an offer to join Project 81. Lee is alert, capable, strong, dependable to a sufficient degree. His training is excellent. He will need little indoctrination. Quinn is to be commended for recommending him to Central Assignment. It is believed that the probable seven-year duration of the trip will not discourage Lee. It is also believed that the calculated risk of one in four of returning from the Project flight will not deter Lee. Permission is requested to contact Lee and furthermore to sound him out on becoming a colonist, dependent, of course, on his finding a suitable woman to accompany him."

Allison, who had been listening with interest, said: "Good work! You have the authority you request."

"Have you got a line on the executive officer for Project 81 yet, Frank?"

Allison frowned. "Not yet, Shane. But something will turn up. Foster and Brady have filled most of the remaining slots. Denvers will go along as head physicist for the refinement of the drive brick for the return. Central Astro had given us the takeoff date as, let me see, ninety-three days from today."

"Pushing us, hey?"

"Can't be helped. It's either then or about three years from then. Say, Shane, instead of returning right away, see what you can find there in the line of an executive officer. Report if you get a line on anybody. Good-by, Shane."

"Good-by, Frank."

As the screen went blank, Shane sighed, cut the switch and walked out. At the front exit he went up the stairs to the platform, stepped into the waiting monorail suspension bus, found an empty seat. He felt drained and weary. Frank Allison was a difficult taskmaster. His personal affection for Allison made the job no easier.

At the scheduled time the bus slid smoothly away from Solaray, and braked to a stop in Allada seventy miles away in fifteen minutes. Shane Brent realized with a tight smile that it was the first time he had made any trip on Venus without paying any attention to the lush bluish-black vegetation below. The vegetation had standards of vitality and growth completely different from Earth vegetation. If the port city of Allada hadn't been originally constructed on a vitrified surface, thousands of laborers would have been required to slash the tendrils which would have grown each day. In fact, when the spot for

Allada had been originally vitrified, it had only been done to a two-foot depth. Tendrils broke through on the third day, heaving and cracking the surface. After that experience, spaceships had hung, tail down, over the Allada site for ten days. When the molten rock had finally cooled, the experts had estimated that the black soil was vitrified to a depth of sixty feet. No plant life had broken through since that time. The electrified cables surrounding Allada constantly spit and crackled as the searching vine tips touched them.

Shane Brent went up to his room in Hostel B, shut the door wearily, listlessly pushed the News button under the wall screen and watched the news of the day with little interest as he slowly undressed. Crowds demonstrating in Asia-Block against the new nutrition laws. Project 80, two years out, said to be nearing Planet K. Skirts once again to be midway between knee and hip next season. The first bachelor parenthood case comes up to decide whether a child born of the fertilization of a laboratory ovum can legally inherit. Brent frowned. Soon a clear definition of the legal rights of "Synthetics" would have to be made. He stopped suddenly as he had an idea. He decided to submit it to Frank. Why not get Inter-Federal Aid for a project to develop Synthetics to fill personnel requirements for future project flights? But would humanity agree to colonization by Synthetics? It still wasn't clearly understood whether or not they'd breed true.

He turned off the news, took a slow shower and dressed in fresh clothes. It was a nuisance changing the insignia. He wadded up the clothes he had removed and shoved them into the disposal chute.

At five o'clock he got on the call screen and got hold of the general manager at Allada. The man recognized him immediately. "What can I do for you, Brent?"

"As soon as Hiram Lee gets off duty, send him in to see me at Hostel B."

"I hope you don't steal him away from us, Brent. He's the best man we've got with the Harids. He doesn't scare easy."

Brent grinned. "I'll try to scare him away from me, sir."

He walked away from the screen, went into the shower room and examined the drinkmaster. It was one of the old type. No choice of brands. He set the master dial to one ounce. He pushed the gin button three times, the dry vermouth button once. He turned the stir lever and held it on for a few seconds before he turned it off. He looked in the side compartment and found no lemon, no olives, no pickled onions. That was the trouble with Central Assignment only approving the second-class places. He took the right size glass off the rack, put it under the spout and lifted it until the rim tripped the lever. The Martini poured smoothly into the glass, beading the outside of it with moisture. Down in the lobby the centralized accounting circuit buzzed and the price of the Martini was neatly stamped on his bill.

He walked back into the other room, sat in the deep chair and sipped the Martini, thinking it odd that with all the scientific experimentation in taste effects, no one had yet come up with any substitute for the delicacy and aroma of a dry Martini.

Hiram Lee arrived as he was sipping his third.

Twenty minutes later Hiram Lee stood at the windows, his lips compressed, pounding his fist into his palm in monotonous rhythm.

He turned suddenly. "I don't know what I'm waiting for, Shane. Yes! Count me in. When do we leave?"

"Hold up there, boy. You've got to go to school for a while. And how about the colonization angle. Will you want to stay?"

Lee grinned. "If I could talk that little Seattle blonde into going along, three years would be a short, short trip."

"Providing she could pass."

"Oh, sure. I think she'd pass. But she's too smart to tie up with me. Maybe. At least I'll give it a try. When have I got to tell you about whether or not I want to stay on this brand new world you boys have located?"

"Let me see. Ninety-three days from now is takeoff. Thirty days would be needed to approve and train a woman. You have sixty-three days to convince this blonde of yours that you're a very attractive guy. And then you'll have to talk her into taking a little three-year trip and settling down in the brush with you."

Lee looked at him curiously. "You knew all this early this afternoon and you gave me that song and dance with a straight face."

"That's my profession, Hiram."

"You're good at it, but I still have got an urge to bust you one."

"We'll arrange that some time. Right now I'm looking for recommendations for somebody to fill the slot of executive officer aboard the Project flight. Any ideas?"

Lee frowned. "None of those boys at Solaray will do. I can tell you that quick. They're either slowly congealing in their own juice or they're making too good a thing out of their job. Better hunt around in the other plantations. There's a guy named Mosey over at Factri-grown on the other side of Allada that has a good reputation."

"I'll take a look. And by the way, Hiram. All this is under the hat."

"Natürlich, *mein herr*. May I respectfully recommend that we embark on an evening of wine and song? I hold out little hope for the other ingredient."

ONE BIG MEAL and two hours later, Shane Brent and Hiram Lee walked into the club on the strip—the club called Brownie's.

The air was chilled, thinned and scented with the crispness of pine. The place was lighted by glowing amber disks set into the walls. It was packed with the usual type of crowd. Bug-eyed tourists trying to pretend that it was old stuff to them; hard-drinking, hard-fisted men from the plantations; neat, careful kids from the ship crews in Allada port; the odd-job drifters who had become parasites on the social structure of Allada; a big party of Allada politicos, wining and dining two inspectors from Asia-Block.

By luck they found an empty table for two not far from

the dance floor. Hiram Lee was on hard liquor and Brent, feeling his limit near, had shifted to beer.

Lee said, slurring his words: "You're smart to get over onto beer, friend. You got to drink in this climate quite a while before you pick up a good head for the stuff." He glanced at his watch. "Floor show in ten minutes. Then you can see my blondie."

Shane Brent felt the artificial gayety draining out of him. He looked around at the other tables, seeing suddenly the facial lines of viciousness and stupidity and greed. He remembered his reading of history and guessed that there must have been faces just like these in the early days of the American West. California in 1849 and 1850. Easy money attracted those who had been unable to make a proper adjustment to their accustomed environment. Actually it was the result of exploitation. The Harids, with their ant culture, had put up suicidal defense until General Brayton had discovered the wave length of the beamed thought waves which directed the Harids of each colony. Science had devised stronger sending devices than the colony waves and suddenly the Harids were servants.

Each foreman, such as Hiram Lee, carried one of the wave boxes and directed his crew. Central Economics had proven that the use of Harids in the culture—picking and drying of the herbs—was cheaper than any mechanical devices which could be set up.

Several couples danced to the music which came directly from New York. The oversize screen, a special three-dimensional job with good color values, covered most of the wall beyond the dance floor, showed a full orchestra. Brent guessed that when the floor show came on the management would either use live music or cut off the New York program and feed recordings onto the screen.

The second guess proved right. The screen darkened and the couples left the floor. It brightened again, showing a canned vision of a small group completely equipped with electrical instruments. The M.C. walked out as the spot came on. He carried a small hand mike. After the initial fanfare, the music gave him a soft background and he said: "This show costs a lot of money to put on. All you folks drinking beer kindly turn your chairs around with your backs toward the floor. It is my pleasure to present a young lady who doesn't belong out here on Venus, wasting her time and talents on you space-burnt wanderers. On the other hand, Venus is a very appropriate spot for her to be. I give you Caren Ames and her famous Dance of a New World!" He grinned and backed out of the spot which widened until it covered most of the small dance floor.

The music shifted into a low, throbbing beat, an insistent jungle rhythm. Brent smiled cynically at the buildup, thought it was pretty fancy for what would probably turn out to be an aging stripper.

She backed slowly onto the floor, staring into the shadows from which she backed. Brent's breath caught in his throat. She was a faintly angular girl who should have had no grace. She wore a stylized version of the jungle clothes of the foremen on the plantations. Across her shoulder was slung a glittering replica of one of the thought boxes. She carried in her right hand a shining knife of silver.

She moved with such an intense representation of great fear that Brent felt the uneasy shifting of the crowd. The music was a frightened heartbeat. Her grace was angular, perfect and beautiful. Her face was a rigid mask of fear, her blond hair a frozen gout of gold that fell across one shoulder.

The throng gasped as the thing followed her into the middle of the floor, stood weaving, with its eyes on her. At first glance Brent thought that it was actually one of the Harids, but then he realized that it was a clever costume, worn by a rather small person. It had all the swaying obscenity of one of the tiny praying mantises of Earth. The swollen abdomen, the little triangular head, the knotted forearms held high—all of it covered with the fine soft gray scales of a Harid. The three digits of each hand waved aimlessly about like the antennae of a mammoth insect.

The expanding spot showed a small bush covered with the blue-black oily foliage of Venus. The girl stood her ground, lifted the thought box to her lips. She swayed slightly in rhythm with the Harid and her shoulders straightened as the Harid turned away from her, went over toward the bush. It began to pluck at the leaves with the perky, incredibly fast motions of the genuine Harid. Her dance of fear turned slowly into a dance of joy of release from fear. The tempo of the music increased and she danced ever closer to the squat form of the Harid, the knife in her hand cutting joyous sparkling arcs in the flood of tinted light.

She danced ever faster, and Brent said to Lee out of the corner of his mouth: "What is she doing here? She's wonderful!"

"I told you she was, boy."

A movement to Brent's right caught his eye. A bulky man from one of the plantations, very drunk, wavered on his chair as he watched the dance with slitted eyes. The lines around his mouth were taut. Brent felt wonder that the girl's artistry could have such an effect on one of the hardened foremen.

The music increased to a crescendo, and suddenly stopped. The girl stood motionless, her arms widespread. A very slow beat began. The Harid began to sway its head slowly from side to side in time with the beat. A woman in the darkness screamed softly. Head swaying, the Harid turned slowly and faced the girl. Her face once again became a face of fear. The knotted arms of the thing lifted high. The girl took a slow step backward. The tension was a physical thing—it could be felt in the utter silence of the audience.

At that moment the man whom Brent had noticed earlier roared, and jumped to his feet. There was a knife in his hand. He started for the mock Harid. Shane Brent left his chair in a quick smooth motion. His shoulder slammed against the thick thigh of the man with the knife and the two of them fell and slid across the polished floor. The room was in an uproar. The foreman bounded up, his drunken face twisted with rage. He drew the knife hand back to slash at Brent. Brent fell inside the thrust and struck the man a hammer blow across the side of his throat with the edge of his palm. The lights came on as the man dropped heavily onto his face. No one had thought of the music. It continued on. The mock Harid stood up and turned into a pale slight man who held the head portion of his costume in his hand. His pale lips trembled. He said, with great wonder: "That fellow would have cut my head off!"

The M.C. came out and said to the girl: "Want to try again from scratch, Miss Ames?"

Her eyes were still wide with shock. "No . . . I couldn't. Not right now. The next show maybe."

The M.C. turned to Brent. "Your check will be on the house, of course. The management is grateful."

The pale young man said: "I'm a little more grateful than the management."

"Thank you," Caren said simply.

Brent grinned at her. "You can return the favor by coming to our table after you change, Miss Ames. We're right over there."

She looked uncertain for a moment. "I don't usually—"

"Just this time, Miss Ames," the M.C. said.

Her smile was brilliant as she turned and left the floor. "See you in a few minutes Mr.—."

"Brent. Shane Brent."

By that time the foreman was back on his feet, pale and shaking. He didn't understand what had happened. His friends led him back through the tables and out the door. He was protesting plaintively.

SHE SAT QUIETLY at the table between them and talked generalities in a quiet, cultured voice. Her between-acts dress was dark and conservative, her blond hair pulled back with determined severity.

She rebuffed the clumsy verbal advances of Hiram Lee very politely. By the time Shane Brent sat through the next show, enthralled anew by her artistry, Hiram Lee had his head on the table and was snoring softly.

During the dull act which followed Caren's, two heavily

built men came over to the table and shook their heads sadly. "Poor ole Hiram! *Tch! Tch!* You mind, mister, if we lug ole Hiram back with us to Solaray. The poor boy needs a nice soft bunk."

Hiram protested feebly, but walked unsteadily between them, half supported by them as he left. Caren came back a few moments later.

They sat and talked of many things. At last she smiled and said: "I was silly when I was afraid to sit with you. Usually such things become a bit . . . messy."

He grinned. "I'm harmless. It does seem a little funny to me to find somebody like you in . . . this place."

Her eyes hardened. "I know how it goes from here on. Caren, you're too nice for a place like this. Let me take you away with me. I know the whole routine, Mr. Brent."

"It's not like that, Caren. Honestly. If I've asked a clumsy question, I'm sorry. It wasn't a buildup."

She looked into his eyes for long seconds. "All right, Shane. I believe you. I'll tell you how it happened. I was trained for ballet. When I was nineteen I married a very rich and very weak young man. After two years life became impossible. I managed to get a divorce. Every minute I spend on Earth is spent keeping out of his way. He manages to queer me in every dancing job I get. He has a weak heart. They won't accept him for space travel. I'm safe here. I can keep this job. But I can't ever go back."

She didn't ask for pity as she told him. It was as though she spoke of someone else.

"What kind of a career can you have here, Caren?"

She smiled and for once it wasn't a pretty smile. "I can make a living here. Some day there will be other cities beside Allada. Some day there will be a civilization on Venus which will be cultured enough so that my kind of career can exist here. But I won't live to see it."

"What do you want out of your life?" he asked gently.

"Peace. Freedom to do as I please." Her eyes were troubled.

"Is that all?" he asked insistently.

"No!" she flared. "I want more than that, but I don't

know what I want. I'm just restless." She stopped and looked at him for long moments. "You are too, Shane. Aren't you?"

He tried to pass it off lightly. "Things have been a little dull lately."

"Take me for a walk through the city, Shane. When I feel like this I have to walk it off."

They walked to the edge of the wire near the constant sparking and crackling as the electricity crisped the searching tendrils. Above them the strange stars shone dimly through the constant heavy mist.

She stood with her head tilted back, her eyes half shut. On an impulse he reached out and unclasped the heavy pin that bound her hair so tightly. It fell in a shining flood over her shoulders.

"Why—" she said, startled.

"It just had to be. I feel like we've both been caught up in something outside of us and we're being hurtled along. Everything from here on will be because it has to be."

Without another word she came quickly into his arms. She was as intensely alive as during the intricate figures of her strange dance.

ONCE AGAIN the pretty clerk pointed out the small room to Shane Brent. He walked slowly, reluctantly, shut the door quietly behind him. In a short time he had a closed circuit to Central Assignment and moments later the alert face of Frank Allison filled the screen.

"What's the matter, Shane? You look done in. Rough night?"

"You could call it that I guess."

"How about Lee?"

"Everything is set, Frank. He'll leave on Flight Seven a week from today. Have somebody meet him and get him cleared and out to the school, will you?"

"Sure thing. What else have you got on your mind? From your tone that isn't all you called about."

"It isn't. I've got an exec for you, Frank."

"Good! A competent man?"

"I guess so. At least he's had the proper background for it."

"Don't keep me in suspense. Who is the man?"

"Me," Shane said flatly.

Frank Allison looked at him for long seconds, no trace of expression on his face. "Are you serious, Shane?"

"Completely, Frank."

Allison moved away from the screen. Shane waited impatiently. In a few moments Allison was back and Shane was mildly shocked to see that the man was smiling broadly. "I had a little detail to attend to, Shane. I had to collect ten bucks. You see, I had a bet with West. We had you picked for the job for the last seven months, but in order for you to qualify for it, the idea had to originate with you. If it didn't, Psycho wouldn't approve your arbitrary assignment to the spot. Congratulations!"

Shane Brent wanted to laugh as he realized Allison had been playing almost the same game with him that he had been playing with Hiram Lee.

"I won't be back, Frank," he said quietly.

Allison sobered. "I had hoped you would, Shane. It's your privilege to make your own choice. I had hoped that seven years from now, with your experience on this project, you'd be fitted to come in here and take my job."

"I'm sorry, Frank," Shane said.

Allison sighed. "So be it. When will you be in?"

"I'll wait until she can come with me. It'll be Flight Eight probably. I'll confirm."

There was deep affection in Allison's smile. "Whoever she is, boy, I'm sure that she's a very lovely person. See you when you get here."

The screen darkened. He stood for a moment and looked at its opaque dead grayness. He didn't see the screen. He saw, instead, a distant planet. He saw himself standing in a clearing, his hands hardened with pioneer labor. Above him was an alien sky. Beside him was a tall girl. Her hair of purest gold blew in the soft breeze.

Shane Brent turned and walked quickly from the small room. Caren would be waiting.

"Ring Around the Redhead" is an alternate universe story—a fine representative of what used to be a very important theme in science fiction. It was selected for inclusion in Groff Conklin's pioneer thematic anthology **Science Fiction Adventures in Dimension.** The story is also noteworthy for its emphasis on criminal detection, a forerunner of things to come from John D. MacDonald's typewriter.

RING AROUND THE REDHEAD

Startling Stories
November, 1948

THE prosecuting attorney was a lean specimen named Amery Heater. The buildup given the murder trial by the newspapers had resulted in a welter of open-mouthed citizens who jammed the golden oak courtroom.

Bill Maloney, the defendant, was sleepy and bored. He knew he had no business being bored. Not with twelve righteous citizens who, under the spell of Amery Heater's quiet, confidential oratory were beginning to look at Maloney as though he were a fiend among fiends.

The August heat was intense and flies buzzed around the upper sashes of the dusty windows. The city sounds drifted in the open windows, making it necessary for Amery Heater to raise his voice now and again.

But though Bill Maloney was bored, he was also restless and worried. Mostly he was worried about Justin Marks, his own lawyer.

Marks cared but little for this case. But, being Bill Maloney's best friend, he couldn't very well refuse to handle it. Justin Marks was a proper young man with a Dewey mustache and frequent daydreams about Justice Marks of the Supreme Court. He somehow didn't feel that the Maloney case was going to help him very much.

Particularly with the very able Amery Heater intent on getting the death penalty.

The judge was a puffy old citizen with signs of many good years at the brandy bottle, the hundreds of gallons of which surprisingly had done nothing to dim the keenness of eye or brain.

Bill Maloney was a muscular young man with a round face, a round chin and a look of sleepy skepticism. A sheaf of his coarse, corn-colored hair jutted out over his forehead. His eyes were clear, deep blue.

He stifled a yawn, remembering what Justin Marks had told him about making a good impression on the jury. He singled out a plump lady juror in the front row and winked solemnly at her. She lifted her chin with an audible sniff.

No dice there. Might as well listen to Amery Heater.

". . . . and we, the prosecution, intend to prove that on the evening of July tenth, William Howard Maloney did murderously attack his neighbor, James Finch and did kill James Finch by crushing his skull. We intend to prove there was a serious dispute between these men, a dispute that had continued for some time. We further intend to prove that the cause of this dispute was the dissolute life being led by the defendant."

AMERY HEATER droned on and on. The room was too hot. Bill Maloney slouched in his chair and yawned.

He jumped when Justin Marks hissed at him. Then he remembered that he had yawned and he smiled placatingly at the jury. Several of them looked away, hurriedly.

Fat little Doctor Koobie took the stand. He was sworn in and Amery Heater, polite and respectful, asked questions which established Koobie's name, profession and presence at the scene of the "murder" some fifty minutes after it had taken place.

"And now, Dr. Koobie, would you please describe in your own words exactly what you found."

Koobie hitched himself in his chair, pulled his trousers up a little over his chubby knees and said, "No need to make this technical. I was standing out by the hedge between the two houses. I was on Jim Finch's side of the hedge. There was a big smear of blood around. Some of it was spattered on the hedge. Barberry, I think. On the ground there was some hunks of brain tissue, none of them bigger than a dime. Also a piece of scalp maybe two inches square. Had Jim's hair on it all right. Proved that in the lab. Also found some pieces of bone. Not many." He smiled peacefully. "Guess old Jim is dead all right. No question of that. Blood was his and the hair was his."

Three jurors swallowed visibly and a fourth began to fan himself vigorously.

Koobie answered a few other questions and then Justin Marks took over the cross-examination.

"What would you say killed Jim Finch?"

Many people gasped at the question, having assumed that the defence would be that, lacking a body, there was no murder.

Koobie put a fat finger in the corner of his mouth, took it out again. "Couldn't rightly say."

"Could a blow from a club or similar weapon have done it?"

"Good Lord, no! Man's head is a pretty durable thing. You'd have to back him up against a solid concrete wall and bust him with a full swing with a baseball bat and you still wouldn't do that much hurt. Jim was standing right out in the open."

"Dr. Koobie, imagine a pair of pliers ten feet long and proportionately thick. If a pair of pliers like that were to have grabbed Mr. Finch by the head, smashing it like a nut in a nut-cracker, could it have done that much damage?"

Koobie pulled his nose, tugged on his ear, frowned and said, "Why, if it clamped down real sudden like, I imagine it could. But where'd Jim go?"

"That's all, thank you," Justin Marks said.

Amery Heater called other witnesses. One of them was Anita Hempflet.

Amery said, "You live across the road from the defendant?"

Miss Anita Hempflet was fiftyish, big-boned, and of the same general consistency as the dried beef recommended for Canadian canoe trips. Her voice sounded like fingernails on the third grade blackboard.

"Yes I do. I've lived there thirty-five years. That Maloney person, him sitting right over there, moved in two years ago, and I must say that I . . ."

"You are able to see Mr. Maloney's house from your windows?"

"Certainly!"

"Now tell the court when it was that you first saw the red-headed woman."

She licked her lips. "I first saw that . . . that woman in May. A right pleasant morning it was, too. Or it was until I saw her. About ten o'clock, I'd say. She was right there in Maloney's front yard, as bold as brass. Had on some sort of shiny silver thing. You couldn't call it a dress. Too short for that. Didn't half cover her the way a lady ought to be covered. Not by half. She was . . ."

"What was she doing?"

"Well, she come out of the house and she stopped and looked around as though she was surprised at where she was. My eyes are good. I could see her face. She looked all around. Then she sort of slouched, like she was going to keel over or something. She walked real slow down toward the gate. Mr. Maloney came running out of the house and I heard him yell to her. She stopped. Then he was making signs to her, for her to go back into the house. Just like she was deaf or something. After a while she went back in. I guessed she probably was made deaf by that awful bomb thing the government lost control of near town three days before that."

"You didn't see her again?"

"Oh, I saw her plenty of times. But after that she was always dressed more like a girl should be dressed. Far as I could figure out, Mr. Maloney was buying her clothes in town. It wasn't right that anything like that should be going on in a nice neighborhood. Mr. Finch didn't think it was right either. Runs down property values, you know."

"In your knowledge, Miss Hempflet, did Mr. Maloney and the deceased ever quarrel?"

"They started quarreling a few days after that woman showed up. Yelling at each other across the hedge. Mr. Finch was always scared of burglars. He had that house fixed up so nobody could get in if he didn't want them in. A couple of times I saw Bill Maloney pounding on his door and rapping on the windows. Jim wouldn't pay any attention."

Justin cross-examined.

"You say, Miss Hempflet, that the defendant was going down and shopping for this woman, buying her clothes. In your knowledge, did he buy her anything else?"

Anita Hempflet sniggered. "Say so! Guess she must of been feeble minded. I asked around and found out he bought a blackboard and chalk and some kids' books."

"Did you make any attempt to find out where this woman came from, this woman who was staying with Mr. Maloney?"

"Should say I did! I know for sure that she didn't come in on the train or Dave Wattle would've seen her. If she'd come by bus, Myrtle Gisco would have known it. Johnny Farness didn't drive her in from the airport. I figure that any woman who'd live openly with a man like Maloney must have hitchhiked into town. She didn't come any other way."

"That's all, thank you," Justin Marks said.

MALONEY sighed. He couldn't understand why Justin was looking so worried. Everything was going fine. According to plan. He saw the black looks the jury was giving him, but he wasn't worried. Why, as soon as they found out what had actually happened, they'd be all for him. Justin Marks seemed to be sweating.

He came back to the table and whispered to Bill, "How about temporary insanity?"

"I guess it's okay if you like that sort of thing."

"No. I mean as a plea!"

Maloney stared at him. "Justy, old boy. Are you nuts? All we have to do is tell the truth."

Justin Marks rubbed his mustache with his knuckle and made a small bleating sound that acquired him a black look from the judge.

Amery Heater built his case up very cleverly and very thoroughly. In fact, the jury had Bill Maloney so definitely electrocuted that they were beginning to give him sad looks—full of pity.

It took Amery Heater two days to complete his case. When it was done, it was a solid and shining structure, every discrepancy explained—everything pinned down. Motive. Opportunity. Everything.

On the morning of the third day, the court was tense with expectancy. The defense was about to present its case. No one knew what the case was, except, of course, Bill Maloney, Justin Marks, and the unworldly red-head who called herself Rejapachalandakeena. Bill called her Keena. She hadn't appeared in court.

Justin Marks stood up and said to the hushed court, "Your Honor. Rather than summarize my defense at this point, I would like to put William Maloney on the stand first and let him tell the story in his own words."

The court buzzed. Putting Maloney on the stand would give Amery Heater a chance to cross-examine. Heater would rip Maloney to tiny shreds. The audience licked its collective chops.

"Your name?"

"William Maloney, 12 Braydon Road."

"And your occupation?"

"Tinkering. Research, if you want a fancy name."

"Where do you get your income?"

"I've got a few gimmicks patented. The royalties come in."

"Please tell the court all you know about this crime of which you are accused. Start at the beginning, please."

Bill Maloney shoved the blonde hair back off his forehead with a square, mechanic's hand and smiled cheerfully at the jury. Some of them, before they realized it, had smiled back. They felt the smiles on their lips and sobered instantly. It wasn't good form to smile at a vicious murderer.

Bill slouched in the witness chair and laced his fingers across his stomach.

"It all started," he said, "the day the army let that rocket get out of hand on the seventh of May. I've got my shop in my cellar. Spend most of my time down there.

"That rocket had an atomic warhead, you know. I guess they've busted fifteen generals over that affair so far. It exploded in the hills forty miles from town. The jar upset some of my apparatus and stuff. Put it out of kilter. I was sore.

"I turned around, cussing away to myself, and where my coal bin used to be, there was a room. The arch leading into the room was wide and I could see in. I tell you, it really shook me up to see that room there. I wondered for a minute if the bomb hadn't given me delusions.

"The room I saw didn't have any furniture in it. Not like furniture we know. It had some big cubes of dull silvery metal, and some smaller cubes. I couldn't figure out the lighting.

"Being a curious cuss, I walked right through the arch and looked around. I'm a great one to handle things. The only thing in the room I could pick up was a gadget on top of the biggest cube. It hardly weighed a thing.

"In order to picture it, you've got to imagine a child's hoop made of silvery wire. Then right across the wire imagine the blackest night you've ever seen, rolled out into a thin sheet and stretched tight like a drumhead on that wire hoop.

"As I was looking at it I heard some sort of deep vibration and there I was, stumbling around in my coal bin. The room was gone. But I had that darn hoop in my hand. That hoop with the midnight stretched across it.

"I took it back across to my workbench where the light was better. I held it in one hand and poked a finger at that black stuff. My finger went right through. I didn't feel a thing. With my finger still sticking through it, I looked on the other side.

"It was right there that I named the darn thing. I said, 'Gawk!' And that's what I've called it ever since. The Gawk. My finger didn't come through on the other side. I stuck my whole arm through. No arm. I pulled it back out. Quick. Arm was okay. Somehow it seemed warm on the other side of the gawk.

"Well, you can imagine what it was like for me, a tinkerer, to get my hands on a thing like that. I forgot all about meals and so on. I had to find out what it was and why. I couldn't see my own hand on the other side of it. I put it right up in front of my face, reached through from the back and tried to touch my nose. I couldn't do it. I reached so deep that without the gawk there, my arm would have been halfway through my head . . ."

"Objection!" Amery Heater said. "All this has nothing to do with the fact . . ."

"My client," Justin said, "is giving the incidents leading up to the alleged murder."

"Overruled," the judge said.

MALONEY said, "Thanks. I decided that my arm had to be someplace when I stuffed it through the gawk. And it wasn't in this dimension. Maybe not even in this time. But it had to be someplace. That meant that I had to find out what was on the other side of the gawk. I could use touch, sight. Maybe I could climb through. It intrigued me, you might say.

"I started with touch. I put my hand through, held it in front of me and walked. I walked five feet before my hand rammed up against something. I felt it. It seemed to be a smooth wall. There wasn't such a wall in my cellar.

"There has to be some caution in science. I didn't stuff my head through. I couldn't risk it. I had the hunch there might be something unfriendly on the other side of the gawk. I turned the thing around and stuck my hand through from the other side. No wall. There was a terrible pain. I yanked my hand back. A lot of little bloodvessels near the surface had broken. I dropped the gawk and jumped around for a while. Found out I had a bad case of frostbite. The broken bloodvessels indicated that I had stuffed my hand into a vacuum. Frostbite in a fraction of a second indicated nearly absolute zero. It seemed that maybe I had put my hand into space. It made me glad it had been my hand instead of my head.

"I propped the thing up on my bench and shoved lots of things through, holding them a while and bringing them back out. Made a lot of notes on the effect of absolute zero on various materials.

"By that time I was bushed. I went up to bed. Next day I had some coffee and then built myself a little periscope. Shoved it through. Couldn't see a thing. I switched the gawk, tested with a thermometer, put my hand through. Warm enough. But the periscope didn't show me a thing. I wondered if maybe something happened to light rays when they went through that blackness. Turns out that I was right.

"By about noon I had found out another thing about it. Every time I turned it around I was able to reach through into a separate and distinct environment. I tested that with the thermometer. One of the environments I tested slammed the mercury right out through the top of the glass and broke the glass and burned my hand. I was glad I hadn't hit that one the first time. It would have burned my hand off at the wrist.

"I began to keep a journal of each turn of the gawk, and what seemed to be on the other side of it. I rigged up a jig on my work bench and began to grope through the gawk with my fireplace tongs.

"Once I jabbed something that seemed to be soft and alive. Those tongs were snatched right through the gawk. Completely gone. It gave me the shudders, believe me. If it had been my hand instead of the tongs, I wouldn't be here. I have a hunch that whatever snatched those tongs would have been glad to eat me.

"I rigged up some grappling hooks and went to work. Couldn't get anything. I put a lead weight on some cord and lowered it through. Had some grease on the end of the weight. When the cord slacked off, I pulled it back up. There was fine yellow sand on the bottom of the weight. And I had lowered it thirty-eight feet before I hit sand.

"On try number two hundred and eight, I brought an object back through the gawk. Justy has it right there in his bag. Show it to the people, Justy."

Justin looked annoyed at the informal request, but he unstrapped the bag and took out an object. He passed it up to the judge who looked at it with great interest. Then it was passed through the jury. It ended up on the table in front of the bench, tagged as an exhibit.

"You can see, folks, that such an object didn't come out of our civilization."

"Objection!" Heater yelled. "The defendant could have made it."

"Hush up!" the judge said.

"Thanks. As you can see that object is a big crystal. That thing in the crystal is a golden scorpion, about five times life size. The corner is sawed off there because Jim Finch sawed it off. You notice that he sawed off a big enough piece to get a hunk of the scorpion's leg. Jim told me that leg was solid gold. That whole bug is solid gold. I guess it was an ornament in some other civilization.

"Now that gets me around to Jim Finch. As you all know, Jim retired from the jewelry business about five years ago. Jim was a pretty sharp trader. You know how he parlayed his savings across the board so that he owned a little hunk of just about everything in town. He was always after me to let him in on my next gimmick. I guess those royalty checks made his mouth water. We weren't what you'd call friends. I passed the time of day with him, but he wasn't a friendly man.

"Anyway, when I grabbed this bug out of the gawk, I thought of Jim Finch. I wanted to know if such a thing could be made by a jeweler. Jim was home and his eyes popped when he saw it. You know how he kept that little shop in his garage and made presents for people? Well, he cut off a section with a saw. Then he said that he'd never seen anything like it and he didn't know how on earth it was put together. I told him that it probably wasn't put together on earth. That teased him a little and he kept after me until I told him the whole story. He didn't believe it. That made me mad. I took him over into my cellar and showed him a few things. I set the gawk between two boxes so it was parallel to the floor, then dropped my grapples down into it. In about three minutes I caught something and brought it up. It seemed to be squirming."

MALONEY drew a deep breath.

"That made me a shade cautious. I brought it up slow. The head of the thing came out. It was like a small bear—but more like a bear that had been made into a rug. Flat like a leech, and instead of front legs it just seemed to have a million little sucker disks around the flat edge. It screamed so hard, with such a high note, that it hurt my ears. I dropped it back through.

"When I looked around, old Jim was backed up against the cellar wall, mumbling. Then he got down on his hands and knees and patted the floor under the gawk. He kept right on mumbling. Pretty soon he asked me how that bear-leech and that golden bug could be in the same place. I explained how I had switched the gawk. We played around for a while and then came up with a bunch of stones. Jim handled them, and his eyes started to pop out again. He began to shake. He told me that one of the stones was an uncut ruby. You couldn't prove it by me. It would've made you sick to see the way old Jim started to drool. He talked so fast I could hardly understand him. Finally I got the drift. He wanted us to go in business and rig up some big machinery so we could dig through the gawk and come back with all kinds of things. He wanted bushels of rubies and a few tons of gold.

"I told him I wasn't interested. He got so mad he jumped up and down. I told him I was going to fool around with the thing for a while and then I was going to turn it over to some scientific foundation so the boys could go at it in the right way.

"He looked mad enough to kill me. He told me we could have castles and cars and yachts and a million bucks each. I told him that the money was coming in faster than I could spend it already and all I wanted was to stay in my cellar and tinker.

"I told him that I guessed the atomic explosion had dislocated something, and the end product belonged to science. I also told him very politely to get the devil home and stop bothering me.

"He did, but he sure hated to leave. Well, by the morning of the tenth, I had pretty well worn myself out. I was bushed and jittery from no sleep. I had made twenty spins in a row without getting anything, and I had begun to think I had run out of new worlds on the other side of the gawk.

"Like a darn fool, I yanked it off the jig, took it like a hoop and scaled it across the cellar. It went high, then dropped lightly, spinning.

"And right there in my cellar was this beautiful red-head. She was dressed in a shiny silver thing. Justy's got that silver thing in his bag. Show it to the people. You can see that it's made out of some sort of metal mesh, but it isn't cold like metal would be. It seems to hold heat and radiate it."

The metal garment was duly passed around. Everybody felt of it, exclaimed over it. This was better than a movie. Maloney could see from Amery Heater's face that the man wanted to claim the metal garment was also made in the Maloney cellar.

Bill winked at him. Amery Heater flushed a dull red.

"Well, she stood there, right in the middle of the gawk which was flat against the floor. She had a dazed look on her face. I asked her where she had come from. She gave me a blank look and a stream of her own language. She seemed mad about something. And pretty upset.

"Now what I should have done was pick up that gawk and lift it back up over her head. That would have put her back in her own world. But she stepped out of it, and like a darn fool, I stood and held it and spun it, nervous like. In spinning it, I spun her own world off into some mathematical equation I couldn't figure.

"It was by the worst or the best kind of luck, depending on how you look at it, that I made a ringer on her when I tossed the gawk across the cellar. Her makeup startled me a little. No lipstick. Tiny crimson beads on the end of each eyelash. Tiny emerald green triangles painted on each tooth in some sort of enamel. Nicely centered. Her hairdo wasn't any wackier than some you see every day.

"Well, she saw the gawk in my hands and she wasn't dumb at all. She came at me, her lips trembling, her eyes pleading, and tried to step into it. I shook my head, hard, and pushed her back and set it back in the jig. I shoved a steel rod through, holding it in asbestos mittens. The heat beyond the blackness turned the whole rod cherry red in seconds. I shoved it on through the rest of the way, then showed her the darkened mitten. She was quick. She got the most horrified look on her face.

"Then she ran upstairs, thinking it was some sort of joke, I guess. I noticed that she slammed right into the door, as though she expected it to open for her. By the time I got to her, she had figured out the knob. She went down the walk toward the gate.

"That's when nosey Anita must have seen her. I shouted and she turned around and the tears were running right down her face. I made soothing noises and she let me lead her back into the house. I've never seen a prettier girl or one stacked any . . . I mean her skin is translucent, sort of. Her eyes are enormous. And her hair is a shade of red that you never see.

"She had no place to go and she was my responsibility.

I certainly didn't feel like turning her over to the welfare people. I fixed her up a place to sleep in my spare room and I had to show her everything. How to turn on a faucet. How to turn the lights off and on.

"She didn't do anything except cry for four days. I gave her food that she didn't eat. She was a mess. Worried me sick. I didn't have any idea how to find her world again. No idea at all. Of course, I could have popped her into any old world, but it didn't seem right.

"On the fourth day I came up out of the cellar and found her sitting in a chair looking at a copy of See Magazine. She seemed very much interested in the pictures of the women. She looked up at me and smiled. That was the day I went into town and came back with a mess of clothes for her. I had to show her how a zipper worked, and how to button a button."

HE LOOKED as if that might have been fun.

"After she got all dressed up, she smiled some more and that evening she ate well. I kept pointing to things and saying the right name for them.

"I tell you, once she heard the name for something, she didn't forget it. It stayed right with her. Nouns were easy. The other words were tough. About ten that night I finally caught her name. It was Rejapachalandakeena. She seemed to like to have me call her Keena. The first sentence she said was, 'Where is Keena?'

"That is one tough question. Where is here and now? Where is this world, anyway? On what side of what dimension? In which end of space? On what twisted convolution of the time stream? What good is it to say 'This is the world'? It just happens to be our world. Now I know that there are plenty of others.

"Writing came tougher for her than the sounds of the words. She showed me her writing. She took a piece of paper, held the pencil pointing straight up and put the paper on top of the rug. Then she worked that pencil like a pneumatic hammer, starting at the top right corner and going down the page. I couldn't figure it until she read it over, and made a correction by sticking in one extra hole in the paper. I saw then that the pattern of holes was very precise—like notes on a sheet of music.

"She went through the grade school readers like a flash. I was buying her some arithmetic books one day, and when I got back she said, 'Man here while Billy gone.' She was calling me Billy. 'Keena hide,' she said.

"Well, the only thing missing was the gawk, and with it, Keena's chance to make a return to her own people. I thought immediately of Jim Finch. I ran over and pounded on his door. He undid the chain so he could talk to me through a five-inch crack, but I couldn't get in. I asked him if he had stolen the little item. He told me that I'd better run to the police and tell them exactly what it was that I had lost, and then I could tell the police exactly how I got it. I could tell by the look of naked triumph in his eyes that he had it. And there wasn't a thing I could do about it.

"Keena's English improved by leaps and bounds and pretty soon she was dipping into my texts on chemistry and physics. She seemed puzzled. She told me that we were like her people a few thousand years back. Primitives. She told me a lot about her world. No cities. The houses are far apart. No work. Everyone is assigned to a certain cultural pursuit, depending on basic ability. She was a designer. In order to train herself, she had had to learn the composition of all fabricated materials used in her world.

"I took notes while she talked. When I get out of this jam, I'm going to revolutionize the plastics industry. She seemed bright enough to be able to take in the story of how she suddenly appeared in my cellar. I gave it to her slow and easy.

"When I was through, she sat very still for a long time. Then she told me that some of the most brilliant men of her world had long ago found methods of seeing into other worlds beyond their own. They had borrowed things from worlds more advanced than their own, and had thus been able to avoid mistakes in the administration of their own world. She told me that it was impossible that her departure should go unnoticed. She said that probably at the moment of her disappearance, all the resources of a great people were being concentrated on that spot where she had been standing talking to some friends. She told me that some trace of the method would be found and that they would then scan this world, locate her and take her back.

"I asked her if it would be easier if we had the gawk, and she said that it wasn't necessary, and that if it was, she would merely go next door and see Jim Finch face to face. She said she had a way, once she looked into his eyes, of taking over the control of his involuntary muscles and stopping his heartbeat.

"I gasped, and she smiled sweetly and said that she had very nearly done it to me when I had kept her from climbing back through the gawk. She said that everybody in her world knew how to do that. She also said that most adults knew how to create, out of imagination, images that would respond to physical tests. To prove it she stared at the table. In a few seconds a little black box slowly appeared out of misty nothingness. She told me to look at it. I picked it up. It was latched. I opened it. Her picture smiled out at me. She was standing before the entrance of a white castle that seemed to reach to the clouds.

"Suddenly it was gone. She explained that when she stopped thinking of it, it naturally disappeared, because that was what had caused it. Her thinking. I asked her why she didn't think up a doorway to her own world and then step through it while she was still thinking about it. She said that she could only think up things by starting with their basic physical properties and working up from there, like a potter starts with clay.

"So I stopped heckling Jim Finch at about that time. I was sorry, because I wanted the gawk back. Best toy I'd ever had. Once I got a look in Jim's garage window. He'd forgot to pull the shade down all the way. He had the gawk rigged up on a stand, and had a big arm, like the bucket on a steam shovel rigged up, only just big enough to fit through the hoop. He wasn't working it when I saw him. He was digging up the concrete in the corner of his cellar. He was using a pick and he had a shovel handy. He was pale as death. I saw then that he had a human arm in there on the floor and blood all over. The bucket was rigged with jagged teeth. It didn't take much imagination to figure out what Jim had done.

"Some poor innocent character in one of those other worlds had had a massive contraption come out of nowhere and chaw his arm off. I thought of going to the police, and then I thought of how easy it would be for Jim Finch to get me stuck away in a padded cell, while he stayed on the outside, all set to pull more arms off more people."

HEATER glanced uneasily at the jury. They were drinking it in.

"I told Keena about it and she smiled. She told me that Jim was digging into many worlds and that some of them were pretty advanced. I gradually got the idea that old Jim was engaging in as healthy an occupation as a small boy climbing between the bars and tickling the tigers. I began to worry about old Jim a little. You all know about that couple of bushels of precious stones that were found in his house. That's what made him tickle the tigers. But the cops didn't find that arm. I guess that after he got the hole dug, Jim got over his panic and realized that all he had to do was switch the gawk around and toss the arm through. Best place for old razor blades I ever heard of.

"Well, as May turned into June and June went by, Keena got more and more confident of her eventual rescue. As I learned more about her world, I got confident of it too. In a few thousand years we may be as bright as those people. I hope we are. No wars, no disease.

"And the longer she stayed with me, the more upset I got about her leaving me. But it was what she wanted. I guess it's what I'd want, if somebody shoved me back a thousand years B.C. I'd want to get home, but quick.

"On the tenth of July, I got a phone call from Jim Finch. His voice was all quavery like a little old lady. He said, 'Maloney, I want to give that thing back to you. Right away.' Anything Jim Finch gave anybody was a spavined gift horse. I guessed that the gobblies were after him like Keena had hinted.

"So I just laughed at him. Maybe I laughed to cover up the fact that I was a little scared, too. What if some world he messed with dropped a future type atomic bomb back through the gawk into his lap? I told him to burn it up if he was tired of it.

"I didn't know Jim could cuss like that. He said that it wouldn't burn and he couldn't break it or destroy it anyway. He said that he was coming out and throw it across the hedge into my yard right away.

"As I got to my front door, he came running out of his house. He carried the thing like it was going to blow up.

"Just as he got to the hedge, I saw a misty circle in the air over his head. Only it was about ten feet across. A pair of dark blue shiny pliers with jaws as big as the judge's desk there swooped down and caught him by the head. The jaws snapped shut so hard that I could hear sort of a thick, wet, popping sound as all the bones in old Jim's head gave way all at once.

"He dropped the gawk and hung limp in those closed jaws for a moment, then he was yanked up through that misty circle into nothingness. Gone. Right before my eyes. The misty circle drifted down to grass level, and then faded away. The gawk faded right away with it. You know what it made me think of? Of a picnic where you're trying to eat and a bug gets on your arm and bothers you. You pinch it between your thumb and forefinger, roll it once and throw it away. Old Jim was just about as important to those blue steel jaws as a hungry red ant is to you or me. You could call those gems he got crumbs, I guess.

"I was just getting over being sick in my own front yard when Timmy came running over, took one look at the blood and ran back. The police came next. That's all there is to tell. Keena is still around and Justy will bring her in to testify tomorrow."

Bill Maloney yawned and smiled at the jury.

Amery Heater got up, stuck his thumbs inside his belt and walked slowly and heavily over to Bill.

He stared into Bill's smiling face for ten long seconds. Bill shuffled his feet and began to look uncomfortable.

In a low bitter tone, Amery Heater said, "Gawks! Golden scorpions! Tangential worlds! Blue jaws!" He sighed heavily, pointed to the jury and said, "Those are intelligent people, Maloney. No questions!"

The judge had to pound with his gavel to quiet the court. As soon as the room was quiet, he called an adjournment until ten the following morning.

When Bill Maloney was brought out of his cell into court the next morning, the jurors gave each other wise looks. It was obvious that the young man had spent a bad night. There were puffy areas under his eyes. He scuffed his heels as he walked, sat down heavily and buried his face in his hands. They wondered why his shoulders seemed to shake.

Justin Marks looked just as bad. Or worse.

Bill was sunk in a dull lethargy, in an apathy so deep that he didn't know where he was, and cared less.

Justin Marks stood up and said, "Your Honor, we request an adjournment of the case for twenty-four hours."

"For what reason?"

"Your Honor, I intended to call the woman known as Keena to the stand this morning. She was in a room at the Hotel Hollyfield. Last night she went up to her room at eleven after I talked with her in the lounge. She hasn't been seen since. Her room is empty. All her possessions are there, but she is gone. I would like time to locate her, your Honor."

The judge looked extremely disappointed.

He pursed his lips and said, in a sweet tone, "You are sure that such a woman actually exists, counsellor?"

Justin Marks turned pale and Amery Heater chuckled.

"Of course, your Honor! Why, only last night . . ."

"Her people came and got her," Bill Maloney said heavily. He didn't look up. The jury shifted restlessly. They had expected to be entertained by a gorgeous redhead. Without her testimony, the story related by Maloney seemed even more absurd than it had seemed when they had heard it. Of course, it would be a shame to electrocute a nice clean young man like that, but really you can't have people going about killing their neighbors and then concocting such a fantasy about it . . .

"What's that?" the judge asked suddenly.

IT BEGAN as a hum, so low as to be more of a vibration than a sound. A throb that seemed to come from the bowels of the earth. Slowly it increased in pitch and in violence, and if the judge had any more to say on the subject, no one heard him. He appeared to be trying to beat the top of his desk in with the gavel. But the noise couldn't be heard.

Slowly climbing up the audible range, it filled the court. As it passed the index of vibration of the windows, they shattered, but the falling glass couldn't be heard. A man who had been wearing glasses stared through empty frames.

The sound passed beyond the upper limits of the human ear, became hypersonic, and every person in the courtroom was suddenly afflicted with a blinding headache.

It stopped as abruptly as a scream in the night.

For a moment there was a misty arch in the solid wall. Beyond it was the startling vagueness of a line of blue hills. Hills that didn't belong there.

She came quickly through the arch. It faded. She was not tall, but gave the impression of tallness. Her hair was the startling red of port wine, her skin so translucent as to seem faintly bluish. Her eyes were half-way between sherry and honey. Tiny crimson beads were on the tip of each eyelash. Her warm full lips were parted, and they could all see the little green enameled triangles on her white teeth. Her single garment was like the silver metallic garment they had touched. But it was golden. Without any apparent means of support, it clung to her lovely body, following each line and curve.

She looked around the court. Maloney's eyes were warm blue fire. "Keena!" he gasped. She ran to him, threw herself on him, her arms around his neck, her face hidden in the line of jaw, throat and shoulder. He murmured things to her that the jury strained to hear.

Amery Heater, feeling his case fade away, was the first to recover.

"Hypnotism!" he roared.

It took the judge a full minute of steady pounding to silence the spectators. "One more disturbance like this, and I'll clear the court," he said.

Maloney had come to life. She sat on his lap and they could hear her say, "What are they trying to do to you?"

He smiled peacefully. "They want to kill me, honey. They say I killed Jim Finch."

She turned and her eyes shriveled the jury and the judge.

"Stupid!" she hissed.

There was a little difficulty swearing her in. Justin Marks, his confidence regained, thoroughly astonished at finding that Bill Maloney had been telling the truth all along, questioned Keena masterfully. She backed up Maloney's story in every particular. Maloney couldn't keep his eyes off her. Her accent was odd, and her voice had a peculiar husky and yet liquid quality.

Justin Marks knuckled his mustache proudly, bowed to Amery Heater and said, "Do you wish to cross-examine?"

Heater nodded, stood up, and walked slowly over. He gave Keena a long and careful look. "Young woman, I congratulate you on your acting ability. Where did you get your training? Surely you've been on the stage."

"Stage?"

"Oh, come now! All this has been very interesting, but now we must discard this dream world and get down to facts. What is your real name?"

"Rejapachalandakeena."

Heater sighed heavily. "I see that you are determined to maintain your silly little fiction. That entrance of yours was somehow engineered by the defendant, I am sure." He turned and smiled at the jury—the smile of a fellow conspirator.

"Miss So-and-so, the defense has all been based on the idea that you come from some other world, or some hidden corner of time, or out of the woodwork. I think that what you had better do is just prove to us that you do come from some other world." His voice dripped with sarcasm. "Just do one or two things for us that we common mortals can't do, please."

Keena frowned, propped her chin on her fist. After a few moments she said, "I do not know completely what you are able to do. Many primitive peoples have learned through a sort of intuition. Am I right in thinking that those people behind that little fence are the ones who decide whether my Billy is to be killed?"

"Correct."

She turned and stared at the jury for a long time. Her eyes passed from face to face, slowly. The jurors were oddly uncomfortable.

She said, "It is very odd. That woman in the second row. The second one from the left. It is odd that she should be there. Not very long ago she gave a poison, some sort of vegetable base poison, to her husband. He was sick for a long time and he died. Is that not against your silly laws?"

The woman in question turned pale green, put her hands to her throat, rolled her eyes up and slid quietly off the chair. No one made a move to help her. All eyes were on Keena.

Some woman back in the courtroom said shrilly, "I knew there was something funny about the way Dave died! I knew it! Arrest Mrs. Watson immediately!"

Keena's eyes turned toward the woman who had spoken. The woman sat down suddenly.

Keena said, "This man you call Dave. His wife killed him because of you. I can read that in your eyes."

Amery Heater chuckled. "A very good trick, but pure imagination. I rather guess you have been prepared for this situation, and my opponent has briefed you on what to do should I call on you in this way."

Keena's eyes flashed. She said, "You are a most offensive person."

She stared steadily at Amery Heater. He began to sweat. Suddenly he screamed and began to dance about. Smoke poured from his pockets. Blistering his fingers, he threw pocketknife, change, moneyclip on the floor. They glowed dull red, and the smell of scorching wood filled the air.

A wisp of smoke rose from his tie clip, and he tore that off, sucking his blistered fingers. The belt buckle was next. By then the silver coins had melted against the wooden floor. But there was one last thing he had to remove. His shoes. The eyelets were metal. They began to burn the leather.

At last, panting and moaning he stood, surrounded by the cherry red pieces of metal on the floor.

Keena smiled and said softly, "Ah, you have no more metal on you. Would you like to have further proof?"

Amery Heater swallowed hard. He looked up at the open-mouthed judge. He glanced at the jury.

"The prosecution withdraws," he said hoarsely.

The judge managed to close his mouth.

"Case dismissed," he said. "Young woman, I suggest you go back wherever you came from."

She smiled blandly up at him. "Oh, no! I can't go back. I went back once and found that my world was very empty. They laughed at my new clothes. I said I wanted Billy. They said they would transport him to my world. But Billy wouldn't be happy there. So I came back."

Maloney stood up, yawned and stretched. He smiled at the jury. Two men were helping the woman back up into her chair. She was still green.

He winked at Keena and said, "Come on home, honey."

They walked down the aisle together and out the golden oak doors. Nobody made a sound, or a move to stop them.

Anita Hempflet, extremely conscious of the fact that the man who had left her waiting at the altar thirty-one years before was buried just beyond the corn hills in her vegetable garden, forced her razor lips into a broad smile, beamed around at the people sitting near her and said, in her high, sharp voice:

"Well! That girl is going to make a lovely neighbor! If you folks will excuse me, I'm going to take her over some fresh strawberry preserves."

Children have always been important in the history of science fiction. They have starred in some of the most famous novels in the genre, and a number of fine anthologies have been done on the subject. "A Child is Crying" gives us a little terror who is both villain **and** hero, functioning in an example of what was to become known as the "Atomic Warning Story." It is one of the best of a large number of stories on this theme published in the late 1940s.

A CHILD IS CRYING

Thrilling Wonder Stories
December, 1948

HIS mother, who was brought to New York with him, said, at the press conference, "Billy is a very bright boy. There isn't anything else we can teach him."

The school teacher, back in Albuquerque, shuddered delicately, looking at the distant stars, her head on the broad shoulder of the manual training teacher. She said, "I'm sorry, Joe, if I talk about him too much. It seems as if everywhere I go and everything I do, I can feel those eyes of his watching me."

Bain, the notorious pseudo-psychiatrist, wrote an article loaded with clichés in which he said, "Obviously the child is a mutation. It remains to be seen whether or not his peculiar talents are inheritable." Bain mentioned the proximity of Billy's birthplace to atomic experimentation.

Emanuel Gardensteen was enticed out of his New Jersey study where he was putting on paper his newest theories in symbolic logic and mathematical physics. Gardensteen spent five hours in a locked room with Billy. At the end of the interview Gardensteen emerged, biting his thin lips. He returned to New Jersey, locked his house, and took a job as a section hand repairing track on the Pennsy Railroad. He refused to make a statement to the press.

John Folmer spent four days getting permission to go ninety feet down the corridor of the Pentagon Building to talk to a man who was entitled to wear five stars on his uniform.

"Sit down, Folmer," the general said. "All this is slightly irregular."

"It's an irregular situation," Folmer retorted. "I couldn't trust Garrity and Hoskins to relay my idea to you in its original form."

The lean little man behind the mammoth desk licked his lips slowly. "You infer that my subordinates are either stupid or self-seeking?"

Folmer lit a cigarette, keeping his movements slow and unhurried. He grinned at the little gray man. "Sir, suppose you let me tell you what I'm thinking, and after you have the story, then you can assess any blame you feel is due."

"Go ahead."

"You have read about Billy Massner, General?"

THE gray man snorted. "Read about him! I've read about him, listened to newscasts about him, watched his monstrous little face in the newsreels. The devil with him! A confounded freak."

"But is he?" Folmer queried, his eyes fixed on the general's face.

"What do you mean, Folmer. Get to the point."

"Certainly. It is of no interest to you or to me, General, to determine the reason for the kid's talents. What do we know about those talents? Just this. The kid could read and write and carry on a conversation when he was thirteen months old. At two and a half he was doing quadratic equations. At four, completely on his own, he worked out theories regarding non-Euclidian geometry and theories of relativity that parallel the work of Einstein. Now he is seven. You read the Beach Report after the psychologists got through with him. He can carry a conversation on mathematical concepts right on over the heads of our best men who have given their life to such things.

"The thing that happened to Gardensteen is an example. The Beach Report states that William Massner, age 7, is the most completely rational being ever tested. The factor of imagination is so small as not to respond to any known test. The kid gets his results by taking known and observed data and extrapolating from that point, proving his theories by exhaustive cross checks."

"So what, Folmer? So what?" the general snapped.

"What is our weapon of war, General? The top weapon?" Folmer asked meaningly.

"The atom bomb, of course!"

"And the atom bomb was made possible by the work of physicists in the realm of pure theory. The men who made the first bomb compare to Billy Massner the way you and I compare to those men."

"What are you getting at?" The general's tone showed curiosity and a little uneasiness.

"Just this, General. Billy Massner is a national resource. He is our primary weapon of offense and defense. As soon as our enemy realize what we have in this kid, I have a hunch they'll have him killed. Inside that head of his is our success in the war that's coming up one of these days."

The general placed his small hard palm on a yellow

octagonal pencil and rolled it back and forth on the surface of his huge desk. The wrinkles between his eyebrows deepened. He said gently, "Folmer, I'm sort of out of my depth on this atomic business. To me it's just a new explosive—more effective than those in use up to this time."

"And it will be continually improved," Folmer asserted. "You know what a very small portion of the available energy is released right now. I'll bet you this kid can point out the way to release all the potential energy."

"Why haven't you talked this over with the head physicist?"

"But I have! He sneered at the kid at first. I managed to get him an interview with Billy. Now he's on my side. He's too impressed to be envious. The kid fed him a production shortcut."

The general shrugged in a tired way. "What do we have to do?"

"I've talked to the boy's mother and last week I flew out and saw the father. They only pretend to love the kid. He isn't exactly the sort of person you can love. They'll be willing to let me adopt him. They'll sign him over. It will cost enough dough out of the special fund to give them a life income of a thousand a month."

"And then what?" the general wanted to know.

"The kid is rational. I explain to him what we want. If he does what we want him to do, he gets anything in the world *he* wants. Simple."

The general straightened his shoulders. "Okay, Folmer," he snapped. "Get under way. And make sure this monster of yours is protected until we can get him behind wire."

Folmer stood up and smiled. "I took the liberty of putting a guard on him, sir."

"Good work! I'll be available to iron out any trouble you run into. I'll have a copy disc of this conversation cut for your file. . . ."

IN SPITE of the general's choice of words, William Massner was not a monster. He was slightly smaller than average for his age, fine-boned and with dark hair and fair skin. His knuckles had the usual grubby childhood look about them. At casual glance he seemed a normal, decent-looking youngster. The difference was in the absolute immobility of his face. His eyes were gray and level. He had never been known, since the age of six months, to show fear, anger, surprise or joy.

After the brief ten minutes in court, John Folmer brought Billy Massner to his hotel room. Folmer sat on the bed and Billy sat on a chair by the windows. John Folmer was a slightly florid man of thirty, with pale thinning hair and a soft bulge at the waistline. His hands were pink and well-kept. Though he had conducted all manner of odd negotiations with the confidence of an imaginative and thorough-going bureaucrat, the quiet gray-eyed child gave him a feeling of awe.

"Bill," he said, "are you disappointed in your parents for signing you away?"

"I made them uncomfortable. Their affection was a pretense. It was an obvious move for them to trade me for financial security." The boy's voice had the flat precision of a slide rule.

Folmer tried to smile warmly. "Well, Bill, at least the sideshow is over. We've gotten you away from all the publicity agents. You must have been getting sick of that."

"If you hadn't stopped it, I would have," the boy stated.

Folmer stared. "How would you do that?"

"I have observed average children. I would become an average child. They would no longer be interested."

"You could fake possessing their mentality?"

"It wouldn't be difficult," the boy said. "At the present time I am faking an intelligence level as much lower than my true level as the deviation between a normal child and the level I am faking."

Folmer uncomfortably avoided the level gray eyes. He said heartily, "We'll admit you're pretty . . . unusual, Bill. All the head doctors have been trying to find out why and how. But nobody has ever asked you for your opinion. Why are you such a . . . deviation from the norm, Bill?"

The boy looked at him for several motionless seconds. "There is nothing to be gained by giving you that information, Folmer."

Folmer stood up and walked over to the boy. He glared down at him, his arm half lifted. "Don't get snippy with me, you little freak!"

The level gray eyes met his. Folmer took three jerky steps backward and sat down awkwardly on the bed. "How did you do that?" he gasped.

"I suggested it to you."

"But—"

"I could just as well have suggested that you open the window and step out." And the child added tonelessly, "We're on the twenty-first floor."

Folmer got out a cigarette with shaking hands and lit it, sucking the smoke deep into his lungs. He tried to laugh. "Then why didn't you?"

"I don't like unnecessary effort. I have made a series of time-rhythm extrapolations. Even though you are an unimportant man, your death now would upset the rhythm of one of the current inevitabilities, changing the end result. With your death I would be forced to isolate once again all variables and re-establish the new time-rhythm to determine one segment of the future."

Folmer's eyes bulged. "You can tell what will happen in the future?"

"Of course. A variation of the statement that the end pre-exists in the means. The future pre-exists in the present, with all variables subject to their own cyclical rhythm."

"And my going out the window would change the future?"

"One segment of it," the boy replied.

Folmer's hands shook. He looked down at them. "Do—do you know when I'm supposed to die?"

"If I tell you, the fact of your knowledge will make as serious an upset in time-rhythm as the fact of your stepping out the window. Your probable future actions would be conditioned by your knowledge."

Folmer smiled tightly. "You're hedging. You don't know the future."

"You called me up here to tell me that we are taking a plane today or tomorrow to a secret research laboratory in Texas. We will take that plane. In Texas the head physicist at the laboratory will set up a morning conference system whereby each staff member will bring current research problems to a roundtable meeting. I will answer the questions they put to me. No more than that. I will not indicate any original line of research, even though I will be asked to do so."

"And why not?"

"For the same reason that you are not now dead on the pavement two hundred feet below that window. Any interference with time-rhythm means laborious re-calculations. Since by a process of extrapolation I can determine the future, my efforts would be conditioned by my knowledge of that future."

FOLMER tried to keep his voice steady as he asked, "You could foresee military attacks?"

"Of course," the child said.

"Do you know of any?"

"I do."

"You will advise us of them so that we can prepare, so that we can strike first?" In spite of himself Folmer sounded eager.

"I will not. . . ."

Folmer took William Massner to Texas. They landed at San Antonio where an army light plane took them a hundred miles northwest to the underground laboratories of the government where able men kept themselves from thinking of the probable results of their work. They were keen and sensitive men, the best that the civilized world had yet produced—but they worked with death, with the musty odor of the grave like a gentle touch against their lips. And they didn't stop to think. It was impossible to think of consequences. Think of the job at hand. Think of CM. Think in terms of unbelievable temperatures, of the grotesque silhouette of a man baked into the asphalt of Hiroshima. . . .

Billy was given a private suite, his needs attended to by two WAC corporals who had been given extensive security checks. The two girls were frightened of the small boy. They were frightened because he spent one full hour each day doing a series of odd physical exercises which he had worked out for himself. But that didn't frighten them as much as the fact that during the rest of his free time he sat absolutely motionless in a chair, his eyes half closed, gazing at a blank wall a few feet in front of him. At times he seemed to be watching something, some image against the flat white wall.

Folmer was unable to sleep. He didn't eat properly. He had told no one of his talk with Billy at the New York hotel. His knowledge ate at him. As his cheeks sagged and turned sallow, as his plump body seemed to wither, the fear in his eyes became deeper and more set.

The research staff made more progress during the first month of roundtable meetings than they had during the entire previous year. The younger men went about with an air of excitement thinly covered by a rigid control. The older men seemed to sink more deeply into fortified battlements of the mind. William Massner's slow and deliberate answers to involved questions resulted in the scrapping of two complete lines of research and a tremendous spurt of progress in other lines.

Folmer could not forget the attack which Billy had spoken of and, moreover, could not forget the fact that Billy knew when the attack would occur. As Folmer lay rigid and unsleeping during the long hours of night, he felt that the silver snouts of mighty rockets were screaming through the stratosphere, arching and falling toward him, reaching out to explode each separate molecule of his body into a hot whiteness.

On the twenty-third of October, after William Massner had been at the Research Center for almost seven weeks, Folmer, made bold by stiff drinks, sought out Burton Janks, the Security Control Officer. They went together to a small soundproofed storeroom and closed the door behind them. Janks was a slim, tanned man with pale milky eyes, dry brown hair and muscular hands. He listened to Folmer's story without any change in expression.

When Folmer had finished, Janks said, "I'm turning you over to Robertson for a psycho."

"Don't be a fool, Burt! Give me a chance to prove it first!" Folmer pleaded.

"Prove that nonsense! How?"

"Will you grant that if any part of my story is true, all of it is true?"

Janks shrugged. "Sure."

"Then do this one thing, Burt. The kid'll be coming out of conference in about ten minutes. He'll go along the big corridor and take the elevator up to his apartment level. Meet him in the corridor, walk up to him and pretend that you are going to slap him. Your guards will be with you. You're the only man who could try such a thing and get away with it."

Janks stretched lazily. "I'd enjoy batting the little jerk's ears back. Maybe I won't pretend."

Ten minutes later Janks stood beside Folmer. They leaned against the wall of the corridor. The door at the end opened and Billy came out, closely followed by the two young guards who were always with him whenever he was out of his apartment. Billy walked slowly and steadily, no expression on his small-boy face, no glint of light in his ancient gray eyes.

JANKS said, "Here goes," and walked out to intercept them. He nodded at the guards, drew one hand back as though to strike the boy. For a second Janks stood motionless. Then he went backward with odd, wooden steps, his back slamming against the corridor wall with a force that nearly knocked him off his feet. Billy stared at him for a moment without expression before continuing toward his apartment. The two guards stood with their mouths open, staring at Janks, and then hurried to their proper position a few feet behind William Massner.

Janks was pale. He looked toward the small figure of

Billy, turned to Folmer and said, "Come on. We'll report to W. W. Gates."

Gates was an unhappy man. He had been a reasonably competent physicist, blessed with a charming personality and an ability to handle administrative details. As a consequence, he was no longer permitted to do research, but had become the buffer between the military and the research staff. His nominal position was head of research, but his time was spent on reports in quadruplicate and in soothing the battered sensibilities of the research staff. Gates loved his profession and continually told himself that he was helping it more by staying out of it. His rationalization didn't make him feel any better. He looked like a bald John L. Lewis without the eyebrows. And without the voice. Gates talked in a plaintive squeak.

He sat very still and listened while Folmer told the complete story and Janks substantiated it. Little beads of sweat appeared on Gates' upper lip in spite of the air conditioning.

He said slowly, "If I had never sat in on the conferences, I wouldn't believe it. Science has believed that the future is the result of an infinite progression of possibilities and probabilities with a factor of complete randomnesss. If you quoted him properly, Folmer, this time-rhythm he spoke of indicates some kind of a pattern in the randomness, so that if you can isolate all the possibilities and probabilities and determine the past rhythm, you can extend that pattern. It's sort of a statistical approach to metaphysics and quite beyond our current science. I wish you hadn't told me."

"I've got an idea, sir," Folmer said. Both men looked at him. "I've spent a long time watching the kid. This reading the future is okay for big stuff, but little things fool him. Once he stumbled and fell against a door. Another time one of the men accidentally tramped on his foot. It hurt the kid."

"What does that mean?" Janks said.

"It means that the kid can avoid big stuff if he wants to, but not minor accidents. I don't think we can carry this much further. The three of us right here are carrying the ball. It's up to us. The future is locked up in the kid's mind. Now, here's what we do. . . ."

Corporal Alice Dentro was nervous. She knew that she had to forget her personal fears and carry out her orders. An order was an order, wasn't it? She was in the army, wasn't she? After all, her superiors must know what they're doing.

She aimlessly dusted the furniture and glanced toward the chair where William Massner sat motionless, staring at a blank wall. Her lips were tight, and little droplets of cold sweat trickled down her body. She moved constantly closer to the boy. Five feet from him, she reached into her blouse pocket and pulled out the hypodermic. It slid easily out of the aseptic plastic case. Quickly she held it up to the light, depressed the plunger until a drop of the clear liquid appeared at the needly tip.

A few feet closer. Now she could reach out and touch him. He didn't move. She held herself very still, the needle poised. A quick thrust. The boy jumped as the needle slid through the fabric of his sleeve and penetrated the smooth skin. She pushed the plunger before he twisted away. She backed across the room, dropping the hypodermic. It glistened against the thick pile of the rug. She stood with her back against the door. Billy tried to stand, but slumped back. In a few seconds his chin dropped on his chest, and he began to snore softly.

She glanced at her watch. With a trembling hand she unlocked the door. Gates, Janks and Folmer came in quickly and quietly. With them was Dr. Badloe from the infirmary. He carried a small black case. Janks nodded at Alice Dentro. She slipped out into the corridor and walked quickly away, her shoulders squared. Behind her she heard the click of the lock on the steel door.

AS THE results of the first drug went away, Billy was given small increments of a derivative of scopolamine. They had turned his chair around, loosened his clothing. Only one light shone in the apartment. It was directed at his face. Dr. Badloe sat near him, fingers on the boy's pulse. Janks, Gates and Folmer stood just outside the circle of light.

"He's ready now," Badloe said, "Just one of you ask the questions."

Both Janks and Folmer looked at Gates. He nodded. In his thin, high voice he said, "Billy, is it true that you can read the future?"

The small lips twitched. In a small, sleepy voice Billy said, "Yes. Not every aspect of the future. Merely those segments of it which interest me. The method is subject to a standard margin of error."

"Can you explain that margin of error?" Gates asked.

"Yes. One segment of the future concerns my relationship with this organization. My study of the future indicated that Folmer, knowing my ability to read the future, would interest others and that a successful attempt would be made to render me powerless to keep my readings to myself."

The three men stared at each other in sudden shock. Gates, with a quaver in his voice said, "Then you knew that we would—do this thing?"

"Yes?"

"Why didn't you anticipate it and avoid it?"

"To do so would have been to alter the future," the sleepy voice responded.

"Are you a mutation caused by atomic radiation?"

"No."

"What are you?"

"A direct evolutionary product. There are precedents in history. The man who devised the bow and arrow is a case in point. He was necessary to humanity because otherwise humanity would not have survived. He was more capable than his fellows." The boy's droning voice halted.

"Are we to assume then that your existence is necessary to the survival of humanity?" Gates questioned.

"Yes. The factor missing from man's intellect is the ability to read the future. To do so requires a more lucid mind than has hitherto existed. The use of atomic energy makes a knowledge of the future indispensable to survival. Thus evolution has provided humanity with a new species of man able to anticipate the results of his own actions."

"Will we be attacked?"

"Of course. And you will counterattack again and again. As a result of this plan of yours, you hope to be able to attack first, but your military won't credit my ability to see into the future."

"When will the attack come?" Gates prodded.

"No less than forty, not more than fifty-two days from today. Minor variables that cannot be properly estimated give that margin for error."

"Who will win?"

"Win? There will be no victory. That is the essential point. In the past the wars between city states ceased because the city states became too small as social units in a shrinking world. Today a country is too small a social unit. This war will be the terminal point for inter-country warfare, as it will dissolve all financial, linguistic and religious barriers."

"What will the population of the world be when this war is over?" was Gates' next question.

"Between fifty and a hundred and fifty millions. There will be an additional fifty per cent shrinkage due to disease before population begins to climb again."

There was silence in the darkened room. The boy sat motionless, awaiting the next query. Badloe had taken his fingers from the boy's pulse and sat with his face in his hands.

GATES said slowly, "I don't understand. You spoke as though your type of individual has come into the world as an evolutionary answer to atomics. If this war will happen, in what sense are you saving mankind?"

"My influence is zero at this point," was the boy's answer. "I will be ready when the war is over. I will survive it, because I can anticipate the precautions to be taken. After it is over the ability to read the future will keep mankind from branching off into a repetition of militarism and fear. I have no part in this conflict."

"But you have improved our techniques!" Gates protested.

"I have increased your ability to destroy," Billy corrected him. "Were I to increase it further, you would be enabled to make the earth completely uninhabitable."

"Then your work is through?"

"Obviously. The result of the drug you have administered to me will be to impair the use of my intellect. I will be sent away. My abilities will return in sufficient time to enable me to survive."

Gates' voice became a whisper. "Are there others like you?"

"I estimate that there are at least twenty in the world today. Obviously many have managed to conceal their gifts. The oldest should be not more than nine. They are scattered all over the earth. They all have an excellent chance of survival. Thirty years from now there will be more than a thousand of us."

Gates glanced over at Janks, saw the fear and the obvious question. Folmer had the same expression on his face. With a voice that had in it a small touch of madness, Gates said, "What is the future of those of us in this room? Will we survive?"

"I have not explored the related probabilities. I knew in New York that it was necessary for Folmer to survive to bring me here and to tell you of my abilities. It can be calculated."

"Now?"

"Give me thirty seconds."

Again the room was silent. Badloe had lifted his face, his eyes naked with fear. Janks shifted uneasily. Folmer stood, barely breathing. Gates twisted his fingers together. The seconds ticked by. Four men waited for the word of death or life.

Billy Massner licked his lips. "Not one of you will live more than three months from this date." It was a flat, calm statement. Badloe made a sound in his throat.

"He's crazy!" Janks snarled.

They wanted to believe Janks. They had to believe the boy.

Gates whispered, "How will we die?"

They watched the small-boy face. Slowly the impassivity of it melted away. The gray eyes opened and they were not the dead gray eyes the men had grown accustomed to. They were the frightened eyes of boyhood. There was fear on the small face. Fear and indecision.

The voice had lost its flat and deadly calm.

"Who are you?" the boy asked, close to tears. "What do you want? What are you doing to me? I want to go home!"

In the darkened room four men stood and watched a small boy cry.

"Flaw" was a rather bold story for its time because it challenged several basic rules of formula science fiction—first, it was intensely and unsubtly pessimistic, even despairing, at a time when writers took a more cautious approach to the subject of failure, and second, it challenged the whole idea of reaching for the stars. Its uniqueness was recognized at the time, and it was selected for **The Best Science Fiction Stories: 1950.**

FLAW

**Startling Stories
January, 1949**

I rather imagine that I am quite mad. Nothing spectacular, you understand. Nothing calling for restraint, or shock therapy. I can live on, dangerous to no one but myself.

This beach house at La Jolla is comfortable. At night I sit on the rocks and watch the distant stars and think of Johnny. He probably wouldn't like the way I look now. My fingernails are cracked and broken and there are streaks of gray in my blonde hair. I no longer use makeup. Last night I looked at myself in the mirror and my eyes were dead.

It was then that I decided that it might help me to write all this down. I have no idea what I'll do with it.

You see, I shared Johnny's dreams.

And now I know that those dreams are no longer possible. I wonder if he learned how impossible they were in the few seconds before his flaming death.

There have always been people like Johnny and me. For a thousand years mankind has looked at the stars and thought of reaching them. The stars were to be the new frontier, the new worlds on which mankind could expand and find the full promise of the human soul.

I never thought much about it until I met Johnny. Five years ago. My name is Carol Adlar. At that time I was a government clerk working in the offices at the rocket station in Arizona. It was 1959. The year before the atomic drive was perfected.

Johnny Pritchard. I figured him out, I thought. A good-looking boy with dark hair and a careless grin and a swagger. That's all I saw in the beginning. The hot sun blazed down on the rocks and the evenings were cool and clear.

There were a lot of boys like Johnny at the rocket station—transferred from Air Corps work. Volunteers. You couldn't order a man off the surface of the earth in a rocket.

The heart is ever cautious. Johnny Pritchard began to hang around my desk, a warm look in his eyes. I was as cool as I could be. You don't give your heart to a man who soars up at the tip of a comet plume. But I did.

I told myself that I would go out with him one evening and I would be so cool to him that it would cure him and he would stop bothering me. I expected him to drive me to the city in his little car. Instead we drove only five miles from the compound, parked on the brow of a hill looking across the moon-silvered rock and sand.

AT first I was defensive, until I found that all he

wanted to do was to talk. He talked about the stars. He talked in a low voice that was somehow tense with his visions. I found out that first evening that he wasn't like the others. He wasn't merely one of those young men with perfect coordination and high courage. Johnny had in him the blood of pioneers. And his frontier was the stars.

"You see, Carol," he said, "I didn't know a darn thing about the upstairs at the time of my transfer. I guess I don't know much right now. Less, probably than the youngest astronomer or physicist on the base. But I'm learning. I spend every minute I can spare studying about it. Carol, I'm going upstairs some day. Right out into space. And I want to know about it. I want to know all about it.

"We've made a pretty general mess of this planet. I sort of figure that the powers-that-be planned it that way. They said, 'We'll give this puny little fella called man a chance to mess up one planet and mess it up good. But we'll let him slowly learn how to travel to another. Then, by the time he can migrate, he will be smart enough to turn the next planet into the sort of a deal we wanted him to have in the beginning. A happy world with no wars, no disease, no starvation.' "

I should have said something flip at that point, but the words weren't in me. Like a fool, I asked him questions about the galaxies, about the distant stars. We drove slowly back. The next day he loaned me two of his books. Within a week I had caught his fervor, his sense of dedication.

After that it was, of course, too late.

All persons in love have dreams. This was ours. Johnny would be at the controls of one of the first interplanetary rockets. He would return to me and then we would become one of the first couples to become colonists for the new world.

Silly, wasn't it?

He told me of the problems that would be solved with that first interplanetary flight. They would take instruments far enough out into space so that triangulation could solve that tiresome bickering among the physicists and astronomers about the theory of the exploding universe as against the theory of "tired light" from the distant galaxies.

And now I am the only person in the world who can solve that problem. Oh, the others will find the answer soon enough. And then they, too, can go quietly mad.

They will find out that for years they have been in the position of the man at the table with his fingers almost touching the sugar bowl and who asks why there isn't any sugar on the table.

That year was the most perfect year of my life.

"When are you going to marry me, Johnny?" I asked him.

"This is so sudden," he said, laughing. Then he sobered. "Just as soon as I come back from the first one, honey. It isn't fair any other way. Don't you see?"

I saw with my mind, but not with my heart. We exchanged rings. All very sentimental. He gave me a diamind and I gave him my father's ring, the one that was sent home to my mother and me when Dad was killed in Burma in World War II. It fit him and he liked it. It was a star ruby in a heavy silver setting. The star was perfect, but by looking closely into the stone you could see the flaws. Two dark little dots and a tiny curved line which together gave the look of a small and smiling face.

With his arm around me, with the cool night air of Arizona touching our faces, we looked up at the sky and talked of the home we would make millions of miles away.

Childish, wasn't it?

Last night after looking in the mirror, I walked down to the rocks. The Government money was given to me when Johnny didn't come back. It is enough. It will last until I die and I hope it will not be too long before I die.

The sea, washing the rocks, asked me the soft, constant question. "Why? Why? Why?" I looked at the sky. The answer was not there.

Fourteen months after I met Johnny, a crew of two in the *Destiny I* made the famous circuit of the moon and landed safely. Johnny was not one of them. He had hoped to be.

"A test run," he called it. The first step up the long flight of stairs.

You certainly remember the headlines given that flight of *Destiny I*. Even the New York *Times* broke out a new and larger type face for the headlines. Korby and Sweeny became the heroes of the entire world.

The world was confident then. The intervening years have shaken that confidence. But the world does not know yet. I think some suspect, but they do not know. Only I know for a certainty. And I, of course, am quite mad. I know that now.

Call it a broken heart—or broken dreams.

JOHNNY was selected for *Destiny II*. After he told me and after the tears came, partly from fear, partly from the threat of loneliness, he held me tightly and kissed my eyes. I had not known that the flight of *Destiny II*, if successful, would take fourteen months. The fourteen months were to include a circuit of Mars and a return to the takeoff point. Fourteen months before I would see him again. Fourteen months before I would feel his arms around me.

A crew of four. The famous Korby and Sweeny, plus Anthony Marinetta and my Johnny. Each morning when I went to work I could see the vast silver ship on the horizon, the early sun glinting on the blunt nose. Johnny's ship.

Those last five months before takeoff were like the five months of life ahead of a prisoner facing execution. And Johnny's training was so intensified after his selection that I couldn't see him as often as before.

We were young and we were in love and we made our inevitable mistake. At least we called it a mistake. Now I know that it wasn't, because Johnny didn't come back.

With the usual sense of guilt we planned to be married, and then reverted to our original plan. I would wait for him. Nothing could go wrong.

Takeoff was in the cold dawn of a February morning. I stood in the crowd beside a girl who worked in the same office. I held her arm. She carried the bruises for over a week.

The silver hull seemed to merge with the gray of the dawn. The crowd was silent. At last there was the blinding, blue-white flare of the jets, the stately lift into the air, the moment when *Destiny II* seemed to hang motionless fifty feet in the air, and then the accelerating blast that arrowed it up and up into the dark-gray sky where a few stars still shone. I walked on leaden legs back to the administration building and sat slumped at my desk, my mouth dry, my eyes hot and burning.

The last faint radio signal came in three hours later.

"All well. See you next year."

From then on there would be fourteen months of silence.

I suppose that in a way I became accustomed to it.

I was numb, apathetic, stupefied. They would probably have got rid of me had they not known how it was between Johnny and me. I wouldn't have blamed them. Each morning I saw the silver form of *Destiny III* taking shape near where *Destiny II* had taken off. The brash young men made the same jokes, gave the office girls the same line of chatter.

But they didn't bother me. Word had got around.

I found a friend. The young wife of Tony Marinetta. We spent hours telling each other in subtle ways that everything would come out all right.

I remember one night when Marge grinned and said:

"Well anyway, Carol, nobody has ever had their men go quite so far away."

There is something helpless about thinking of the distance between two people in the form of millions of miles.

After I listened to the sea last night, I walked slowly back up the steep path to this beach house. When I clicked the lights on Johnny looked at me out of the silver frame on my writing desk. His eyes are on me as I write this. They are happy and confident eyes. I am almost glad that he didn't live to find out.

The fourteen months were like one single revolution of a gigantic Ferris wheel. You start at the top of the wheel, and through seven months the wheel carries you slowly down into the darkness and the fear. Then, after you are at your lowest point, the wheel slowly starts to carry you back up into the light.

Somewhere in space I knew that Johnny looked at the small screen built into the control panel and saw the small bright sphere of earth and thought of me. I knew all during that fourteen months that he wasn't dead. If he had died, no matter how many million miles away from me, I would have known it in the instant of his dying.

The world forgets quickly. The world had pushed *Destiny II* off the surface of consciousness a few months after takeoff. Two months before the estimated date of return, it began to creep back into the papers and onto the telescreens of the world.

Work had stopped on *Destiny III*. The report of the four crewmen might give a clue to alterations in the interior.

It was odd the way I felt. As though I had been frozen under the transparent ice of a small lake. Spring was coming and the ice grew thinner.

Each night I went to sleep thinking of Johnny driving down through the sky toward me at almost incalculable speed. Closer, closer, ever closer.

It was five weeks before the date when they were due to return. I was asleep in the barracks-like building assigned to the unmarried women of the base.

The great thud and jar woke me up and through the window I saw the night sky darkening in the afterglow of some brilliant light.

WE gathered by the windows and talked for a long time about what it could have been. It was in all of our minds that it could have been the return of *Destiny II,* but we didn't put it into words, because no safe landing could have resulted in that deathly thud.

With the lights out again, I tried to sleep. I reached out into the night sky with my heart, trying to contact Johnny.

And the sky was empty.

I sat up suddenly, my lips numb, my eyes staring. No.

It was imagination. It was illusion. Johnny was still alive. Of course. But when I composed myself for sleep it was as though dirges were softly playing. In all the universe there was no living entity called Johnny Pritchard. Nowhere.

The telescreens were busy the next morning and I saw the shape of fear. An alert operator had caught the fast shape as it had slammed flaming down through the atmosphere to land forty miles from the base in deserted country making a crater a half-mile across.

"It is believed that the object was a meteor," the voice of the announcer said. "Radar screens picked up the image and it is now known that it was far too large to be the *Destiny II* arriving ahead of schedule."

It was then that I took a deep breath. But the relief was not real. I was only kidding myself. It was as though I was in the midst of a dream of terror and could not think of magic words to cause the spell to cease.

After breakfast I was ill.

The meteor had hit with such impact that the heat generated had fused the sand. Scientific instruments proved that the mass of the meteor itself, nine hundred feet under the surface was largely metallic. The telescreens began to prattle about invaders from an alien planet. And the big telescopes scanned the heavens for the first signs of the returning *Destiny II*.

The thought began as a small spot, glowing in some deep part of my mind. I knew that I had to cross the forty miles between the base and the crater. But I did not know why I had to cross it. I did not know why I had to stand at the lip of the crater and watch the recovery operations. I felt like a subject under post-hypnotic influence—compelled to do something without knowing the reason. But compelled, nevertheless.

One of the physicists took me to the crater in one of the base helicopters after I had made the request of him in such a way that he could not refuse.

Eleven days after the meteor had fallen, I stood on the lip of the crater and looked down into the heart of it to where the vast shaft had been sunk to the meteor itself. Dr. Rawlins handed me his binoculars and I watched the mouth of the shaft.

Men working down in the shaft had cut away large pieces of the body of the meteor and some of them had been hauled out and trucked away. They were blackened and misshapen masses of fused metal.

I watched the mouth of the shaft until my eyes ached and until the young physicist shifted restlessly and kept glancing at his watch and at the sun sinking toward the west. When he asked to borrow the binoculars, I gave them up reluctantly. I could hear the distant throb of the hoist motors. Something was coming up the shaft.

Dr. Rawlins made a sudden exclamation. I looked at the mouth of the shaft. The sun shone with red fire on something large. It dwarfed the men who stood near it.

Rudely I snatched the binoculars from Dr. Rawlins and looked, knowing even as I lifted them to my eyes what I would see.

Because at that moment I knew the answer to something that the astronomers and physicists had been bickering about for many years. There is no expanding universe. There is no tired light.

As I sit here at my writing desk, I can imagine how it was during those last few seconds. The earth looming up in the screen on the instrument panel, but not nearly large enough. Not large enough at all. Incredulity, then because of the error in size, the sudden application of the nose jets. Too late. Fire and oblivion and a thud that shook the earth for hundreds of miles.

No one else knows what I know. Maybe soon they will guess. And then there will be an end to the proud dreams of migration to other worlds. We are trapped here. There will be no other worlds for us. We have made a mess of this planet, and it is something that we cannot leave behind us. We must stay here and clean it up as best we can.

Maybe a few of them already know. Maybe they have guessed. Maybe they guessed, as I did, on the basis of the single object that was brought up out of that shaft on that bright, cold afternoon.

YES, I saw the sun shining on the six-pointed star. With the binoculars I looked into the heart of it and saw the two dots and a curved line that made the flaws look like a smiling face. A ruby the size of a bungalow.

There is no expanding universe. There is no "tired light." There is only a Solar system that, due to an unknown influence, is constantly shrinking.

For a little time the *Destiny II* avoided that influence. That is why they arrived too soon, why they couldn't avoid the crash, and why I am quite mad.

The ruby was the size of a bungalow, but it was, of course, quite unchanged. It was I and my world that had shrunk.

If Johnny had landed safely, I would be able to walk about on the palm of his hand.

It is a good thing that he died.

And it will not be long before I die also.

The sea whispers softly against the rocks a hundred yards from the steps of my beach house.

And *Destiny III* has not yet returned.

It is due in three months.

This is the story of a man overwhelmed by his
hobby (in this case also his work), a forerunner of
the more recent "The Man Who Collected the
Shadow" by Bill Pronzini. It is rich in imagery and
happens to contain one of the bitchiest women in
science fiction.

BUT NOT TO DREAM

Weird Tales
May, 1949

SARA, the virtuous wife of Dr. Morgan Nestor of
the Lavery College faculty, situated in Willowville, Ohio,
planted sensible heels on the worn gray paint of the side
porch and thrust off, the rocking chair tipping back almost
to the point of no return.

Each time the chair rocked forward, the low heels
thumped on the boards. Dr. Nestor sat ten feet away, and
with each thump his head sank a millimeter lower over the
paper he was reading. An interesting document—
published by a fellow entomologist at an eastern university. But he couldn't concentrate on it. Being of a statistical

frame of mind, he knew that after fifty determined thumps, his good wife would start a conversation. And he knew that the odds against the conversation being pleasant were roughly ten thousand to one.

Often he tried to associate Sara with the deliciously helpless and winsome little female who had occupied the second seat in the third row in the first classroom of his teaching career, twenty-three years before.

He remembered wide gray eyes, fragile bones, cobweb hair and hands that fluttered. He gave Sara a sidelong glance. The wide gray eyes had narrowed. The fragile bones were buried in all too solid flesh. The cobweb hair had acquired the consistency of fine copper wire, and had turned steel gray. The hands no longer fluttered.

Her voice had the thin sharpness of a fractured flute.

"Who wrote that?" she demanded.

"This?" he asked weakly, waving the paper he had been reading. Morgan Nestor was a big man who had not become soft through years of sedentary life. He had faraway eyes and a lock of hair that consistently fell across the broad dreamer's forehead. Though he did not realize it, he still caused frequent heart flutters among the coed population of Lavery College.

He licked his lips. "Why Brunhardt wrote this. Good man."

"Ha!" she said. The explosive little sound blasted across the porch and seemed to whip down the quiet, shady street, disturbing the leaves of the silent maples.

With great caution and a too innocent expression, Morgan Nestor stood up, taking one step toward the screen door.

"Sit down!" Sara said. He sat. "Something has got to be done, Morgan."

"About what?" He knew very well what she meant.

"About getting your son a job, that's what. Robert is a delicate and sensitive boy, and in the right department he'd be a credit to the faculty. Also, he would probably do a whole lot better in twenty-four years of it than you've managed to do."

MORGAN NESTOR ran a hand through his hair. During the brief moment that his palm touched his forehead he wondered if he were feverish.

"Sara," he said, "I've explained this a dozen times. We sent Robert to four colleges before we found one that would graduate him. One of the colleges he flunked out of was Lavery. Why it's . . . I . . . it's *unthinkable* that the faculty should take on as an instructor a person who could not make the grade here as an undergraduate. Besides, Robert isn't the type for. . . ."

"How do you know what type he is? Have you given him a chance? Have you? I certainly know he's brighter than a lot of fools instructing over there on the hill. Haven't you any influence? What good is it to teach about bugs for twenty-four years if you can't even do a small favor for your own family? What do they have you doing? I thought you were a full professor. Apparently you've been deceiving me, Morgan. Apparently they have you cutting grass or rolling the tennis courts."

"Sara, dear, I tell you that I can't in all honesty. . . ."

She suddenly stopped rocking and fixed him with a narrow gray eye, as penetrating as an insect pin. "You can and you will," she said in a low voice, "even if I have to go see the dean with you. Make no mistake about that."

AT THAT moment Robert appeared in the side yard with a seven iron and a cotton golf ball. He smiled up at the side porch. "Hello, soaks," he said. A psychologist would label Robert as socially immature, with a low attention factor. He was blonde, with a stubble of beard on his ripe jaw, a band of fat around his middle.

He dropped the ball, swung heartily at it. The ball arched just a bit further than the divot he slashed out of the lawn.

Morgan shut his eyes. The lawn had become a sort of retreat. While encouraging and working on the velvety growth, it was sometimes possible to forget . . . many things.

"Robert," he said hesitantly. "The lawn. . . ."

"You want to deny him every pleasure," Sara said. "You go right ahead, Robert."

Robert came up onto the porch and collapsed onto the swing. It creaked under his weight. "Too hot, anyway."

"Your father," Sara said, "has promised to speak to the dean about taking you on as an instructor."

Robert licked his thumb, moistened the palm of his left hand and hit the spot with a chubby fist. "Coeds, here comes Robert!" he said.

"It's possible, my boy, that the dean may not see his way clear to. . . ."

"Morgan," Sara said crisply, "I am not going to give you the chance of speaking too mildly about Robert. I am going to see the dean with you."

"When?" Morgan asked. His voice had a faintly strangled tone.

"Tomorrow after your ten o'clock class. I'll meet you in front of the administration building."

Morgan Nestor found himself wondering if there was any efficient way of guaranteeing a broken leg.

He looked at his son with his usual mild disbelief. Could this vast and amiable child be flesh of his flesh? Surely genetics should not play such a dastardly trick on the one man who had so carefully studied the science as it applied to fruit flies.

From within the house there was a scuffling sound, and the clink of a glass. Sara came to attention like a good bird dog. "Alice!" she shrilled. "What are you doing?"

"Getting a drink of water, Mom," Alice answered sleepily. Alice had followed her usual schedule of arising at ten, eating lunch at noon and going back to bed until four-thirty.

Alice came scuffling out onto the porch carrying the glass. Ever since she had reached fourteen Morgan had seen her become more and more like the Sadie Thompson in a low-budget production of *Rain*. No power on earth seemed to be able to keep Alice out of shiny black dresses, dangling earrings and a mouth painted to resemble a smashed strawberry.

He had long since decided that her faintly unclean look came from putting makeup on top of makeup *ad infinitum*.

She carried her glass as though it were the most precious thing in the world, but about which she was obligated to act negligent and casual.

Morgan Nestor swallowed hard and avoided looking at Sara. If she discovered Alice's latest ruse, there would be a scene. And somehow, at the end of the scene, it would all turn out to be Morgan's fault. Each day, when Alice got up the second time, she dipped into her secret store of gin, filled a water glass, put an ice cube in it and stayed far enough away from her mother to maintain the illusion that it was water.

Unless she actually caught Alice in the act, Mrs. Nestor blithely ignored any strong odor of alcohol that might hang around her only daughter. She also told friends and acquaintances that Charley Nesbitt, her son-in-law, had brought Alice back and had moved in on them because of the "housing shortage."

Actually Charley and Alice had maintained a rather trim little white frame house on the other side of town, but Charley had grown weary of trying to sober up Alice after work each day.

Alice knew that her father knew that the glass held gin. She winked at him. Through long practice, she was able to drink it as though it were, in truth, water.

At dinner, Alice would be gay, flushed and jovial. The life of the party.

"Alice has *such* spirit!" Sara often said.

Morgan knew that his daughter should go to an institution, yet so long as Sara resolutely refused to admit the flaw, there was nothing he could do.

"Charley's about due?" Alice asked.

Morgan glanced at his watch and nodded. Charley, boisterous and muscular manager of Willowville's only supermarket, usually came home at five.

A distant brassy horn played the first few bars of "The Old Grey Mare."

"Here comes Charley," Alice said in a dull tone.

CHARLEY whipped his coupe into the drive sliding to a stop on the gravel. He bounded out and came up onto the porch steps. He was a balding, florid young man with all his features bunched too closely in the middle of a wide face.

He struck a pose on the top step, slapped himself on the chest. "Promoted again, folks! Whadya know about that? Old Charley comes through, he does."

"That's great. That's dandy," Alice said in a flat monotone. Charley gave her an angry look.

But he beamed at Sara, because she clapped her hands together and said, "Oh, Charley! How wonderful!"

"Yep, from a hundred a week to a hundred and a quarter. New responsibilities. Got four stores under my wing now. They are sending in a new manager here. Have to travel a little, you know. They know they got a good man in Charles J. Nesbitt."

Sara turned to Morgan and said, "Charley's been in that business for five years and now he's making, let me see, twelve hundred dollars a year more than you are. And you've been fooling with those dead bugs of yours for nearly thirty years."

Before Morgan could answer, Charley swaggered over to him, slapped him on the shoulder. "You tell her, old boy, that the business I'm in would kill you in a year. It's a high pressure deal, what I mean. Have a cigar?"

Morgan took his pipe out of his jacket pocket. "I'll smoke this, thanks."

"Make sure you don't take that smelly thing in the house, Morgan," Sara said.

CHARLEY had left matches on Morgan's chair arm. He filled his pipe, took the packet of matches and struck one. The match burned with a horrid red flame and a chemical snake came writhing out of the end of it. Morgan stared at it in horror and dropped the match. The four of them roared at him. After a few moments he managed a feeble smile.

"Great gag, hey?" Charley said when he could speak. "Picked those up this afternoon. Almost as good as that dribble glass, hey Doc? You remember the glass?"

"How could he forget?" Robert said.

Sara left the porch and went into the kitchen. Alice sat on the swing beside Robert. Her glass was half-empty. Her face was flushed. Charley sat in the rocker that Sara had vacated. Morgan let their conversation wash around him like the sea washing around rocks. He found it puzzling that he was never able to find anything of the slightest interest in their conversation.

He smoked his pipe and waited for dinner. Sara had a knack of achieving the ultimate in tastelessness from even the freshest garden vegetables. The smells that floated out of the kitchen were vaguely sour.

Morgan smoked his pipe and remembered that after dinner he would be able to go into his study, shut the door and be absolutely alone. In the study he could lick the wounds of the day and steel himself for the morrow.

He sat at the table, huddled over his plate, eating from a sense of duty. He thought of the paper he had been working on for three years. A good paper. When it was published he would get letters from all over the world, congratulating him on his new classification system for the subspecies of butterfly, classification dependent on the timing of the phases of metamorphosis.

Suddenly he realized that he had been asked a question. He looked up. They were all looking at him. "What was that?"

"I'll repeat it, Doc. It's like this. With my new job, I got to have office space. A headquarters. I could rent an office in town, but it would be handier here. I was wondering if you'd give up that room of yours. Hell, you don't seem to use it for anything that I can see."

"No!" Morgan said loudly, his eyes wide. "No!" He thought of the unending evenings when he would be trapped in the bosom of his family, condemned to sit among them, half-alive. How could he work? Where would he find that solitude on which he depended? He looked at Sara with quick appeal. Surely she would stand by him!

"Charles is absolutely correct, Morgan. You use that room as an excuse for being selfish and anti-social. I've been waiting for years for a good excuse to root you out of there. This is it. We can turn that room over to someone who will get some practical use out of it."

Morgan stood up, his hands trembling as he held onto the back of his chair. "No! He can't have it!" he said desperately.

"Look at him!" Sara said with a savage smile. "A little boy losing his candy cane. For heaven's sake, Morgan. Grow up! Where are all the papers you were going to write in that study of yours? Where is the wonderful fame you were going to have? You might as well face things. The best thing you can do is try to hold your job until they're willing to retire you. Now stop acting like a child and march into that study and start packing those silly trays of bugs."

"I won't do it!" Morgan said hoarsely. Charley was looking at him with an injured expression. Robert was frankly enjoying the scene. Alice was battling hiccups.

Sara lost her smile. "Take your choice, Morgan. Either pack that nonsense yourself, or I'll clear that place out tomorrow while you're at class. And I might not be very careful about what goes in the incinerator."

Morgan looked into the eyes of his virtuous wife for three seconds. All the fight went out of him. With heavy tread he went to his study, bolted the door behind him and drew the shades. He turned on the desk light.

He stood by the desk and his eyes had an unaccustomed sting as he looked around at the small and cluttered room in which he spent so many peaceful and happy hours. The huge desk, the crowded bookshelves he had made, the display trays where, under glass, the insect wings glowed with rare and delicate beauty.

A NEW specimen was on the spreading board. The desk lamp picked up the ovals of brilliant turquoise at the base of the wings. They were his creatures, the moths and the butterflies. Small living things, intent with instinct, unaccountably beautiful.

He sat for a long time at the desk, staring down into the drawer he had opened. In the drawer was the metallic blue sheen of an automatic. He touched it with his finger-tips and the chill of the metal entered his soul.

He envied the insects, envied them in the unthinking beauty of their involuntary death.

There was no insect but what struggled against the net, struggled for its small life. And he, Morgan Nestor, would give up life with no struggle.

He shut the desk drawer violently.

For many years he had watched the life cycles of the moths and butterflies, watched the soft worm become inert and hard, watched the splitting, the emergence of a creature of loveliness which perched and slowly dried its mystic wings before the first flight.

His envy of their escape was a roar in his ears. "Unfair!" he thought. "Unfair!" For within one lifespan they existed twice—once earthbound; once creatures of the warm and fragile air.

He knew so well each stage of the process, each instinctive larval transformation.

All thought of packing was gone. He stood near the desk in strange ecstasy, sensing more clearly than ever before the mystic sequence of changes encompassed by the small dusty bodies he had pinned to the frames.

He wished suddenly that he had never used a killing jar, a net, the spreading boards, the insect pins. His kinship with them was clear and distinct.

Vaguely he realized that he was wasting time, that he should try to sort out the things to be saved, the things to be thrown away. He tried to remember what Sara had said, and she seemed an alien being, a creature of another race, another life rhythm. Her features were indistinct.

The green shade of the desk lamp cast a soft light in the room.

All of them out there were alien. He could hear the distant harshness of their voices.

Suddenly he began to undo the buttons of his shirt with fingers that were unruly and awkward. He stripped off all his clothes, stood naked by the desk. He heard a distant humming, as of the vast beating of many wings.

The drone filled his soul, a deep and heady rhythm that spoke to him of freedom and of far places.

He stood very straight, slowly drawing his arms up so that his fists were under his chin, his elbows together at his stomach. There was an itching harshness about his skin, and a sense of urgency.

When he fell it was without shock or pain, and almost without noise. He lay on his stomach on the floor, his arms under him, and both legs had somehow become a unit, a single unit, joined from ankle to hip.

He looked along the floor level, and the fibres of the rug were harsh and strange. Too dry.

They should have been of a moist greenness. He yearned for the grass, dimly remembered some oddly upright creature that had hit at the grass with a club.

A tingling ran down the surface of his skin along the forearms that had merged with his chest, along the tops of the thighs and shins that had joined together.

Holding his head high, he began to cross the rug with a sinuous motion, accepting without question the use of the double row of small legs that had sprouted from the tingling flesh.

THE feeling of urgency was great, and yet it carried with it no particular aim or goal. He accepted the domination of the body, let himself be carried along with the body that so obviously knew its function and purpose.

He reached the wall, and without hesitation raised his head, the small sucker legs getting a grip on the smooth surface, carrying him up until his head was within inches of the ceiling.

From the corner of his eyes he saw that his shoulder was sunken, rounded and a pleasing shade of green. He distantly remembered a disgusting pink and white hue.

His skin was rapidly growing more harsh and irritating. His mouth, which seemed oddly wider, was pulsating rapidly generating a ropy saliva.

Deftly he fastened one bit of the saliva to the wall, stretched back, seeing it turn firm and silklike on exposure to the air. He made a second rope that was attached a foot or so to the left of the first one.

Where his heels had been, there seemed to be an exceptionally strong clamping device.

With all his strength he dug the clamp into the plaster, fastened it tight. Then, with the two silken ropes held in his teeth, he let himself fall back so that he was at an angle to the wall, supported only by the clamp where his feet had been, the two silk ropes.

The itching and tightness of his skin was rapidly becoming unbearable. He writhed, felt the delicious slackening of pressure as his skin slit down the back. The writhing was difficult, but somehow pleasurable. As he bucked and strained against the ropes, the outer skin gradually rolled down from his body. It took with it his eyes, the myriad legs, leaving him a moist green wetness, vulnerable and helpless.

He was dimly conscious of it falling to the floor below him.

Form was changed. The air brushed the moist inner skin, hardening it rapidly, tightening it, turning it into a protective shell around him.

Sleep was a deep well into which he was slipping. Without ears, he heard the sound of the knocking, and the small part of him that yet retained the ghostly memories of humanity knew it for what it was. They would be shouting and hammering on the door. Soon they would break it down. But by then he would be in the darkness of sleep, protected by the cocoon which would be hard and firm around him.

There would be a time of sleep, and one day the cocoon would split and a shining creature, all memory of manhood gone, would awaken to dry the wide, glowing expanse of wings.

Something inside of him smiled as he thought of how they would stare at him.

To the tiny and distant and unimportant accompaniment of breaking wood, Dr. Morgan Nestor slid down into the deep, unthinking sleep that instinct demands of her creatures.

John D. MacDonald was so prolific in the late forties
that he was forced to use a variety of pen names.
In science fiction he most frequently employed
"Peter Reed," usually when he had more than
one story in a magazine. "The Miniature" appeared
under the Reed name because his novelette "Minions
of Chaos" was there by MacDonald. Appropriately
enough, it is perhaps the ultimate version of
the labor theory of value.

THE MINIATURE

Super Science Stories
September, 1949

AS Jedediah Amberson stepped through the bronze,
marble and black-glass doorway of the City National
Bank on Wall Street, he felt the strange jar. It was,
he thought, almost a tremor. Once he had been in
Tepoztlan, Mexico, on a Guggenheim grant, doing research on primitive barter systems, and during the night
a small earthquake had awakened him.

This was much the same feeling. But he stood inside

the bank and heard the unruffled hum of activity, heard no shouts of surprise. And, even through the heavy door he could hear the conversation of passers-by on the sidewalk.

He shrugged, beginning to wonder if it was something within himself, some tiny constriction of blood in the brain. It had been a trifle like that feeling which comes just before fainting. Jedediah Amberson had fainted once.

Fumbling in his pocket for the checkbook, he walked, with his long loose stride, over to a chest-high marble counter. He hadn't been in the main office of the bank since he had taken out his account. Usually he patronized the branch near the University, but today, finding himself in the neighborhood and remembering that he was low on cash, he had decided to brave the gaudy dignity of the massive institution of finance.

For, though Jed Amberson dealt mentally in billions, and used such figures familiarly in dealing with his classes in economics, he was basically a rather timid and uncertain man and he had a cold fear of the scornful eyes of tellers who might look askance at the small check he would present at the window.

He made it out for twenty dollars, five more than he would have requested had he gone to the familiar little branch office.

Jedediah Amberson was not a man to take much note of his surroundings. He was, at the time, occupied in writing a text, and the problems it presented were so intricate that he had recently found himself walking directly into other pedestrians and being snatched back onto the curb by helpful souls who didn't want to see him truck-mashed before their eyes. Just the day before he had gone into his bedroom in midafternoon to change his shoes and had only awakened from his profound thoughts when he found himself, clad in pajamas, brushing his teeth before the bathroom mirror.

He took his place in the line before a window. He was mentally extrapolating the trend line of one of J. M. Keynes' debt charts when a chill voice said, "Well!"

He found that he had moved up to the window itself

and the teller was waiting for his check. He flushed and said, "Oh! Sorry." He tried to push the check under the grill, but it fluttered out of his hand. As he stooped to get it, his hat rolled off.

At last recovering both hat and check, he stood up, smiled painfully and pushed the check under the grill.

The young man took it, and Jed Amberson finally grew aware that he was spending a long time looking at the check. Jed strained his neck around and looked to see if he had remembered to sign it. He had.

Only then did he notice the way the young man behind the window was dressed. He wore a deep wine-colored sports shirt, collarless and open at the throat. At the point where the counter bisected him, Jedediah could see that the young man wore green-gray slacks with at least a six-inch waistband of ocher yellow.

Jed had a childlike love of parties, sufficient to overcome his chronic self-consciousness. He said, in a pleased tone, "Ah, some sort of festival?"

The teller had a silken wisp of beard on his chin. He leaned almost frighteningly close to the grill, aiming the wisp of beard at Amberson as he gave him a careful scrutiny.

"We are busy here," the teller said. "Take your childish little game across street and attempt it on them."

Though shy, Jedediah was able to call on hidden stores of indignation when he felt himself wronged. He straightened slowly and said, with dignity, "I have an account here and I suggest you cash my check as quickly and quietly as possible."

The teller glanced beyond Jedediah and waved the silky beard in a taut half circle, a "come here" gesture.

Jedediah turned and gasped as he faced the bank guard. The man wore a salmon-pink uniform with enormously padded shoulders. He had a thumb hooked in his belt, his hand close to the plastic bowl of what seemed to be a child's bubble pipe.

The guard jerked his other thumb toward the door and said, "Ride off, honorable sir."

Jedediah said, "I don't care much for the comic-opera

atmosphere of this bank. Please advise me of my balance and I will withdraw it all and put it somewhere where I'll be treated properly."

The guard reached out, clamped Jed's thin arm in a meaty hand and yanked him in the general direction of the door. Jed intensely disliked being touched or pushed or pulled. He bunched his left hand into a large knobbly fist and thrust it with vigor into the exact middle of the guard's face.

The guard grunted as he sat down on the tile floor. The ridiculous bubble pipe came out, and was aimed at Jed. He heard no sound of explosion, but suddenly there was a large cold area in his middle that felt the size of a basketball. And when he tried to move, the area of cold turned into an area of pain so intense that it nauseated him. It took but two tiny attempts to prove to him that he could achieve relative comfort only by standing absolutely still. The ability to breathe and to turn his eyes in their sockets seemed the only freedom of motion left to him.

The guard said, tenderly touching his puffed upper lip, "Don't drop signal, Harry. We can handle this without flicks." He got slowly to his feet, keeping the toy weapon centered on Jedediah.

Other customers stood at a respectful distance, curious and interested. A fussy little bald-headed man came trotting up, carrying himself with an air of authority. He wore pastel-blue pajamas with a gold medallion over the heart.

The guard stiffened. "Nothing we can't handle, Mr. Greenbush."

"Indeed!" Mr. Greenbush said, his voice like a terrier's bark. "Indeed! You seem to be creating enough disturbance at this moment. Couldn't you have exported him more quietly?"

"Bank was busy," the teller said. "I didn't notice him till he got right up to window."

Mr. Greenbush stared at Jedediah. He said, "He looks reasonable enough, Palmer. Turn it off."

Jed took a deep, grateful breath as the chill area suddenly departed. He said weakly, "I demand an explanation."

Mr. Greenbush took the check the teller handed him and, accompanied by the guard, led Jed over to one side. He smiled in what was intended to be a fatherly fashion. He said, glancing at the signature on the check, "Mr. Amberson, surely you must realize, or your patrons must realize, that City National Bank is not sort of organization to lend its facilities to inane promotional gestures."

Jedediah had long since begun to have a feeling of nightmare. He stared at the little man in blue pajamas. "Promotional gestures?"

"Of course, my dear fellow. For what other reason would you come here dressed as you are and present this . . . this document."

"Dressed?" Jed looked down at his slightly baggy gray suit, his white shirt, his blue necktie and cordovan shoes. Then he stared around at the customers of the bank who had long since ceased to notice the little tableau. He saw that the men wore the sort of clothes considered rather extreme at the most exclusive of private beaches. He was particularly intrigued by one fellow who wore a cerise silk shirt, open to the waist, emerald green shorts to his knees, and calf-length pink nylons.

The women, he noticed, all wore dim shades of deep gray or brown, and a standard costume consisting of a halter, a short flared skirt that ended just above the knees and a knit cap pulled well down over the hair.

Amberson said, "Uh. Something special going on."

"Evidently. Suppose you explain."

"Me explain! Look, I can show you identification. I'm an Associate Professor of Economics at Columbia and I—" He reached for his hip pocket. Once again the ball of pain entered his vitals. The guard stepped over to him, reached into each of his pockets in turn, handed the contents to Mr. Greenbush.

Then the pressure was released. "I am certainly going to give your high-handed procedures here as much publicity as I can," Jed said angrily.

But Greenbush ignored him. Greenbush had opened his change purse and had taken out a fifty-cent piece. Greenbush held the coin much as a superstitious savage would have held a mirror. He made tiny bleating sounds. At last he said, his voice thin and strained, "Nineteen forty-nine mint condition! What do you want for it?"

"Just cash my check and let me go," Jed said wearily. "You're all crazy here. Why shouldn't this year's coins be in mint condition?"

"Bring him into my office," Greenbush said in a frenzy.

"But I—" Jed protested. He stopped as the guard raised the weapon once more. Jed meekly followed Greenbush back through the bank. He decided that it was a case of mistaken identity. He could call his department from the office. It would all be straightened out, with apologies.

WITH the door closed behind the two of them, Jed looked around the office. The walls were a particularly liverish and luminescent yellow-green. The desk was a block of plastic balanced precariously on one slim pedestal no bigger around than a lead pencil. The chairs gave him a dizzy feeling. They looked comfortable, but as far as he could see, they were equipped only with front legs. He could not see why they remained upright.

"Please sit there," Greenbush said.

Jed lowered himself into the chair with great caution. It yielded slightly, then seemed to clasp him with an almost embarrassing warmth, as though he sat on the pneumatic lap of an exceptionally large woman.

Greenbush came over to him, pointed to Jed's wristwatch and said, "Give me that, too."

"I didn't come for a loan," Jed said.

"Don't be ass. You'll get all back."

Greenbush sat behind his desk, with the little pile of Jed's possessions in front of him. He made little mumbling sounds as he prodded and poked and pried. He seemed very interested in the money. He listened to the watch tick and said, "Mmm. Spring mechanical."

"No. It runs on atomic power," Jed said bitterly. Greenbush didn't answer.

From the back of Jed's wallet, Greenbush took the picture of Helen. He touched the glossy surface, said, "Two-dimensional."

After what seemed an interminable period, Mr. Greenbush leaned back, put the tips of his fingers together and said, "Amberson, you are fortunate that you contacted me."

"I can visualize two schools of thought on that," Jed said stiffly.

Greenbush smiled. "You see, Amberson, I am coin collector and also antiquarian. It is possible National Museum might have material to equip you, but their stuff would be obviously old. I am reasonable man, and I know there must be explanation for all things." He fixed Jed with his sharp bright eyes, leaned slowly forward and said, "How did you get here?"

"Why, I walked through your front door." Jed suddenly frowned. "There was a strange jar when I did so. A dislocation, a feeling of being violently twisted in here." He tapped his temple with a thin finger.

"That's why I say you are fortunate. Some other bank might have had you in deviate ward by now where they'd be needling out slices of your frontal lobes."

"Is it too much to ask down here to get a small check cashed?"

"Not too much to ask in nineteen forty-nine, I'm sure. And I am ready to believe you are product of nineteen forty-nine. But, my dear Amberson, this is year eighty-three under Gradzinger calendar."

"For a practical joke, Greenbush, this is pretty ponderous."

Greenbush shrugged, touched a button on the desk. The wide draperies slithered slowly back from the huge window. "Walk over and take look, Amberson. Is that your world?"

Jed stood at the window. His stomach clamped into a small tight knot which slowly rose up into his throat. His eyes widened until the lids hurt. He steadied himself with his fingertips against the glass and took several deep, aching breaths. Then he turned somehow and walked, with knees that threatened to bend both ways, back to the chair. The draperies rustled back into position.

"No," Jed said weakly, "this isn't my world." He rubbed his forehead with the back of his hand, finding there a cold and faintly oily perspiration. "I had two classes this morning. I came down to look up certain documents. how. . . ."

Greenbush pursed his lips. "How? Who can say? I'm banker, not temporal tech. Doubtless you'd like to return to your own environment. I will signal Department of Temporal Technics at Columbia where you were employed so many years ago. . . ."

"That particular phraseology, Mr. Greenbush, I find rather disturbing."

"Sorry." Greenbush stood up. "Wait here. My communicator is deranged. I'll have to use other office."

"Can't we go there? To the University?"

"I wouldn't advise it. In popular shows I've seen on subject, point of entry is always important. I rather postulate they'll assist you back through front door."

Greenbush was at the office door. Jed said, "Have—have you people sent humans back and forth in time?"

"No. They send neutrons and gravitons or something like those. Ten minutes in future or ten minutes in past. Very intricate. Enormous energy problem. Way over my head."

While Greenbush was gone, Jed methodically collected his belongings from the desk and stowed them away in his pockets. Greenbush bustled in and said, "They'll be over in half hour with necessary equipment. They think they can help you."

Half an hour. Jed said, "As long as I'm here, I wonder if I could impose? You see, I have attempted to predict certain long-range trends in monetary procedures. Your currency would be—"

"Of course, my dear fellow! Of course! Kindred interest, etcet. What would you like to know?"

"Can I see some of your currency?"

Greenbush shoved some small pellets of plastic across the desk. They were made from intricate molds. The inscription was in a sort of shorthand English. "Those are universal, of course," Greenbush said.

Two of them were for twenty-five cents and the other for fifty cents. Jed was surprised to see so little change from the money of his own day.

"One hundred cents equals dollar, just as in your times," Greenbush said.

"Backed by gold, of course," Jed said.

Greenbush gasped and then laughed. "What ludicrous idea! Any fool with public-school education has learned enough about transmutation of elements to make five tons of gold in afternoon, or of platinum or zinc or any other metal or alloy of metal you desire."

"Backed by a unit of power? An erg or something?" Jed asked with false confidence.

"With power unlimited? With all power anyone wants without charge? You're not doing any better, Amberson."

"By a unit share of national resources maybe?" Jed asked hollowly.

"National is obsolete word. There are no more nations. And world resources are limitless. We create enough for our use. There is no depletion."

"But currency, to have value must be backed by something," Jed protested.

"Obviously!"

"Precious stones?"

"Children play with diamonds as big as baseballs," Greenbush said. "Speaking as economist, Amberson, why was gold used in your day?"

"It was rare, and, where obtainable, could not be obtained without a certain average fixed expenditure of man hours. Thus it wasn't really the metal itself, it was the man hours involved that was the real basis. Look, now you've got me talking in the past tense."

"And quite rightly. Now use your head, Mr. Amberson. In world where power is free, resources are unlimited and no metal or jewel is rare, what is one constant, one user of time, one eternal fixity on which monetary system could be based?"

Jed almost forgot his situation as he labored with the

problem. Finally he had an answer, and yet it seemed so incredible that he hardly dared express it. He said in a thin voice, "The creation of a human being is something that probably cannot be shortened or made easy. Is—is human life itself your basis?"

"Bravo!" Greenbush said. "One hundred cents in dollar, and five thousand dollars in HUC. That's brief for Human Unit of Currency."

"But that's slavery! That's—why, that's the height of inhumanity!"

"Don't sputter, my boy, until you know facts."

Jed laughed wildly. "If I'd made my check out for five thousand they'd have given me a—a person!"

"They'd have given you certificate entitling you to HUC. Then you could spend that certificate, you see."

"But suppose I wanted the actual person?"

"Then I suppose we could have obtained one for you from World Reserve Bank. As matter of fact, we have one in our vault now."

"In your vault!"

"Where else would we keep it? Come along. We have time."

THE VAULT was refrigerated. The two armed attendants stood by while Greenbush spun the knob of the inner chamber, slid out the small box. It was of dull silver, and roughly the size of a pound box of candy. Greenbush slid back the grooved lid and Jed, shuddering, looked down through clear ice to the tiny, naked, perfect figure of an adult male, complete even to the almost invisible wisp of hair on his chest.

"Alive?" Jed asked.

"Naturally. Pretty well suspended, of course." Greenbush slid the lid back, replaced the box in the vault and led the way back to the office.

Once again in the warm clasp of the chair, Jed asked, with a shaking voice, "Could you give me the background on—this amazing currency?"

"Nothing amazing about it. Technic advances made all too easily obtainable through lab methods except living humans. There, due to growth problems and due to—certain amount of nontechnic co-operation necessary, things could not be made easily. Full-sized ones were too unwieldy, so lab garcons worked on size till they got them down to what you see. Of course, they are never brought up to level of consciousness. They go from birth bottle to suspension chambers and are held there until adult and then refrigerated and boxed."

Greenbush broke off suddenly and said, "Are you ill?"

"No. No, I guess not."

"Well, when I first went to work for this bank, HUC was unit worth twenty thousand dollars. Then lab techs did some growth acceleration work—age acceleration, more accurate—and that brought price down and put us into rather severe inflationary period. Cup of java went up to dollar and it's stayed there ever since. So World Union stepped in and made it against law to make any more refinements in HUC production. That froze it at five thousand. Things have been stable ever since."

"But they're living human beings!"

"Now you sound like silly Anti-HUC League. My boy, they wouldn't exist were it not for our need for currency base. They never achieve consciousness. We, in banking business, think of them just as about only manufactured item left in world which cannot be produced in afternoon. Time lag is what gives them their value. Besides, they are no longer in production, of course. Being economist, you must realize overproduction of HUC's would put us back into inflationary period."

At that moment the girl announced that the temporal techs had arrived with their equipment. Jed was led from the office out into the bank proper. The last few customers were let out as the closing hour arrived.

The men from Columbia seemed to have no interest in Jed as a human being. He said hesitantly to one, smiling shyly, "I would think you people would want to keep me here so your historians could do research on me."

The tech gave him a look of undisguised contempt. He said, "We know all to be known about your era. Very dull period in world history."

Jed retired, abashed, and watched them set up the massive silvery coil on the inside of the bank door.

The youngest tech said quietly, "This is third time we've had to do this. You people seem to wander into sort of rhythm pattern. Very careless. We had one failure from your era. Garcon named Crater. He wandered too far from point of entry. But you ought to be all opt."

"What do I have to do?"

"Just walk through coil and out door. Adjustment is complicated. If we don't use care you might go back into your own era embedded up to your eyes in pavement. Or again, you might come out forty feet in air. Don't get unbalanced."

"I won't," Jed said fervently.

Greenbush came up and said, "Could you give me that coin you have?"

The young technician turned wearily and said, "Older, he has to leave with everything he brought and he can't take anything other with him. We've got to fit him into same vibratory rhythm. You should know that,"

"It is such nice coin," Greenbush sighed.

"If I tried to take something with me?" Jed asked.

"It just wouldn't go, gesell. You would go and it would stay."

Jed thought of another question. He turned to Greenbush, "Before I go, tell me. Where are the HUC's kept?"

"In refrigerated underground vault at place called Fort Knox."

"Come on, come on, you. Just walk straight ahead through coil. Don't hurry. Push door open and go out onto street."

JED STOOD, faintly dizzy, on the afternoon sidewalk of Wall Street in Manhattan. A woman bounced off him, snarled, "Fa godsake, ahya goin' uh comin"! Late papers were tossed off a truck onto the corner. Jed tiptoed over, looked cautiously and saw that the date was Tuesday, June 14th, 1949.

The further the subway took him uptown, the more the keen reality of the three-quarters of an hour in the bank faded. By the time he reached his own office, sat down behind his familiar desk, it had become like a fevered dream.

Overwork. That was it. Brain fever. Probably wandered around in a daze. Better take it easy. Might fade off into a world of the imagination and never come back. Skip the book for a month. Start dating Helen again. Relax.

He grinned slowly, content with his decision. "HUC's, indeed!" he said.

Date Helen tonight. Better call her now. Suddenly he remembered that he hadn't cashed a check, and he couldn't take Helen far on a dollar.

He found the check in his pocket, glanced at it, and then found himself sitting rigid in the chair. Without taking his eyes from the check, he pulled open the desk drawer, took out the manuscript entitled, "Probable Bases of Future Monetary Systems," tore it in half and dropped it in the wastebasket.

His breath whistled in pinched nostrils. He heard, in his memory, a voice saying, "You would go and it would stay."

The check was properly made out for twenty dollars. But he had used the ink supplied by the bank. The check looked as though it had been written with a dull knife. The brown desk top showed up through the fragile lace of his signature.

This story is a minor classic, praised for its social content by the noted critic H. Bruce Franklin. It concerns the nature of reality, capitalism, and American culture.

SPECTATOR SPORT

Thrilling Wonder Stories
February, 1950

DR. RUFUS MADDON was not generally considered to be an impatient man—or addicted to physical violence.

But when the tenth man he tried to stop on the street brushed by him with a mutter of annoyance Rufus Maddon grabbed the eleventh man, swung him around and held him with his shoulders against a crumbling wall.

He said, "You will listen to me, sir! I am the first man to travel into the future and I will not stand—"

The man pushed him away, turned around and said, "You got this dust on my suit. Now brush it off."

Rufus Maddon brushed mechanically. He said, with a faint uncontrollable tremble in his voice, "But nobody seems to care."

The man peered back over his shoulder. "Good enough, chum. Better go get yourself lobed. The first time I saw the one on time travel it didn't get to me at all. Too hammy for me. Give me those murder jobs. Every time I have one of those I twitch for twenty hours."

Rufus made another try. "Sir, I am physical living proof that the future is predetermined. I can explain the energy equations, redesign the warp projector, send myself from your day further into the future—"

The man walked away. "Go get a lobe job," he said.

"But don't I look different to you?" Rufus called after him, a plaintive note in his voice.

The man, twenty feet away, turned and grinned at him. "How?"

When the man had gone Rufus Maddon looked down at his neat grey suit, stared at the men and women in the street. It was not fair of the future to be so—so dismally normal.

Four hundred years of progress? The others had resented the experience that was to be his. In those last few weeks there had been many discussions of how the people four hundred years in the future would look on Rufus Maddon as a barbarian.

Once again he continued his aimless walk down the streets of the familiar city. There was a general air of disrepair. Shops were boarded up. The pavement was broken and potholed. A few automobiles traveled on the broken streets. They, at least, appeared to be of a slightly advanced design but they were dented, dirty and noisy.

The man who had spoken to him had made no sense. "Lobe job?" And what was "the one on time travel?"

He stopped in consternation as he reached the familiar park. His consternation arose from the fact that the park was all too familiar. Though it was a tangle of weeds the equestrian statue of General Murdy was still there in deathless bronze, liberally decorated by pigeons.

Clothes had not changed nor had common speech. He wondered if the transfer had gone awry, if this world were something he was dreaming.

He pushed through the knee-high tangle of grass to a wrought-iron bench. Four hundred years before he had sat on that same bench. He sat down again. The metal powdered and collapsed under his weight, one end of the bench dropping with a painful thump.

Dr. Rufus Maddon was not generally considered to be a man subject to fits of rage. He stood up rubbing his bruised elbow, and heartily kicked the offending bench. The part he kicked was all too solid.

He limped out of the park, muttering, wondering why the park wasn't used, why everyone seemed to be in a hurry.

IT APPEARED that in four hundred years nothing at all had been accomplished. Many familiar buildings had collapsed. Others still stood. He looked in vain for a newspaper or a magazine.

One new element of this world of the future bothered him considerably. That was the number of low-slung white-panel delivery trucks. They seemed to be in better condition than the other vehicles. Each bore in fairly large gilt letters the legend WORLD SENSEWAYS. But he noticed that the smaller print underneath the large inscription varied. Some read, *Feeder Division*—others, *Hookup Division*.

The one that stopped at the curb beside him read, *Lobotomy Division*. Two husky men got out and smiled at him and one said, "You've been taking too much of that stuff, Doc."

"How did you know my title?" Rufus asked, thoroughly puzzled.

The other man smiled wolfishly, patted the side of truck. "Nice truck, pretty truck. Climb in, bud. We'll take you down and make you feel wonderful, hey?"

Dr. Rufus Maddon suddenly had a horrid suspicion that he knew what a lobe job might be. He started to back away. They grabbed him quickly and expertly and dumped him into the truck.

The sign on the front of the building said WORLD

SENSEWAYS. The most luxurious office inside was lettered, *Regional Director—Roger K. Handriss.*

Roger K. Handriss sat behind his handsome desk. He was a florid grey-haired man with keen grey eyes. He was examining his bank book thinking that in another year he'd have enough money with which to retire and buy a permanent hookup. Permanent was so much better than the Temp stuff you could get on the home sets. The nerve ends was what did it, of course.

The girl came in and placed several objects on the desk in front of him. She said, "Mr. Handriss, these just came up from LD. They took them out of the pockets of a man reported as wandering in the street in need of a lobe job."

She had left the office door open. Cramer, deputy chief of LD, sauntered in and said, "The guy was really off. He was yammering about being from the past and not to destroy his mind."

Roger Handriss poked the objects with a manicured finger. He said, "Small pocket change from the twentieth century, Cramer. Membership cards in professional organizations of that era. Ah, here's a letter."

As Cramer and the girl waited Roger Handriss read the letter through twice. He gave Cramer an uncomfortable smile and said, "This appears to be a letter from a technical publishing house telling Mr.—ah—Maddon that they intend to reprint his book, *Suggestions on Time Focus* in February of nineteen hundred and fifty. Miss Hart, get on the phone and see if you can raise anyone at the library who can look this up for us. I want to know if such a book was published."

Miss Hart hastened out of the office.

As they waited Handriss motioned to a chair. Cramer sat down. Handriss said, "Imagine what it must have been like in those days, Al. They had the secrets but they didn't begin to use them until—let me see—four years later. Aldous Huxley had already given them their clue with his literary invention of the Feelies. But they ignored him.

"All their energies went into wars and rumors of wars

and random scientific advancement and sociological disruptions. Of course, with Video on the march at that time, they were beginning to get a little preview. Millions of people were beginning to sit in front of the Video screens, content even with that crude excuse for entertainment."

Cramer suppressed a yawn. Handriss was known to go on like that for hours.

"Now," Handriss continued, "all the efforts of a world society are channeled into World Senseways. There is no waste of effort changing a perfectly acceptable status quo. Every man can have Temp and if you save your money you can have Permanent, which they say is as close to heaven as man can get. Uh—what was that, Miss Hart?"

"There is such a book, Mr. Handriss, and it was published at that time. A Dr. Rufus Maddon wrote it."

Handriss sighed and clucked. "Well," he said, "have Maddon brought up here."

Maddon was brought into the office by an attendant. He wore a wide foolish smile and a tiny bandage on his temple. He walked with the clumsiness of an overgrown child.

"Blast it, Al," Handriss said, "why couldn't your people have been more careful! He looks as if he might have been intelligent."

Al shrugged. "Do they come here from the past every couple of minutes? He didn't look any different than any other lobey to me."

"I suppose it couldn't be helped," Handriss said. "We've done this man a great wrong. We can wait and reeducate, I suppose. But that seems to be treating him rather shabbily."

"We can't send him back," Al Cramer said.

Handriss stood up, his eyes glowing. "But it is within my authority to grant him one of the Perm setups given me. World Senseways knows that Regional Directors make mistakes. This will rectify any mistake to an individual."

"Is it fair he should get it for free?" Cramer asked. "And besides, maybe the people who helped send him up here into the future would like to know what goes on."

Handriss smiled shrewdly. "And if they knew, what would stop them from flooding in on us? Have Hookup install him immediately."

THE subterranean corridor had once been used for underground trains. But with the reduction in population it had ceased to pay its way and had been taken over by World Senseways to house the sixty-five thousand Perms.

Dr. Rufus Maddon was taken, in his new shambling walk, to the shining cubicle. His name and the date of installation were written on a card and inserted in the door slot. Handriss stood enviously aside and watched the process.

The bored technicians worked rapidly. They stripped the unprotesting Rufus Maddon, took him inside his cubicle, forced him down onto the foam couch. They rolled him over onto his side, made the usual incision at the back of his neck, carefully slit the main motor nerves, leaving the senses, the heart and lungs intact. They checked the air conditioning and plugged him into the feeding schedule for that bank of Perms.

Next they swung the handrods and the footplates into position, gave him injections of local anaesthetic, expertly flayed the palms of his hands and the soles of his feet, painted the raw flesh with the sticky nerve graft and held his hands closed around the rods, his feet against the plates until they adhered in the proper position.

Handriss glanced at his watch.

"Guess that's all we can watch, Al. Come along."

The two men walked back down the long corridor. Handriss said, "The lucky so and so. We have to work for it. I get my Perm in another year—right down here beside him. In the meantime we'll have to content ourselves with the hand sets, holding onto those blasted knobs that don't let enough through to hardly raise the hair on the back of your neck."

Al sighed enviously. "Nothing to do for as long as he lives except twenty-four hours a day of being the hero of the most adventurous and glamorous and exciting stories that the race has been able to devise. No memories. I told them to dial him in on the Cowboy series. There's seven years of that now. It'll be more familiar to him. I'm electing Crime and Detection. Eleven years of that now, you know."

Roger Handriss chuckled and jabbed Al with his elbow. "Be smart, Al. Pick the Harem series."

Back in the cubicle the technicians were making the final adjustments. They inserted the sound buttons in Rufus Maddon's ears, deftly removed his eyelids, moved his head into just the right position and then pulled down the deeply concave shining screen so that Rufus Maddon's staring eyes looked directly into it.

The elder technician pulled the wall switch. He bent and peered into the screen. "Color okay, three dimensions okay. Come on, Joe, we got another to do before quitting."

They left, closed the metal door, locked it.

Inside the cubicle Dr. Rufus Maddon was riding slowly down the steep trail from the mesa to the cattle town on the plains. He was trail-weary and sun-blackened. There was an old score to settle. Feeney was about to foreclose on Mary Ann's spread and Buck Hoskie, Mary Ann's crooked foreman, had threatened to shoot on sight.

Rufus Maddon wiped the sweat from his forehead on the back of a lean hard brown hero's hand.

"Half-Past Eternity" was the lead "novel" in the July, 1950, issue of **Super Science Stories** in an era when twenty thousand words received a book-length designation. Because of its length, it was reprinted only once, by the anthologist William F. Nolan. Chapter Six of the story contains some of the best handling of difficult material that one could hope to find in the sf pulps.

HALF-PAST ETERNITY

Super Science Stories
July, 1950

CHAPTER ONE

Stolen Lives

THE KID didn't talk. Nat February talked. Which is what you might have expected.

The kid had a punch like the business end of a mule, sure, and he kept boring in, shuffling flat-footed, game all the way through. But everybody on the Beach knew that the kid, who, by the way, at thirty-one was a kid no longer, had suffered slow degeneration of the reflexes to the point where his Sunday punch floated in like a big balloon and he could be tagged at will.

The way the bout happened to be set up was on account of Jake Freedon, a fast, vicious young heavy, not being able to get his title bout. The champion was justly leery of young Jake and the only thing for Jake's managers to do was to line up every pug in the country and let Jake knock them over. Sooner or later the pressure would grow heavy enough for the title match to be a necessity.

The Garden crowd was slim. There was no question about Jake Freedon winning. The kid was all through in the fight game although nobody had told him that yet. The odds hovered around twelve to one.

This old man had come to Nat February, having been guided to him after three or four days of asking questions. Nat was hard at work on a cheese blintz and resented the intrusion. He had his usual little group with him and Nat was about to give the brush to the old gentleman when same old gentleman said with tremulous dignity that he wished to speak alone to Nat February. So saying, he pulled a wad of currency out of his wallet that looked entirely capable of choking the fabulous cow.

Nat gave the sign and his cohorts cleared out.

"I," said the old man, "wish to bet on Mr. Goth in the contest tomorrow night."

"Mr. Who?"

"Goth. He is scheduled to box a gentleman named Freedon."

"Oh! The kid! Let me get this. You want to bet on the kid. A poor old guy like you with holes in his socks wants to bet the wrong way. You're going to make me feel like the guy with his mitt in the poor box, uncle."

"Your emotional reaction is of little interest to me, Mr. February. I understood that if I stated my wager clearly, you would take my money and give me a slip of paper testifying as to my wager. I understand that in your—ah—profession, you are considered to be one of the most thoroughly ethical and—ah—well financed."

"What have you got there, uncle?" February asked.

"Thirty-two hundred and fourteen dollars. I had hoped to bet thirty-two hundred and twenty-five, but my expenses were higher than I had planned and it has taken longer to locate you."

"The whole wad on the kid, eh?" February was not at all troubled by removing the funds from the old gentleman. It appeared to him that if he did not do so, someone else would.

"Yes, young man. All of this I would like to bet on the circumstance of Mr. Goth striking Mr. Freedon unconscious during the first three minutes of their engagement."

"Holy mice, uncle! The kid to knock Jake out in the first round?"

"Exactly. They told me you would quote the odds on that particular thing happening."

"I don't want to take your money."

"I insist, Mr. February."

"Okay. Thirty to one."

"You will please write out the paper for me, Mr. February, and tell me where I can find you directly after the fight. I shall expect you to have ninety-six thousand four hundred and twenty dollars with you. I am not—ah—superstitious about thousand-dollar bills."

"You'll bring a satchel, eh? Maybe a carpet bag?"

"If you consider it necessary."

For a fraction of a second Nat February's calm was shaken. But he quickly reviewed the past record of both the kid and Jake Freedon. It seemed highly probable that if the two of them were locked in a phone booth it would take the kid more than three minutes to lay a glove on Freedon, much less chill him.

"What's your name, uncle?"

"Garfield Tomlinson."

Nat wrote out the slip, counted the money, pocketed it, pushed the slip across the table. Tomlinson picked it up, examined it, sighed, put it in his wallet, now almost completely empty.

"And where will I find you?"

"Right here, uncle. In this same booth. They save it for

me. I don't wish you any bad luck, but I hope you won't be looking for me."

Nat February had bad dreams that night. In the morning, trusting more to dreams than to judgment, he shopped around town until he found odds of fifty to one. He placed a thousand of Tomlinson's money there, accepting the jeers of the wise ones. In doing so he cut his maximum profit to twenty-two hundred and fourteen dollars, but his maximum loss went down to forty-six thousand four hundred and twenty. He still felt uneasy. He looked up Lew Karon in the afternoon, talked Lew into offering sixty to one and placed a bet of eight hundred twenty-five. Now, if the old man's bet was bad, he still had a profit of thirteen hundred and eighty-nine. But if the old man had a reliable crystal ball—and he had acted like a man who at least had access to one—Nat would profit to the extent of three thousand and eighty dollars. If the old boy got wise and insisted on getting his original bet back, which he had every right to do, as well as the ninety-six thousand four hundred and twenty, then Nat would be out one hundred and thirty-four bucks. He felt comfortably covered.

He sat in his usual fifth-row ringside and dozed through the preliminary bouts, making a little here, losing a little there—but always more making than losing.

When the main came on and the kid fumbled his way over the ropes, his gray battered face wearing its usual dopy look, Nat cursed himself for cutting his profit with the overlay. Jake Freedon bounced in, smiling, confident, young, alert.

After the usual formalities the house lights dimmed and they came out for the first round. The kid shuffled out, slower and dopier than ever. They touched gloves, Freedon flicked the kid with a searching, stinging left jab and danced back. The kid stood, flatfooted. The referee motioned to him to fight.

Nat's eyes bulged and his hands clamped on the arm of the chair. He shut his eyes and shook his head.

When he opened his eyes again he saw what he thought he had seen in the first place. Freedon, spread-eagled on his face, his mouth in a puddle of blood, the referee jumping out of his stunned shock to pick up the time-keeper's count. The referee counted to eight, then spread his arms wide and Freedon's seconds jumped in to cart him back to the stool.

Nat shook the man beside him. "What'd you see happen?"

"Gosh!" the man said. "Gosh!"

"What happened?"

"Well, the way I see it the kid kinda jumped at Freedon, real fast. Fast as a flyweight. It looked to me like he nailed him with a left fist. I can't be sure. And I don't know how many times he hit him on the way down. Maybe six or nine times. Every one right on the mush. Hell, his fists were going so fast I couldn't see them."

The doctor jumped up into Freedon's corner. Nat read his lips as he shook his head and said, "Broken jaw."

Nat joined the shuffling crowd heading toward the exits. He picked up two boys he sometimes used, arranged with Lew Karon for the transfer of cash in some way that would not pain the Bureau of Internal Revenue boys by focusing their attention on it, and went back to the booth.

Garfield Tomlinson was there. There was relief on his face as he saw Nat February approach.

"Think I stood you up, uncle?"

"I rather hoped you'd be here. I brought this—uh—small suitcase."

Nat whacked the old man on the shoulder. "You're the one! Yes sir, you're the one. Come on, uncle. We gotta go get the sugar."

"I trust this large loss won't disconcert you, Mr. February."

"Uh? Oh, no. Just a fleabite, uncle. Tomorrow I'll have it back."

As they climbed into the taxi, the four of them, Tomlinson said, "Should it make any difference to you, Mr. February, let me state that you could not have lost money to any more worthy venture."

"You win it for a church?"

Tomlinson laughed dryly. "Oh dear me, no! Not at all for a church."

They went to the hotel where February lived. The envelope was taken out of the safe and given to February. At that point the two young men became very wary, very alert.

Nat pulled Tomlinson over into a corner, shielded the transaction with a big padded shoulder. "Uncle, these are tired old thousands because the new ones are poison. I got 'em folded in packages of ten each with the rubber band on 'em. Here's one, three, seven, eight, nine. Now check those."

"Ninety thousand," Tomlinson said. His voice shook a little.

"Plus one, two, three, four, five, six. Now the hundreds. These I get outa my billfold. One, two, three, four. And here's the change. A twenty. Ninety-six thousand four hundred and twenty dollars. Correct?"

"Ah—I'm not acquainted with these things. The wager was at thirty to one. Don't I get my original wager returned?"

"Thirty to one to make it simple. You wanna be that accurate I should have told you twenty-nine to one, plus getting your bet back."

"Oh. Oh, I see. Well, I—ah—hmm, I guess I didn't need the satchel after all. Just a joke, was it?"

"I can see you got a great sense of humor, uncle. Now don't go running away. Don't you think you oughta tell me how you knew that clown was going to clobber Freedon in the first?"

Garfield Tomlinson gave Nat February a look of utter surprise. "But my dear fellow! He couldn't possibly have failed to do otherwise!"

Tomlinson turned and walked out into the night. Nat handed the slimmer envelope back to the desk clerk. One of the guards licked his lips and stared hungrily after the old gentleman.

"Ah-ah-ah!" February said warningly. "No naughty thoughts, children."

He sighed. "Kinda cute, wasn't he?"

And to leave it there would have been fine. But Nat had a reputation as a wit and charming dinner companion.

By noon of the next day he was saying to a table of eight at Lidnik's, "This little old guy comes to me and what does he want but to bet his wad on a knockout by the kid in the first. Naturally I tried to talk him out of it. Candy from babies, yet. And so—"

JAKE was talking in a peculiar way. His teeth were wired together. His two managers, squat men with ugly expressions, stood by his bed.

"I tell yah," Jake mumbled, "I never seen the punch coming. Not at all. I know, I've been hit before, but then I seen it when it was too late to duck. This time I never even knew I was hit. I'm moving in and boom—I'm walking up the aisle with rubber knees."

"An investment we had in you," one of them said with disgust.

"Come on, Joe," the other said.

They walked out and left Jake Freedon staring hopelessly at the ceiling.

IN A GRIMY suite in a Forty-first Street hotel of a little less than third class, a tall young man glowered at Lew Karon. Taken as a whole, Sam Banth's face was well proportioned, almost handsome. But each individual feature was oversized, heavy. The big lips rested together with a hint of ruthlessness and brutality. Pale eyes protruded slightly, and they looked coldly incapable of any change of expression. His neck and sloped shoulders were ox-heavy. In contrast to the extreme cut of sharp-nosed little Lew Karon's clothes, Banth was dressed in quite good taste.

"Just tell me this, Lew," Sam said, "tell me why on a sixty to one shot you didn't cover it the other way."

"Take it easy, kid," Lew said loftily. "Take a look at the record. I hire you to help my collection department. You do good. You get a little stake. So I let you buy in. The piece you got of this business doesn't give you no right to tell me how to handle the bets, does it?"

"Just tell me why, Lew," Banth said. "That's all."

"Look, kid! Some sucker wants you to lay him fifty to one the Empire State Building falls down tomorrow at noon sharp. I ask you, do you cover a bet like that?"

"But it wasn't a sucker, Lew. It was Nat February. Couldn't you smell some kind of a fix?"

"After the investment they got in Freedon? And after the pounding everybody's been giving the kid? It doesn't figure, Sam."

"How do we stand? Can we stall February?"

"I'd rather bust J. Edgar Hoover in the nose. We pay off, in full. That'll drag the kitty down to about eleven thousand. You own a fifth of that."

"Twenty-two hundred," Banth said, disgustedly. "I put in ten thousand."

"These things happen," Lew said philosophically. "All the time they happen. Look, Sam. For your own good. You got an education. Why don't you go back to that steady job you had?"

"Maybe I'm restless."

"I'll give you your twenty-two hundred, Sam. You look like you don't like the way I handle things."

"I don't."

"Here. I'll count them out right here. Three fives and seven ones. Twenty-two hundred. Better luck next time."

Sam studied little Lew Karon for a moment. He knew what the play was. Lew wanted him to back down, refuse the money, continue the arrangement. He picked the money up, folded it casually, shoved it into his pocket.

"Get yourself a new boy, Lew. I can do better with this than you can. I thought you were shrewd."

"Walk out! See if I care! You'll be broke in a week."

Sam Banth realized that he had been restless lately. Progress with Lew Karon had been too slow. The hard ambition that drove him was satisfied at first. Working with Lew had been more interesting and more profitable than work in the brokerage house. But Lew had his limitations. Sam had no intention of halting his climb at the petty gambling level.

"You've taught me a lot, Lew." He moved toward the sharp-featured man.

"Stick around and you'll learn more, kid."

"You're pretty happy about that slim patrician nose of yours, eh, Lew?"

"Huh? Nose?"

"Here's for what you did to my first ten thousand bucks, Lew."

He yanked the man close, striking as he did so. He let go and backed away, smiling without humor. Lew fell to his knees, gasping with the pain. His eyes ran tears and blood came between his fingers as he held his hand flat against the smashed nose.

Sam Banth walked to the door. He ignored the half-screamed threats of Lew Karon. Out in the sunlight he squared his shoulders, smiled warmly at an attractive girl, hailed a cruising cab and gave the name of the restaurant where he was most likely to find February.

"I KNOW you," Nat said. "You're Lew's boy."

"Was. I heard talk about an old man who nicked you for that first-round knockout. I was wondering about him. What's his name?"

"Garfield Tomlinson, he said. He acted like it was the first bet he ever made in his life. He sure had the right dope."

"By the way, where can I find the kid?" Sam asked.

"Over in Jersey someplace. Find Bull Willman at Conover's Gym and he can tell you exact. You looking for a job? I got two horse players give one of my partners bad checks. Shake it out of 'em and you can have ten percent."

"Haven't you got your own people?"

"Sure, but Lew's been bragging so much about how you operate on collections I wanted to see you work."

"Later, maybe."

THE TAXI from the Elizabeth station pulled up in front of a frame house on a quiet street. "The kid did real good in there last night," the driver said.

"He's still got it," Sam said absently. He paid off the cab and walked up to the front porch. The house was jammed full of people, all in various stages of celebration. There was so much noise that Sam couldn't tell whether the bell worked or not. He opened the door and went in. A fat little man lurched against him in the hall, grabbed his shoulder and said, "Greatest li'l ol' battler ever was. Tipped me to bet on a knockout in the first. Spread twenny bucks around and got better'n five hunnert back."

"Sure, sure," said Sam, untangling himself.

Most of the noise seemed to be coming from the kitchen. A tall slatternly girl blundered through the open door, grabbed Sam and kissed him wetly. "Wasn't it wonnerful!" she sighed.

The kid was at the kitchen table, his gray knobbly face wearing a mild permanent grin. The table top was covered with bottles. His eyes were faraway.

"Everybody-have-'nother-drink," the kid said. His voice was high-pitched and he spoke so quickly that it was hard to follow him. "Gonna-be-champ-f'r-sure."

Sam moved through the press of bodies and made himself a drink. He sipped it and watched the kid narrowly. Somebody blundered against the table and a bottle at the kid's elbow tipped and fell. Without seeming to look the kid reached out and caught it an inch from the floor. Everybody applauded.

"Lookit that reaction time," somebody shouted.

Sam pursed his lips. He'd watched the kid work out more than once. The kid was at that stage of punchiness where it was almost painful to watch his slow response to any stimulus. He moved around the table and with what was apparently a dareless sweep of his arm sent another bottle plummeting. As before, the kid's hand flashed out and he plucked the bottle out of the air and replaced it on the table.

Sam left the house, walking slowly, his head bent. He swung onto a bus and sat looking, unseeing, out the smeared window. At three-thirty he turned the corner on Forty-second and went into the Public Library.

At last he found the references he wanted. His hand

began to tremble. Dr. Garfield A. Tomlinson—Pathologist. From the magazine index he located the *Journal of American Medicine* for February, 1946. *Relation Between Hormone Theories and Tissue Entropy in Geriatrics*. He read the article with great care. Much of it was meaningless to him, but he absorbed a few of the basic ideas.

It was no trick to find out that Dr. Tomlinson lived on R.F.D. 2 at Kingston, New York. His next step was to recontact Bull Willman.

"I was wondering where the kid trained for this last go, Bull."

Bull frowned and inspected the wet end of his cigar. "He's an old hand, not one of these kids you got to watch to see they get in shape. The kid always rounded himself out nice, usually right here at Conover's. But this time he said he was going to the country. He didn't say where. I tried once to get him through his wife but she said she didn't know where he went." Bull grinned suddenly. "Maybe I oughta send the whole stable to wherever he went, heh?"

"You've got yourself a property now, haven't you?"

Bull shrugged. "Maybe yes, maybe no. If I'm smart I'll sell the contract right now. For me it looks like the peak of the market. Freedon'll kill him next fight."

"How does a thousand dollars for one percent sound to you?"

"Like twice the market value. I got thirty percent of him. Who wants to buy?"

"I do." He took out his money. "Here's a hundred on account, the balance when the papers are ready for signature."

Bull shook his head sadly. "Everybody's crazy these days." He took the money.

CHAPTER TWO

Elixir of Death

TOMLINSON lived in a rambling farmhouse. The lawn was overgrown with weeds and the fences sagged.

Sam Banth paid the man who had brought him out from Kingston. He walked up the drive carrying a small suitcase. He climbed the sagging porch steps and used the door knocker. After a long wait, just as he was about to try again, the door was yanked open. Sam, in one searching glance before he smiled, took in the straight tallness of her, the wood-smoke eyes which had sooted the lashes heavily, the ripe tautness across the front of the blue work shirt, the lorelei curve of flank which blue jeans couldn't hide, the softness and petulance and discontent in the wide mouth. She was a big girl. A big restless unhappy girl with annoyance at him and the world showing plainly.

"Brushes?" she said. "Or chicken feed? Or maybe children's encyclopedias." Her voice was pleasantly deep, husky-harsh.

"None of those," he said. "Dreams. I sell dreams to visions who come to doors."

"Sell me one, brother. Mine haven't been too good lately."

"I've got a nice little item you might like. Acapulco, surf in the moonlight, dancing on the terrace, and a square-cut emerald the size of a walnut."

Her manner changed. "We're through playing now. What are you selling?"

"Are you Miss Tomlinson?"

"I was. Now I'm Mrs. Knight. But I'm not working at it."

"I came to see your father."

"Say hello to him for me. He's been in the barn ever since I can remember. You can go around the house." She started to slam the door. He put his foot in it.

"I don't like that little trick," she blazed. "Now what?"

"What do you want most in the world, Miss Tomlinson?"

"That's a stupid question. Money. Enough to smother me."

"What would you say if I told you that because I came here you're going to have exactly that?"

"I would say you've got nails in your head, friend."

He removed his foot. "You may now slam the door." She did. He walked around the house, grinning.

The barn was a solid structure and appeared to be in far better shape than the house. A door had been cut into the large original door. He knocked.

The door opened. "Well?" said Dr. Tomlinson. "What is it? You disturbed me at a bad time. Are you selling something?"

"No. Mind if I come in?"

"You can stand right there and state your business."

"You owe the federal government roughly fifty thousand dollars on the bet you collected last night, Dr. Tomlinson."

Tomlinson gave a jump of surprise. "Goodness! I never thought—I never realized that—Oh dear, now I'll have to do it all over again."

"What you did to Kid Goth?"

Tomlinson, in spite of his fussy and pedantic air, had a pair of keen blue eyes. He narrowed them. "Exactly what do you mean, young man?"

Sam Banth pushed by him and into the brightly lighted interior of the barn.

"Here! You can't come in."

Sam looked at the banked cages of experimental animals, at the tables of chemical apparatus, at the binocular microscope, at the shelves of texts and notebooks.

"Nice layout, Dr. Tomlinson."

"I shall complain to your superiors. You have no right to force your way in here."

Sam sighed, put his suitcase next to the microscope, pulled the chair away and turned it around. He sat down, crossed his legs, tapped a cigarette on his thumbnail and smiled gently up into the flushed face of Dr. Tomlinson.

"Independent research takes a lot of money."

"Of course it does. But I don't see how that—"

"Please, doctor. Let me hazard a series of guesses. Your funds are running low. You are at a critical and interesting stage in your experimentation. You have learned to apply new principles, apparently. The usual ways of getting funds are too slow. Maybe you're so far off the beaten path no institution will give you a grant. Maybe they would if you showed them what progress you've made, but you're not ready to do that yet. You contact Goth, manage in some way to give him a set of reflexes faster than any man ought to have, and then you bet all your funds and collect a small fortune. Then you were impractical enough to think you could come right back here, shut the door, and keep on with your work as if nothing had happened."

Tomlinson's shoulders sagged. He walked woodenly over to another chair and sat down listlessly. "I thought nobody would find out," he said in a dulled voice. "I was careful that nobody would see Goth. I trained him so that he wouldn't be—unusual."

"You forgot that he might go and get himself drunk."

Tomlinson looked up sharply. He compressed his lips. "I forgot to warn him about that!"

"You made a nice sum of money."

"I'll give you the tax, in cash. You figure it out for me, please."

For a moment Sam was tempted. But that would be like burning down the house to cook the dinner.

"I'm not a tax man."

"Then who are you?"

"Your new partner, doctor."

"There's no way you can force yourself on me, young man."

"My name is Banth. Samuel Banth. We will now consider my possible courses of action. I could arrange for a detailed medical examination of Goth. I could get so much newspaper coverage that you'd never have a moment's peace from now on. But I imagine that the way to make you unhappy the quickest would be to tell your daughter how much you made last night and how you made it."

WITH each stated alternative Tomlinson's gray head had sunk lower.

Sam laughed. "Come on, now. Cheer up."

"How can I?" Tomlinson said angrily. "You're intruding yourself on a most important work. I sense that you want to profit out of my—methods. My object, sir, is research, not profit."

"You're going about it in a funny way."

"Are you competent to judge that?"

"How much land have you got here?"

"Twenty acres. Why?"

"You've been puttering around with these mice for so long that your plans are mouse size. I want to help you, not hinder you. First, can you do for any athlete what you did for Goth?"

"Yes, but—"

"All right. Listen. We'll form two corporations. One will be called the Tomlinson Research Laboratories, Incorporated. That, for tax purposes, will be classed as a charitable educational institution. You will be the operating head of it. We'll build some dream labs for you and we'll staff them with bright young men from the best schools to handle details of research. You'll make as much progress that way in a week as you do now in six months. The other corporation will be called Champions, Incorporated. Half this property will become a training area. I'll hold fifty percent of the stock in it. You and your daughter will hold the other fifty. No, I'll hold forty-nine percent in both corporations. That gives you and your daughter control, you see."

"But I don't—"

"Simple. We contact a professional athlete. We guarantee, for the maximum percentage of his future gross that we can wangle, to make him the best in the world. We maintain a floating fund and bet heavily on him. If you can do for others what you did for Goth, we can make at the minimum ten million bucks."

"The—the whole idea makes me dizzy, Banth. I don't see how—"

"Let me handle all tax matters, business angles and so on. You just take care of the research angle. Our first job is to pay off Uncle Sam on what you made last night, incorporate, and put the rest of it into the new corporations. We'll set ourselves a minimal salary to begin with and boost it as the money begins to come in."

Tomlinson was silent for a long time. He studied his folded hands.

"I must know that nothing will interfere with my work. It is important."

"Maybe you could tell me in layman's terms what the work is, Dr. Tomlinson. Then I could appreciate its importance."

Eagerness crept into Tomlinson's tone. "I began this line of research six years ago. As a pathologist the phenomenon of age has always fascinated me. I had done research in geriatrics, the study of old people, the study of how to help them physically. Take glandular secretions for example. We know that the flow of secretions from many organs diminishes in both quantity and quality as time passes. Once a duplicate of the flow from a young and healthy gland is injected into the aged patient there is often an almost miraculous increase in vitality. The endocrinologists have done a lot in that field. But basically it is superficial, as it does not get at the root cause of the slow degeneration of the glands and tissues and organs. It is a stop-gap, the same way a salt-free diet is a stop-gap in treating—say—congestive heart failure. The books talk about the ravages of time, yet a single cell, according to all growth and regeneration theories, should be almost eternal. Say that there is a time stream. Must all of us be carried immutably along that stream? Do you know what entropy is?"

Banth shrugged. "The standard example. The gas in a

divided container, and then remove the division and though each molecule moves independently, they will never regain, even for a fraction of a second, their original positions all at once on each side of the non-existent division.

"In its broader sense it refers to the continual, supposedly unalterable progress from order to disorder. Thus we can call it an attribute of time, as we know it. Or a by-product of time. Thus my thinking began to be along the line of attempting to slow up that entropic progress in living tissue. I had no success. When you come up against a blank wall it is often good theory to try the exact opposite direction. Could entropy be speeded? I attacked that problem by an attempt to stimulate every gland and organ in a living organism to the same exact degree. I was clumsy at first. The interrelations are delicate. My laboratory animals died. Finally there was one experiment where there was quite a deviation from the control group. After the injection, what I term the master injection, the life span of the animals, which had the same hereditary and environmental factors, was decreased by one tenth. I performed the same experiment many times, keeping a frequency distribution on the life spans. The next step was pure accident. I was working with cats and by accident a tom from the injected group got into the control group cages. He killed two of the control group with apparent ease. I then began to test reaction time. Do you begin to see?"

Banth rubbed his heavy jaw with his fingertips. "Maybe I see. By increasing the rate of entropy, or by stimulating the organism or whatever you want to call it, you've shortened the life span, but telescoped all normal reactions into the reduced time period."

"Exactly. Take the case of Goth. I selected him rather carefully. A boxer on the down-grade without any other skill or talent by which he could make a living. Inevitably a charity or institution case before long. I speeded him up at first in the ratio of a one tenth decrease in life span. The effect was to make him live sixty-six seconds in every sixty, thus speeding his reaction time by one tenth of a second. I rigged up a reaction time test and found that he was a shade below the norm. Thus the first tenth didn't seem enough. I made it a fifth giving him two tenths of a second advantage. That brought him considerably above the norm and even above extreme cases that have been reported. The most amazing thing to me was the new impression of mental alertness that he gave after treatment, even though I knew that the myriad pinpoint concussions he had suffered had made him—ah—"

"Punchy."

"Yes, that's the word."

"Suppose he was going to live eighty years before old age got him, doctor."

"Now he'll live to be seventy, and show, at seventy, an apparent age of eighty. Goth seemed to feel that it was a very good trade. He had not intended to die of old age anyway. He merely uses up six months of his life every five months."

"How about his habits?"

"Habits? Oh, I see what you mean. He'll get six hours' sleep in five hours. There'll be physiological phenomena—accelerated heartbeat, respiration and so on. And, unless there is a training period, the change will be too noticeable to intimates. I had to keep Goth here and coach him in how to walk, talk, eat and so on. I had to continually urge him to slow down, to make each gesture with a conscious slowness."

"Doc, are we in business?"

"You can honestly do what you said for my research program?"

"Yes. You need more funds and more help."

"Well—then it's a bargain. Come in the house. I believe there is a bottle of fair sherry about somewhere."

They went into the kitchen. The girl turned from the sink. Tomlinson said, "Ah, there you are, Linda. My dear, this is Mr. Banth. He is my new—uh—partner."

"Him?" she said. "Sticking needles in mice?"

"Mr. Banth has ideas which are somewhat more expansive."

"I should imagine," Linda said dryly. She straightened

up, drying her hands on the thighs of the jeans. She stared at Sam for a long, long second. "Keep a close watch on the gold in your teeth, Pop," she said, still staring full into Sam's eyes.

"He seems quite—straightforward, Linda," Tomlinson said. "You know, he might resent such a—"

Linda smiled and nodded. "You win, Pop. He is straightforward. Like the way a snake strikes. Welcome to our happy rustic little group, Mr. Banth."

"You'd better call me Sam, Linda."

"Straightforward Sam, the Confidence Man."

"Do you young people dislike each other on sight?" Tomlinson complained.

Sam finally forced her to drop her eyes. "Not at all, doctor. We just talk like this because we each recognize a kindred spirit."

"That I could resent." Linda said.

"The truth is ever bitter."

CHAPTER THREE

School for Champions

SAM watched the kid in centerfield. He had the expert's knack of starting at the crack of the bat. His name was Wally Christopher. It was the lower half of the eighth. The last man up slammed a hard one over the second baseman's head. Christopher came in fast, took it expertly on the bounce, came around with a greased throwing motion to second, nailing the runner to first. He trudged back out to his position.

It had taken six weeks to locate this boy and Sam Banth liked what he saw. He went over the statistics. Age nineteen, five foot eleven, a hundred and sixty-five pounds. Errors for the season, none. Batting average 166.

Christopher was up in the top of the ninth. He went

down swinging after a ball, two foul tips and a called strike. He walked disconsolate from the batter's box. Banth grinned. He'd been pulling for a hitless day for the kid, to yank the average down a little further.

This was bush-league ball, and even with Christopher's outfield talent, he was slowly but very certainly slipping out of baseball because of that powderpuff batting average.

He left before the inning was over, confident that his note would bring Christopher to the hotel room in this small Pennsylvania city.

"Come right up and knock," he had said in the note.

A few minutes after six there was a hesitant knock on the door. "Come on in," Banth called.

Christopher came in. He was heavy-jointed with good hands and wrists, a reddened complexion, clear eyes and a diffident manner. "You Mr. Banth?"

"Sit down, Christopher. This is just a friendly little chat."

The boy seemed despondent. "Sure."

"You didn't look so sharp out there today."

"I knew that without coming up here, mister. Nothing for four. I've had other news. They're letting me go the end of the week."

Banth felt an inner excitement. This was better than he'd hoped. He sat down facing the boy. "What do you want to do with your life?"

"Play baseball. Ever since I was six years old that's all I ever wanted to do. Fat chance I've got now."

"This is the end of the road. Once they let you out here, you're all done."

Christopher squinted at him. "You trying to make me feel good?"

"How long do you expect to live?"

"Now that's a damn-fool question."

"Okay. We'll try another one. Suppose you played baseball and maintained the best batting average in the country. How long would you last in the game?"

"Hell, up into my forties I suppose. Some do."

"When they let you go, what are you going to do?"

"I don't know. Go back home. Get a job. Bread truck or something."

"Here's my card. I'm the president of a concern called Champions, Incorporated. It's a very hush-hush organization. We run a training course."

"I can't afford anything like that."

"It won't cost you a dime. All you have to do is sign a contract stating that you will pay us fifty percent of all your future earnings in baseball."

"Fifty percent of nothing is nothing."

"We'll take that chance, provide free transportation, give you your training course and give you a chance to show your stuff to a good club after you're trained."

"What's the catch?"

"We think you've got what it takes. But there is one thing. Our training course is very, very strenuous. It won't cut short your active playing career, Christopher, but it may shorten your life a little. We want that understood."

The boy frowned. "But you'll take a chance on me just when I'm getting the can?"

"Yes."

"If you want to be soft in the head, Mr. Banth, I guess I can be crazy too."

"Have you got to finish out the week?"

"I think they'd rather I wouldn't."

"Then clear with them, pack up and meet me in the lobby tomorrow morning at nine o'clock. Here's fifty. Put that against your expenses. There's plenty more coming."

WITH Christopher beside him Banth slowed the powerful convertible for Kingston traffic, then opened it up again. He came around the last bend.

"There's the layout," he said.

The twenty acres had been enclosed with hurricane fence topped by barbed wire and electrified wire. Two trucks loaded with building materials were just turning in at the gate. The gate guard, uniformed in slate blue, saw Banth approaching and yelled to the truckers to move along. A new white stone building stood a hundred yards back of the barn. Two foundations for other buildings were taking shape. Amidst the bustle of activity the sagging farmhouse looked forlorn, forgotten.

Sam pulled up beside it, gave a blast on the horn and said, "End of the line, Christopher."

The boy got out. He looked puzzled. "That sign says Tomlinson Research Foundation."

"Don't worry about it. We've got the right place."

As they reached the foot of the porch steps Linda came out the door. She smiled warmly. "Welcome home, Sam." She wore a soft gray dress that matched her eyes. Her black hair had been done in the latest fashion and her fingernails were long and the color of blood.

"Miss Tomlinson, this is Wally Christopher."

"Nice to meet you, Wally."

"Same here."

"Bring your bag along and I'll show you your room. I'm sorry the new dormitory isn't ready yet. That will be another month."

Sam was waiting at the foot of the stairs when Linda came back down. She paused two stairs from the bottom. He reached up, took her by the waist with his big hands and lifted her lightly down. "Miss me?"

"Mmmm. Hard to tell."

"Was I right in calling you Miss Tomlinson?"

"It came through yesterday. Restoration of maiden name and all."

"Like the looks of our boy Christopher?"

"Poor little lost sheep."

"Poor little lost gold mine. Inside a year he'll be trying to find a lawyer smart enough to find a hole in that contract. But there won't be any. He signed in the city before we came out. Next year they'll be paying him at least sixty thousand. Thirty thousand for us, darling."

"Fifty percent!" Her eyes widened. "You weasel, you!"

"I better go out and pay my respects to the esteemed Doctor Tomlinson. How did that fuddy get a kid like you?"

"Throwback. My great, great, great, great grandfather was a pirate."

"I'll tell him about the Christopher boy. I want this one fixed up fast so he can start bringing in the dough. Expenses are high."

She held him close. "And they're going to be higher, man."

"Acapulco?"

"And the emerald too. I'm holding you to that." She was warm against him. "I missed you, you thief," she whispered. "Oh, how I've missed you!"

"This much?"

"Even more than that, Sam. More than that. You've got cold eyes, Sam. Pale eyes. What goes on behind them?"

"Ideas."

"With me in them?"

"With you in them. I think it's you. A big girl. Black hair, soot on her eyelashes. Eyes the color of campfire smoke."

"Where there's smoke—"

WALLY CHRISTOPHER sat on the edge of the bed. The tall dark girl had explained the schedule. Pretty girl. Wise looking. Made him uncomfortable somehow, as if she was laughing at him inside herself. Lots of girls like that in the world. Get in the big time and all you got to do is whistle. The big time!

She said to come down and eat at six. He looked at his watch. She hadn't said anything about wandering around for a while. It was close to five. He went downstairs and out without seeing anyone. A swarm of men were working on the new buildings. He watched them for a while, wondering what time they'd quit, and then he saw them rigging floodlights so the masons could work at night.

From a distance he saw Mr. Banth coming out of the white stone building beyond the barn. Mr. Banth had his arm around the shoulders of an older man, a small man with gray hair that was nearly white. Mr. Banth was talking excitedly. Quite a guy, that Sam Banth. Convincing.

Banth waved to him casually so Wally guessed that it

was all right to wander around the place. Diagonally off to the left beyond the white stone building he saw a tennis court. A girl and a fellow were talking over the net. The fellow turned and walked away toward the rear of the white stone building. Wally ambled toward the tennis court. She came walking rapidly toward him, slim brown legs twinkling. She wore white shorts and a halter. She was a striking tan, particularly in contrast to her carrot-red hair.

She stopped and stared at Wally. He saw that her small, pert-featured face was older than he had realized. The weather wrinkles were deep at the corners of her eyes, and the lines were stark from snub nostrils to the corners of her mouth.

"You play tennis?" she asked in a remarkably high-pitched voice. She spoke very rapidly.

"Play at it," he said grinning. The grin faded. "Say!" he said. "I've seen you someplace. Wait a minute. Allison? No. Anson. That's it. Barbara Anson."

"Give the boy a cookie," she said.

"I thought you quit tennis a long time ago."

Her voice became slower and dropped in pitch. "I didn't quit on purpose, son. My legs gave out." They walked side by side. She kept getting a few steps ahead and then slowing down.

He gave her a bashful smile. "Gave out? They look good from here."

"Listen to him! What's your name? How old are you? What's your sport?"

"Wally Christopher. Nineteen. Baseball."

"Nineteen, eh? Then I am just barely old enough to be your mother."

"Don't kid me, Miss Anson."

She gave him an odd smile. "What's your trouble in baseball?"

"Can't hit. Do you think they'll be able to straighten me out?"

"You don't know how it's done?"

"Nobody's told me a thing yet."

"I'll let them tell you, Wally. Don't worry about it.

Don't worry about a thing. Every little kid in the country will know your name inside of two years."

AT NINE o'clock in the morning Miss Tomlinson sent Wally to the white stone building. The old man he had seen Banth talking to was there. And some young men in white coats with high collars.

He was told to strip and then they had him climb onto a table and lie down. There was a long and uncomfortable period of tubes and needles and a thing wrapped around his arm. Then they had him breathing into a tube while a pen drew lines on a piece of graph paper wrapped around a cylinder, behind glass. They took all sorts of samples. They used words to each other that were strange. Wally had heard a few of them but he couldn't remember what they meant. They put gunk on his temples, stuck metal things into the gunk and another pen drew a different sort of line. After he came back from lunch they waited thirty minutes and then pumped the lunch out of his stomach. It made him sick for a little while and then he was famished again. Another gadget, once it was fastened onto him, made a pen line that had a peak for every time his heart beat.

"Come back here at three in the afternoon the day after tomorrow," Dr. Tomlinson said. "Your time is your own until then."

During the two days he played tennis with Barbara. She was amazing; she seemed to know where the ball was going to go the instant he hit it. Banth had gone away again. The buildings were roofed, both of the new ones, and interior work had begun. The dark girl, Miss Tomlinson, wandered around looking glum. There was a lake ten miles away. He drove Barbara's car and they went swimming. Later he kissed her and she pretended to think it was funny and called him a silly kid, but he guessed from the way her eyes looked that she enjoyed it all right. She didn't kick the second time or from then on.

He went back at the time Tomlinson had said and they gave him two capsules with a glass of water. The room swung slowly back and forth and darkened and was gone.

When he woke up it was night. He was back in his room. He was very sleepy. He tried to think and remember, but his head hurt. He went back to sleep.

In the morning he got dressed and went downstairs. It was the same as any other morning except that he managed to break the laces in both shoes and that annoyed him. Miss Tomlinson was the only one in the dining room.

"Come and sit with me, Wally," she said. Her voice was deep and slow.

"Have you got a cold?" he asked.

"That's what Barbara Anson asked the first morning. No, I'm just as I've always been, Wally."

"You're different. You act sleepy and slow."

"Look at the clock, Wally. Look at the pendulum."

"It's running down, isn't it? About to stop?"

"No. It's just the same. You're different, Wally. The world is the same. You're speeded up. Do you know how you've changed?"

"What is this?"

"Your voice is so high that you sound almost like a girl, Wally. Every move you make is too fast. You look and act like a man with a bad case of jitters."

"What's happened to me? What is this?"

"Everything in the world will look as though it has slowed down, Wally. So will that baseball floating down toward the batter's box."

Slowly he began to understand. "They—Dr. Tomlinson, he speeded me up?"

"That's right. Now don't look so upset. It will work out just the way you want it. But now your real work starts. You must learn to walk and talk and smile all over again. You must learn how to eat and how to drive a car. Then you'll have to learn how to play baseball. You must start all over again and learn timing from the ground up. You can start right now. Keep saying to yourself every moment, 'Slowly, slowly.' See, you're stirring your coffee right over the sides of the cup. Now move at the same speed I do. That's right. Slow your hand down as you raise the cup. When you speak to me pretend you're imitating a slow deep western drawl. Pitch your voice as low as you can. Only fair, Wally. Try again."

IT WAS a difficult ten days. They made him stay away from Barbara. Those who had been treated had to associate with people who had normal timing. That way it came faster. At the end of ten days his slips were very infrequent. His habits changed. Each night, at ten, he was exhausted and his body yearned for sleep. Yet by six in the morning he was slept out. He was ravenous an hour before lunch, an hour before dinner. And slowly he learned always to walk as though he were wasting an idle hour in a park, move his hands like a sleepwalker.

One of the young men took movies of him standing, sitting, talking, walking. He found that his head movements were too rapid, too jerky, and he had to learn that when he heard a sound behind him he must give himself a slow count as he turned around.

Banth came back with two glum young recruits. Wally found out later that one of them was a discouraged pro basketball player, the other a pro hockey player who had slowed down to the point where none of the top teams would have anything to do with him.

That night, at dinner, Sam Banth said, "Wally, you've done well. Tomorrow morning you and I have an appointment at Yankee Stadium. I want to get some bids for you. I've wangled three top managers into being there. I guess curiosity is bringing them around. Paul Paris will pitch to you."

"Paris! Mr. Banth, he's the hottest arm in the game right now! He's hanging up new records. How about that no-hitter out in Cleveland?" Even in his excitement he managed to keep his voice pitched low and say the words slowly.

"I don't think he'll worry you any. I'm paying him five hundred to pitch ten times. That's fifty a pitch. If I was worried, Wally, I wouldn't pay out that much."

"Yes, but—"

"Now you've got some memorizing to do. He'll throw ten pitches. I want the first one lined out of the park. I want a clean miss on the second one. I want the next two hit deep. Another miss, another homer, two more strikes and then another one out of the park. That's nine. Then see if you can bang the last one for a long foul."

"Mr. Banth, nobody can call their shots that way when—"

"Now tell me what you're going to do on each pitch."

"It doesn't work that way. He won't throw the whole ten right across the sack."

"His control is good. If he throws a wild one, it won't count. But if they're a little bit outside, go after them."

IT WAS a misty morning. Wally felt the sweat running down his sides. He wore spikes, but Mr. Banth hadn't wanted him to put on a uniform. There was a fill-in catcher. Lean Paul Paris, with a smirk on his face, was warming up. Banth stood over at the side laughing and joking with the three managers. One of them had remembered seeing a scout's report on Wally and had wanted to leave right away, but Sam Banth had talked him out of it.

The vast empty stadium was filled with a hard silence. When Banth laughed an echo came back from centerfield. The ball thwacked against the mitts. Wally sweated and swung the bat a few times.

Banth said quietly, "Okay, Wally." Wally walked to the box, tapped the dirt out of his spikes. The catcher pulled the mask down over his face and said, "Now I seen everything."

Paris went into a windup that looked very slow to Wally. His long arm slanted down and the ball came down the groove. It was a fine, fat pitch. Wally tightened and swung. Usually the ball disappeared completely when it was within six feet of the bag. But this time he watched it the whole way and he saw the bat swinging to meet it. He saw that the swing was too fast and too soon and a shade high. He pulled the swing a little and moved the bat down a trifle. There was a fine deep-throated crack and the ball soared away. Paris turned and put his hands on his hips and watched it. It went into the left-field stands, fair by inches.

"Lucky," the catcher grunted. Paris put a new ball into play. It was another fat pitch. The temptation was too strong. The bat stung his hands. Paris ducked after the ball was already beyond him. Wally glanced guiltily over at Banth. Sam was scowling at him. He looked back in time to see the ball hit the center-field wall hard enough to rebound half way back to second base.

He made himself miss the third one. It was an outside pitch, but he swung anyway. Banth looked relieved. Paris was wild on the next one. Wally slammed the next into deep right center, then swung and missed, put the next into the right-field stands, racked up two strikes, dropped the next into the left-field stands and banged the last one high and foul into the right-field stands. Paul Paris looked seriously shaken. He tore his glove off and glared toward Wally.

"Brother," the catcher said with deep sincerity, "some of those were the best hit balls I seen in a long time."

Wally moved over toward the three managers and Banth. Banth told him to go take the spikes off. When he came back out only one of the managers was left. He had a smug look and a happy gleam in his eyes. He slapped Wally on the shoulder. "Welcome aboard, son."

CHAPTER FOUR

Empire of the Damned

THE meeting was held in a room so new that it still smelled of damp plaster. Dr. Tomlinson walked briskly in, pushing the door open. Linda looked quickly over her shoulder and pushed herself away from Sam Banth. Her eyes had a heavy-lidded look. Her lips were parted and her face and throat were flushed. It troubled Tomlinson to see her like that. Banth gave him an impudent grin.

"Prader'll be along any minute, doc," Sam said. Prader was the combination lawyer and accountant hired by Sam when the two corporations were being formed.

The three of them sat at the board table. Linda kept her smoky eyes on Sam Banth. Dr. Tomlinson sorted his papers.

Prader came in with a short mincing stride, his briefcase under his arm. He apologized profusely for the delay. He found his chair, unbuckled the briefcase and took out a minute book. He was a giant of a man down to the waist, but his legs were absurdly short. Once he sat down he had a commanding presence, emphasized by a jutting jaw and black, unwinking eyes. Afoot he merely looked absurd.

"Let's take Dr. Tomlinson's pet first," Sam said. "The meeting of the Board of the Tomlinson Research Foundation, Incorporated, will please come to order. We better take the financial report first, doctor."

Tomlinson found the proper page. "Ah, yes. The donation this month from Champions, Incorporated, was thirty-seven thousand, five hundred. Twenty-six hundred and ten went for salaries and wages. Twenty-four thousand was applied against the building. Eighteen thousand, three hundred of new equipment was ordered. The total comes to forty-four thousand nine hundred and ten. There was thirteen hundred and three on hand from the previous month. Thus the deficit to date is six thousand one hundred and seven, plus, of course, the additional fourteen thousand outstanding on the lab. I've given the figures to the nearest dollar for simplicity's sake."

Sam said harshly, "The purpose of the large donation was to build up a cash reserve. Instead you spent every dime of it and more too. I don't know as I care for that. What's that eighteen thousand three hundred for equipment?"

"Let's take things in order, Mr. Banth," Prader said smoothly. "I see you have the progress sheets on your phase of construction, Dr. Tomlinson. If you'll pass them over I'll enter the pertinent data in the minute book. I—ah—believe that we can dispense with the reading of the minutes of the previous meeting. Any new business?"

Tomlinson interrupted. "Yes. We're on the track of a new method of excitation. Rather than go into detail I'll merely say that rather than the concocting of the precise stimulants for the secretion pattern of the individual, it is based on placing the individual at the focal point of a vibrating magnetic field. Nerve tissue so stimulated has shown an almost incredible impulse speed. Our barrier in the injection method was a speed-up of fifty percent. So far we cannot determine the barrier in the new method."

"I don't see any particular excuse for any new method," Banth said.

Tomlinson gave him a surprised look. "But this is a research group! There is always a reason for research, Banth."

Sam looked down at his big fists for a moment. He looked up quickly. "I would like the privilege, as a large stockholder, to countersign all checks issued by the Tomlinson Research Foundation, and approve all orders for materials."

"I was told I would have a free hand."

"To milk Champions, Inc., of every dime, eh?" Banth said. "Not so fast, doc. Not quite so fast. Maybe it was agreed, but it can be put to a vote." He looked meaningfully at Linda. "So let's vote on it, doc. My forty-nine percent votes that one Sam Banth be dealt into your financial picture."

"And my forty-one percent," said Tomlinson "is, of course, against such a change in our picture. Really, you disappoint me, Banth."

Both men looked at Linda. She had turned a bit pale. She looked quickly at Sam and then, more shyly, at her father. "Some compromise, maybe," she said weakly.

"Vote, baby," Sam said.

She gave him a look of anger. "Don't try to tell me what to do! I'll vote with my father. Against you."

Sam's eyes narrowed dangerously. Then he grinned.

"Good girl. I like a good loyal girl. You win, doc. But let's have a gentleman's agreement. Let's turn over the same amount this month and you see if you can hang onto some of it."

"That will suit me," Tomlinson said quietly.

"That should wind up the foundation," Prader said. "Now, Mr. Banth. How did your enterprise function? Financial report first, of course."

"Our cut of the wages of all eleven employed graduates came to seventy-eight hundred. That end is chicken feed so far. Eventually it'll be the big end of the stick. Income from wagers amounted to one hundred nine thousand, three hundred and five."

Prader whistled involuntarily. Tomlinson's eyebrows went up.

"Now think it out for a minute," Banth said. "This month was the end of the gravy train on wagers. The boys are on guard now. I'm going to have to bet through dummies. The bets will have to be smaller. At the beginning of the month there was eight thousand two hundred in the kitty, after turning over the thirty-seven five to the foundation. That, plus income, equals one hundred twenty-five thousand, three hundred and five. Another thirty-seven five to the foundation leaves eighty-seven, eight oh five. Expenses were fourteen two. Reserve for taxes twenty, leaving fifty-three, six oh five. I suggest a twenty buck dividend on each of the thousand outstanding shares. It will take us down to thirty-three, six oh five, enough to cover operating expenses for the coming month. Eighty-two hundred bucks for the doctor, ninety-eight hundred for me and two thousand for Linda. Shall we vote? Hands up? Done.

"Now for the progress report. As I said before we have eleven 'graduates.' There are twelve in training and we ought to have four of those out bringing in income by the end of the month and an additional six or seven lined up. The twelve consist of three boxers in three different weight divisions, a professional magician whose hand wasn't quicker than the eye, a pro miler—his income will be peanuts but the side bets might be all right on a four-minute mile, one golfer whose trouble was not enough distance on the drives, a baseball pitcher who had lost his fast stuff, a team of three circus acrobats, and two pro footballers who were about through.

"Every one of them and also our 'graduates' understand that if they do any talking we can flood their particular specialty with graduates and put them right back where they started. We've kept the press from finding out anything. Sooner or later they'll suspect and track it down, of course. Then we'll have to throw up some smoke screens. As to future plans, I want to go down to Mexico and grab a couple of bullfighters. Headliners in that trade make thousands for an afternoon's work and reflexes are pretty important. Collections and accounting may be a problem, but I think we can handle it all right. I have—some experience in making collections."

Prader organized the minutes into proper form. The dividend checks were drawn up and distributed. Salaries were given an upward boost.

The meeting broke up and Tomlinson went back to his research in the labs.

SAM AND LINDA walked slowly down toward the farmhouse. She held the folded check in her hand.

"You're the girl who wanted to be smothered with money," he said, giving her a crooked smile.

"Two thousand isn't going to smother me, Sam."

"There's a lot more in the picture."

"How do you mean that?"

"Take those two payments to the foundation. They total seventy-five thousand. Ten percent of that is seventy-five hundred, plus what you've got in your hand would make your take for two months total ninety-five hundred."

She stopped. He turned and faced her. "What are you trying to tell me, Sam? What are you trying to get across? The whole agreement was made because you showed dad how it would help his work. If you cut off all funds—"

"Let's not get sentimental, Linda honey."

"I'm being practical. He treats the people you bring

here. If he didn't get the agreed money, he might stop treatments, and then where would you be?"

Sam scuffed the ground with his toe. "Have you taken a look at the kids he hired? Have you seen that one named Howard Dineen? Have you seen him looking at you?"

She flushed. "I guess I have."

"He's a big dumb-looking towhead and his red ears stick out but the doc says he's the keenest one in the group. And if *you* told Dineen to jump up in the air and land on his head, he'd knock himself out."

"Sam, darling, you're—frightening me."

He shrugged. "I don't know why. I was just showing you that if we're smart and if your old man should decide to walk out on the deal, Dineen could be made to go along with us. You'd just have to smile at him every Tuesday. That's all."

"Why would dad walk out?"

"If you should vote with me a few times, honey, he might get sore. But that would be a shame because he'd walk out with forty-one percent of the stock and forty-one percent of the profits. You'd inherit, I suppose. Eventually."

"Don't talk like that!" she whispered. "Don't!"

He gave an elaborate shrug. "Now why act like that? I didn't say a word. I was just thinking that if you ever did inherit we could keep Dineen working for peanuts. You'd take fifty-one percent each month of the total. Our target is one hundred 'graduates.' After we get to that point, we won't treat any more of them. Some will make a lot, some won't make much. They will average a gross of twelve thousand a year. And we'll average forty percent of that. Call it an even half million a year. And little Linda would be getting a quarter million a year, all her very own before Uncle Sugar's cut. I'm just thinking out loud. Would that smother you?"

She laughed nervously. "It might bring on shortness of breath."

"He's an old guy. What is he? Close to seventy?"

"Don't, Sam. Don't!"

"You act like I might be trying to talk you into something, kid."

"Sam! Are you?"

He shut the kitchen door behind them, swung her around and backed her against the closed door. His mouth was an inch from hers. He said softly, "How do I know whether I'm talking you into anything? Can you be talked into anything?"

"I'm frightened, Sam. Scared green. Hear my heart. It's pounding."

He took a small box out of his pocket, opened it with his thumbnail. The stone was a living and perfect green. "Remember that dream I tried to sell you? Will you buy it?"

"Oh, Sam!"

"There was more to the dream. I got to go line up a couple of bullfighters. Acapulco is maybe an hour and a half, two hours, by air from Mexico City."

"But I couldn't leave with you," she whispered.

"Go visit a girl friend. A girl friend in Seattle, or New Orleans. You got two thousand. Take yourself a vacation."

She bit her lip. "I might do that."

"If you want to write me or anything, I'll be at a hotel called the Del Prado in Mexico City. I'll get there next Tuesday."

"I'll send you a special delivery."

"You do that."

HOWARD DINEEN crouched and looked moodily in at the cage of white mice. One would stop for a moment and he could see it. Then it would completely disappear and reappear on the opposite side of the cage. He knew that this group had been speeded to a point where the eye could not follow their normal movements. Dr. Tomlinson had fretted about the possible structural damage that would be self-inflicted by the mice through their mere velocity of movement, but it was beginning to appear that the new vibration-born acceleration also caused a compensation in the structural qualities of bone and tissue so that the expected damage did not result.

Dineen was moody about the changes which this past seven months had made in him. Before coming here there had been nothing but the work, the intense, almost feverish devotion to the work of research. And now another factor had intruded. Linda Tomlinson. Even as he stared into the cage he seemed to see her walking toward him.

He had tried all manner of things to chase her out of his mind. He lay at night picturing her in the embrace of that crude Banth person, and instead of making it better, it made it worse so that he heard himself groan aloud. He had walked the nearby roads and fields until he was exhausted, and still he dreamed of Linda. He had forced himself into an intrigue with one of the new lab girls who had recently reported, but it had been awkward and tawdry and utterly disappointing.

She had been gone for ten days now. And so had Banth. He tortured himself with conjectures about whether they were together. Dr. Tomlinson had said that Linda was visiting a school friend. Dr. Tomlinson did not seem to be worried.

Howard Dineen knew that it was hindering his work, his powers of concentration. He made mistakes in timing and in recording and found it necessary to repeat an awkward number of experiments. He told himself a thousand times that she was a tramp, Banth's girl, a divorced woman. Nothing worked.

"Hello, Howard," her voice said, close behind him. He thought how odd it was that his imagination could consistently give him such convincing impressions of her.

"Didn't you hear me?" Linda asked.

He spun around awkwardly, rapping his elbow smartly against the side of the cage. He rubbed it and said vacuously, "You're back!"

She wore a dark suit, so severely tailored that it accented rather than concealed the intense femaleness of her. Her dark hair had been cropped fashionably short. Her eyes puzzled him. They had lost a certain awareness while she had been away. They had an almost glazed look, as though she were an automaton set in motion by a superior force for a specific purpose.

"Yes, I'm back, Howard. How has the work been going?"

"The work? Oh, fine. Great. How was your trip, Miss Tomlinson?"

"Do you have to be so formal? My name is Linda. It was a nice trip."

"I'm glad—Linda." He flushed, knowing that the way he had said her name, the way he had mouthed it so gently had told her too much.

"I'm glad to see you again, Howard. Dad is always so engrossed, and Mr. Banth is so busy. It seems like you're the only real friend I have here."

The suspicions of Sam Banth melted like snow in a furnace. He grinned. "I want to be your friend, Linda. Your—good friend."

"I don't see any reason why you can't be, Sam. Dad says you're ever so clever."

He flushed again. "He overrates me, Linda."

"I don't want you to think I'm too bold."

"I won't."

"I have a new car and I'm timid about driving it into New York at night. I wondered if tonight you and I could —I mean it would be nice to—"

"I'd love it, Linda!"

"At seven, then. No, make it six, so the evening will be long."

"At six, then," he said reverently. She left. Howard turned back to the cage and spoke tender words to the uncomprehending mice who flitted back and forth like rays of soft white light.

SAM arrived the next day, in the afternoon. He sought out Linda. He spoke a few words to her and later she came to his room. He shut the door.

"How did the kid react?"

"How did you expect?" she said bitterly. "He's nice, Sam. Too nice for what we're doing to him."

He held her shoulders. "Come on, now! Don't go soft on me. We've got to keep the kid in line and know he's going to stay in line before we do—the other thing."

"You're cold, Sam. You're cold and hard and cruel."

His hands tightened on her shoulders and his mouth curled. "Duckling, I was protecting your sensibilities. I used nice words. I could have said before we kill your father. I was being delicate."

Her eyes half closed. She swayed. "Sam, maybe I—can't—"

"I made you a promise in Acapulco, duckling. I told you that you'd follow through—all the way—or you'd never see me again. It still stands that way."

"Please, Sam."

"Don't forget we're married, duckling. We're gay newlyweds. Remember? I'm your staunch and loyal husband. Between us we'll own a hundred percent of this business. You said you wanted that."

"All right, Sam. All right," she said wearily. "I'll be all right—afterward."

"You better be. Now get out of here."

CHAPTER FIVE

The Iron Maiden

IT was a most unfortunate accident. Lieutenant Klatsa of the state police, who handled the investigation, saw how it had happened. The daughter—a nice item, that one, even with her tear-puffed eyes—told how Tomlinson had left the dinner table saying that he wanted to take a look at progress on the small addition to the main lab building. It was dusk, a fool time of day for an old duffer like that to be out climbing ladders.

The ladder had been tilted up against the cinderblock wall, with the legs in soft sand. It was clear how the ladder had shifted and slid. It came down with the old boy and he would have survived the fall had it not been for the cinderblock. The edge of it caught him at the temple.

The man named Banth was pretty upset about the whole thing. An odd setup: the old man working with rabbits and cats and rats right on the same property where this Banth operated a health camp or something.

He made his report and the body was taken to a Kingston funeral home and buried two days later in a local cemetery, at a service attended by the weeping daughter, a grim-faced Sam Banth and the entire staff.

AFTER dark, as Howard was heading back to the dormitory, he passed Linda's car in the drive. He did not notice her sitting in it. "Howard!" she called. He turned back and she said, "Get in, Howard. Sit beside me for a little while." He sensed the tears behind her words.

She began to sob softly as he got in. She leaned against his shoulder. A scalding tear fell on the back of his hand, and her helplessness turned his heart over and over.

"There, there," he said. He held her in his arms. He wished she would keep crying forever so that he could hold her.

At last she was under control. She sat up and moved away from him.

"What is it? Anything I can do, Linda?"

"I don't think so, Howard. There was a board meeting today. That horrible Mr. Prader and Mr. Banth and me. I thought things were going so well. I thought dad had left me a little money. But it doesn't look that way."

"What do you mean?"

"Mr. Prader says that we're over-extended. We expanded too fast. Notes have to be met. The only thing to do, they say, is disband the staff and close the labs."

"They can't do that!" Howard said hotly.

"But we can't afford to keep them up. No one man could handle the treatments, you know. I guess it's all over."

"But that's silly! I could handle them by myself. The big staff was for research."

"You could do it by yourself. Would you do that for me? I think we could keep on paying you the same amount."

"They should have had me in that meeting. What do they know about what Dr. Tomlinson was doing? In another three days I'll have the new equipment set up so that an idiot child could operate it. Dr. Tomlinson and I were working on making the outfit both portable and equipped with fool-proof controls. I don't know why he wanted it that way, but now maybe I understand."

"Oh, Howard! If you'll only stay there's a chance that the gamble will pay off. After all dad did, it seems a shame to give it all up."

"I thought Banth was making a good thing out of all this. I thought those athletes were bringing in a good return. I don't approve of what you people were using Tomlinson's discoveries for, but I thought that it was at least profitable. To me it has always seemed like monkeying with people's life spans, which could be a second cousin to murder. What's the matter? Did I say something wrong?"

"No. Go on."

"You keep giving athletes miraculous reaction times and they automatically become tops in each sport. It destroys the basic idea of competition. When the world knows, and some day it will, they'll either outlaw the 'graduates' of this place, or competitive sport will be dead."

"But in the meantime it's profitable, Howard. But not profitable enough. The return hasn't been big enough to cover the investment."

"That surprises me. It doesn't seem logical the way Banth tosses the coin around. But I guess that's none of my business. I'd do anything in the world to help you. Fire the rest of the research staff and I'll stay on and run the new gismo once I get it hooked up. If you have to cut down even further, I could show you how to operate it in twenty minutes."

Her arms slipped around his neck and her lips were insistent. It was not the sort of tender kiss that he had expected. In some obscure way it disappointed him.

"Thank you, darling," she whispered.

SAM BANTH walked into the smallest lab building, the only one that was not closed when the rest of the staff departed. Howard looked up and nodded distantly.

"That the works?" Banth asked, pointing at the apparatus. It was a framework sarcophagus, an iron maiden formed of metal tubes, hinged to open and admit the patient. Affixed to the tubing at what appeared to be random points were cup-sized discs. The back of each disc was an exposed maze of wiring and tiny tubes.

"That's it," Dineen said absently.

"How does it work?"

"We don't know. Dr. Tomlinson abandoned his previous line of conjecture a few weeks before he died. If it was pure stimulation, the body structure could not withstand the increased speed. We were working on the theory that in some unknown way it put the individual out of phase with normal time. In other words it creates for each individual an entire universe of accelerated time in which he is the sole example."

"I don't mean *why* does it work, Dineen," Banth said. "I mean how do you make it work?"

"Here's the control box. You can see that the wiring passes through it before leading to the discs. Note that there are two dials, calibrated, on the slanted side of the box. You translate the subject's weight into kilograms and set the left-hand dial carefully. There's a mass problem involved. The right-hand dial works much the same way as a rheostat control. You can see that it is calibrated with a diminishing interval between markings. Those markings are in percentages. The dial must be turned slowly. It is geometric. The first centimeter gives you a ten percent acceleration, the next centimeter twenty. Then forty, eighty, one sixty, three twenty and so on. It goes so high because we used it on lab animals. For humans this little stop should be slid over so that there is no chance of the acceleration going beyond twenty percent. Anything beyond that and the individual cannot be trained to simulate normalcy."

"Have you turned the dial over all the way on an animal?"

"Once. It was a bit—terrifying. We filled a cage with ample food for the lifetime of a mouse. The mouse disappeared for the smallest fraction of a second and then reappeared, quite dead on the bottom of the cage. Most of the food and the water was gone. We were able to tell that it had died of old age. There was a distinct malformation of the nostrils and lungs that had not been there before, showing that in the first part of its accelerated life span it had trouble sucking the air into its lungs with sufficient speed to maintain life. You see, it had to overcome the inertia of the air."

"Almost anybody could operate the thing the way it's set up, eh?"

Howard smiled. "If you're thinking of firing me, I'd advise against it. I'm committing a criminal act using this process on human beings, even with their consent. You don't know yet what the potential after-effects may be. I'm trying to find out. If you block me, I'll go directly to the authorities. You see, I'm the only person with the exception of Dr. Tomlinson among the research staff who knew what you've been doing here."

Banth pursed his lips. "That's pretty big talk. Feeling tough, eh?"

"No sir. Just practical. My salary is small. I think you'll see that it's best to keep me around. I'll even be frank with you. If it weren't for Miss Tomlinson I would have quit six months ago when I first found out what was really happening here."

Banth looked back at the apparatus for a long moment. It looked absurdly like some skeletal robot.

"Keep working, Dineen," he said. "Any after-effects you can isolate will be helpful. I'll send two more boys around this afternoon. They're young enough so that ten percent ought to do it."

WALLY CHRISTOPHER caught the signal and shifted left. He adjusted his sun glasses. He saw the pitch go down and the lusty swing. The ball was an unslanting streak. He gauged it and moved over, careful not to move too fast. It came down, ridiculously slow. He moved toward it, as slowly as he dared, then dived, gloved hand outstretched. The ball smacked into the pocket and stuck. He rolled over and over, hearing the full-throated roar of the crowd. In days gone by it would have given him a lift. Now it was just too easy. He jogged in toward the dugout and he realized with something close to fear that baseball just wasn't very much fun any more. . . .

The girl across the net from Barbara Anson was playing with taut despair. They were into the second set after Barbara's 6-1 win in the first. It was four games to one, Barbara's favor and she had this game at deuce. Barbara's serve. She softened the serve and let the opponent return it. She forced herself to place her own return within easy reach of the younger woman's powerful forehand. Barbara made herself lose the return, smacking it into the net. She walked back to serve. It would have looked silly to win without giving up a single point in any game. Yet she knew she could do it. She had always loved the tense competition of the game. Now it was like playing with children, humoring them along, encouraging them. She wondered if she should give up the game—for good. The old thrill was gone. . . .

The seventeenth had always bothered him. Four hundred and sixty-five yards, par four. Before, it had been a case of getting the second wood close enough so that the approach could be played up to one-putt the green for a possible par. The only chance of a birdie was to sink the approach. Now he was alone on the hole in the graying dusk. He teed the ball, took a limbering swing and then addressed it. He swung with every ounce of effort and speed at his command, breaking his wrists at the right point for that final snap. Club-head against ball made the deepest, heaviest crack he had ever heard on a golf course. The ball went out and it looked slow to him, *but it rose, floating, fading. When at last he walked up to it he saw that he was not more than thirty yards from the edge of the green. He looked at it for a long time and then picked the ball up and trudged back in the direction of the clubhouse. . . .*

And all over the country, sports figures, doing at last, with ease, the things of which they had so long dreamed, became discontented. Now the ability was there, and yet it had been gained too easily, with too little effort. It was suspect, as are all gifts. Records were broken. The sportswriters talked about "the new crop of immortals" and when they talked among each other they marveled at the comebacks that had been made. They speculated. They did not guess the answer. There were new champions. Bored champions. Wealthy, yawning champions. Restless and lonely. They were the new strangers in a strange land. There was no need to train, to practice. The only goal was to refrain from winning too flagrantly. There was no competition for them. And thus all the games became work.

SAM BANTH spent less and less time on the property and more time in the city. Linda's devotion bored him. He would not have said that he was in any way a moralist, and yet he was oddly troubled that Linda was so unaffected by the death of her father. She had planned it with him and had correctly given her testimony which made it all the more obvious that it had been an accident.

Sam felt no special guilt at having committed the crime with his own hands. It had been absurdly easy, once the plan had been made. And Tomlinson, at best, had very few years left to him. It was not like killing a young person—hardly, to Sam, like killing a person at all.

Yet there was something almost obscene about the placid and untroubled way that Linda treated it, as though it were an unfortunate incident.

When she was unattainable she had been an excitement to him. Now she cloyed and sated and smothered him.

Two factors entered into his planning. The apparatus was portable and could just as well be set up in New

York. Without Linda the entire take would be his. He woke up often in the middle of the night thinking about those two factors. The puzzling additional factor was Howard Dineen. How would Dineen react if he and Linda made their marriage public? Linda wanted it made public. Sam had demurred with the reason that to do so would alienate Dineen. But now Linda knew how to run the apparatus. In fact, she had treated two "students" with almost no supervision from Dineen. She was growing more insistent in her demands.

From a practical point of view it would be wise to publicize their relationship before Linda met with an "accident." Then the marriage license, reposing in his safe-deposit box, would not be in the least suspect. It would be accepted as a legitimate document, which it was.

But to alienate Dineen might mean his running to the newspapers with the full account. It might cut the throat of the golden goose. "Graduates" might be barred from competition.

He worried the problem around in his mind for several weeks. The golden flow of money from the "graduates" increased. Instead of sating his needs it merely seemed to increase his itch to gather in all of it, not forty-nine percent.

And at last he had his plan, and it pleased him. It depended on how trusting Linda was. He covered his motive by a confusing monologue on tax structure.

"If you say so, dear," Linda said. There was no suspicion in her now. She signed over her own stock and that which she had inherited from her father for the consideration of one dollar. The forms were duly notarized and recorded. Prader wore a wise look. Sam made a private vow to unload Prader and take on a new accountant-attorney.

The next day he went to a cheap rooming house and paid in advance for a room. That night, at dinner, he said to Howard and Linda, "I've got a pretty special customer who doesn't want to be seen coming out here. It's a profitable deal. Maybe we could take the thing into town. You said you could make it run on a house circuit."

"It will take a few hours' work."

"Could you do that tonight? Then we can take it in in the morning."

"Okay with me." Dineen said.

Linda said just what Sam had hoped and expected. "Oh, can I come along?"

"If you want to, Linda. Sure." He smiled at her. Inside he was laughing.

THE furnished room was on East Ninety-third. It was dismal, with rug, walls, one overstuffed chair in varying shades of dirty brown. The two windows looked out onto an airshaft. No sun ever reached it. The low-wattage bulbs had to be kept on at all times.

"Charming setup," Linda said.

Sam carried the iron maiden over by the table. He unwrapped the blankets from around it. Howard busied himself with the connections. Sam sat on the bed and smoked until at last Howard sighed and backed away. "All set."

"When will this Important Person be along?" Linda asked.

"Any minute now."

He put his hand in his pocket and, as he stepped close to Howard Dineen, he pulled out a worn leather sap. Back in hungrier days he had taken it away from a recalcitrant bookie customer. He planted the lead weight delicately behind Howard Dineen's ear. Dineen sagged and fell.

Linda stood, her mouth open, her eyes wide. Horror and realization replaced surprise as Sam swung at her. The lead struck the corner of her jaw. He caught her as she fell.

It was awkward getting her inside the tubular iron maiden. He shut the hinged front of it and she slumped down inside it until her knees struck the front and she remained partially propped up. He pulled the control box toward him, set it at an approximation of her weight and twisted the other dial. As he did so he leaned against the front of the case to keep her from bursting it open. She began to move around inside so rapidly that she was blurred. He could not focus on her. If Dineen had not been lying it should take only a few moments before she became still, dead of thirst. At times he could see her and he guessed that she slept. When he was certain she was dead he would haul her out and put Dineen in there. It would be a mystery the police would never solve. Two people dead of thirst after a dozen witnesses had seen them alive earlier the same day. . . .

He was totally unprepared for Dineen's heavy step behind him, for the smashing blow against his jaw that drove him down into blackness. . . .

CHAPTER SIX

The Endless Twilight

HE stirred and shook his head. He was looking out through the tubing at Howard Dineen. Dineen stood like a man carved of stone, thumb and forefinger on the right-hand dial. Tears seemed to be frozen on his face.

In panic Sam Banth pushed against the front of the iron maiden. He could barely lift his arm. It was as though he were imbedded in sticky oil. His arm seemed to take interminable seconds to reach the tubing. He pushed hard and nothing happened. He leaned his whole weight against it. He could look down and see that it wasn't latched, that the hinges seemed free. He pushed mightily, panting with the effort. It was enormously difficult to breathe. The air felt like a solid substance. Yet when he tried to breathe the hardest, the air seemed to scorch his lips and nostrils.

He pushed again and saw a tiny gap. No matter how hard he thrust he could not hasten the speed of its opening. Howard stood there, completely motionless. No man could stand like that for so long. Sam wondered if he were dead. There was no question about Linda's being dead. He could see her on the floor. Her body was shrunken and cracked, swollen lips protruded. Her eyes were sunk back into her head.

Time after time he was forced to stop and rest. He had no idea how many hours passed before the door was opened wide enough for him to squirm through. The room was changeless and eternal. He tried to move toward the door, but it was a prolonged struggle to take each step. He tried harder and saw that both pants legs had split completely down the front. It was then that he realized the constriction of his clothes.

When he pulled at his clothes the material came apart, with agonizing slowness, in his hands. Hunger and thirst began to torture him. He knew that he had been in that room for the passing of an entire day and a night. He began to grow weak. The shoes were the last. And finally he stood naked; he could move once more. He went to the door with quick steps and found that he couldn't turn the knob. He gave a fearful look at Howard Dineen. During the past hours the position of his head had changed a bit. Sam went into the small bathroom. The window was open. He eeled through, knowing that public nakedness was preferable to the sure and certain charge of murder should he be captured in the room. He dropped twelve feet to the alley level, falling with a lightness that surprised him, as though something had cushioned his drop through the air.

He trotted cautiously down the alley with a half-made plan to grab someone and strip him of clothing. He came out and peered cautiously at the street. At that moment he realized, for the first time, the complete and utter soundlessness of the city. Pedestrians' feet were frozen in mid-stride. All traffic was halted. An absurd pigeon hung motionless in the air. Across the street a woman had tripped, She was falling forward, her hands outstretched, a startled look on her face. Sam looked at her narrowly. He could detect no movement.

The fear of pursuit, of being captured and convicted of murder, faded and died in the face of this newer, greater fear. His sensations, except for the breathing difficulty and an odd heat against his body when he moved quickly, seemed normal to him. Yet the world had changed in some grotesque way. Howard Dineen had turned the dial. . . .

Sam Banth was not an emotional man. He forced himself to stand very still despite thirst and hunger and weakness. He would have to weigh his own situation from the point of view of the outside normal world. If he could detect no movement then undoubtedly his own movements would be too fast to be detected by the naked eye.

He puzzled over the problem of the clothes. Evidently it had been inertia. He was capable of moving at a vastly greater speed than the clothes could be moved. Thus they would split and, while clinging, hinder every movement. And that explained why he could not force the door of the iron maiden open except with an agonizing slowness.

He looked back at the falling woman. He narrowed his eyes. Her angle of inclination seemed subtly different. The city was soundless, a vast tomb. The thing was to find something he could measure, some way he could find out just how far he had been speeded up, just how far he was out of phase. A falling woman seemed an inadequate yardstick. He stepped onto the sidewalk. No eye turned toward him. He realized how fortunate he was that it happened to be a warm day. A man was poised a few feet away, frozen in the process of taking a step. Sam walked up to him and hit him in the stomach with all his strength. It was like hitting marble. The painful shock ran up his arm. The inertia of the flesh prevented it from giving under the force of the blow. Yet Sam knew how terrible that blow had been. He went behind the man, bent and wedged his finger between the angle of shoe sole and sidewalk. In several long minutes he sensed that the pressure was increasing. Yes, the man was being driven backward by the force of the blow. It seemed likely that he would eventually end up a dozen feet from the point where he had been struck. Sam went around and looked into the man's open eyes. There was a subtle change in the expression. He knew that the man was dead where he stood.

Suddenly Sam Banth had a wild sense of power. He turned and touched the bare arm of a girl. It was warm, yet marble-hard. He kissed her lips. They were like sun-warmed stone. He laughed wildly in the silent city and his voice soared shrill in the stone canyon and was gone.

He remembered his hunger. And with it came caution. If hours passed for him at the rate of seconds for the rest of the world, then it would be wise not to be trapped in any closed place. He trotted down the sidewalk to Park Avenue and turned south. In the second block he found a cafeteria with the door wedged open because of the heat of the day. Two men were emerging, fixed in stasis, one grinning back over his shoulder at the other. Just inside a fat woman was reaching for the punch slip. Sam ducked under her extended arm. Thirst was the most pressing need. A girl was filling a water glass from the fountain. The stream of water looked like ice. A few drops that had spattered were perfect spheres hanging in the air.

There were long moments of panic until he found a way that he could drink. It had to be done in precisely one way, and no other. He had to turn so that he was looking straight up and then force his cheek against the still column of water. By exerting a long steady pressure he could move his head through the column. Then, with the end of the broken column directly above his mouth he pushed upward, thrusting the column down to the back of his throat. He bit a length off and it was like biting through a stick of rubbery taffy. He swallowed, gagging at its solidity, but feeling it change in his throat to the fluid he needed so badly. He went to four other fountains and did the same. It seemed to him that an hour passed before his thirst was partially satisfied.

Eating was a simpler problem. At first the method gave him a moment of nausea. There were at least a hundred persons eating. The process was to find forks that were raised halfway to lips. He could fold his mouth over the food and taking what seemed to be a full three minutes in each case, pull it away from the fork. It came reluctantly as though it were frozen to the fork and his action melted it slowly. He found that attempting to chew the food was too prolonged a process, and thus he was forced to find those morsels that he could swallow whole.

It seemed to take hours. When he left he saw that the man who had been smiling over his shoulder had turned his head a full inch. The fat woman had pulled the slip almost free of the machine.

He was enormously weary, his body starved for sleep. Weariness drugged him so that he staggered as he walked. He found an alley, a small dim corner near a barred window. He curled up like a dog and went to sleep.

SAM BANTH awakened with a great start. He jumped to his feet, knowing at once where he was, remembering what had happened. He was hungry. He went furtively to the alley mouth and saw the sunlit street still in its frozen state. He trotted back to the cafeteria.

He stopped suddenly and sobbed aloud. The two men were still emerging. The man in front had turned his head so that he faced straight ahead and he had taken one more step. The fat woman was another step closer to the pile of trays and the slip was free of the machine.

Panting to suck the solid air into his lungs, he walked rapidly back to the street he had first seen. The pigeon had moved a full thirty feet and, feet outstretched, it was frozen in the act of landing on the pavement. The man he had struck had taken two steps backwards. His eyes bulged and his mouth was open and he had lifted his arms.

Sam walked back to the cafeteria. The streams of water that he had bitten off had replaced themselves and the same persons stood filling the water glasses. The forks he had emptied seemed not to have moved and he realized that they had been carried up to the lips and were now on the return journey to the plates.

He spent long hours satisfying thirst and hunger, and then he was face to face with the problem of finding some measuring stick to compare his time with outside time. He walked all the way down to Fortieth Street, seeking some method he could use. No motion was perceptible to his naked eye. He leaned in at the window of a cab and saw that according to the speedometer it was traveling at twenty-four miles an hour. He figured out that, in outside time, it would go thirty-five feet a second. He found that the left rear wheel was resting directly on a small crack in the asphalt. For a moment he thought he had a method of computation and then he realized that he had no certain way of keeping track of his own time. He could go only by "sleep times." He memorized the license plate of the cab.

After he slept again, this time in the back seat of the empty cab after worming his way in at the open window, he climbed out and paced off the distance that had been traveled. He estimated it at thirty feet. He looked at the speedometer again. The cab was traveling twenty-eight miles an hour now. The variables had defeated him.

But after he ate another idea came to him. He found a penny arcade on Seventh. A young boy had a .22 rifle at his shoulder, the trigger depressed. Sam climbed over the counter and searched down the line of fire until he found the tiny slug, suspended in midair. He knew from the loads on the counter that the boy was firing a .22 short. The slug was a dozen feet from the muzzle and he estimated that it was traveling at a thousand feet per second according to outside time.

The most precious thing about it was that he could see the slug move. He could touch it very lightly with his finger and feel it move. He lined it up with an object on the side wall, shut his eyes and counted off a minute— "one thousand one, one thousand two, one thousand three, one thousand four. . . ." He opened his eyes. The little lead pellet had moved what appeared to be a good two feet. He measured it more carefully. Less than two feet. He rechecked, using longer intervals. For a little time it ceased to be such an intensely personal matter and became an abstract problem.

He said, aloud, with satisfaction, "Close enough. One

second outside time equals ten hours subjective time."
He carried it further. "Let me see. Five of my minutes
equal one hundred twentieth of a second for Them.
Conversely, thirty-six hundred seconds in an hour, eighty-
six thousand, four hundred seconds in a twenty-four hour
day, multiplied by ten to give the number of subjective
hours—divided by twenty-four is thirty-six thousand days,
or—"

He fell to his knees as the full import struck him. He
beat his thighs with his fists. He shouted at the deathly
stillness of the city and at the frozen people. He ran
through the streets then, cursing them and the motionless
sun and the unseeing, unknowing faces.

THOSE were the early years. The sunlit years, the
years when his beard grew full and tangled and his belly
was gaunt and his legs knotted and stringy from trotting
through the city.

As he grew more adept at eating it took up less of his
time, and he estimated that he cut it down to half his
waking hours. He learned craft. If he saw someone in
the act of pushing a door open, a heavy door, he knew
that before the door swung shut again he could spend
long hours inside the building. It became a dangerous
game.

Once he barely slid through in time and he was afraid,
because if ten objective seconds passed before the door
was opened again, it would be one hundred hours for
him. Thus he learned caution.

He got a childlike pleasure from the department stores.

He roamed all over the city. In the city were many
women. He saw the fresh young faces, the skirts sculp-
tured and frozen by the breeze, the legs striding. He
found them in the dressing rooms of the department
stores, on the rubbing tables, in the beauty salons, and
their flesh was to him like the stone of a garden bench
in the sun. He found one girl warm-eyed, smiling into the
face of her beloved, and he returned to that girl many
times to put his face in the line of her vision and imagine

that she smiled at him rather than at the stone man behind him. But he tired of that.

Several years later, it seemed, he found himself in a neighborhood that looked vaguely familiar. A shattered man lay on the sidewalk, crumpled in death and the blood around him was like a dark red mirror. It took a long time to remember. He seemed to remember having struck that man a long time ago, and yet he did not know why. People stood around the fallen man, with horror fixed on their faces.

Once he heard a deep sustained sound. It took four "sleep times" before he found it. It was a subway train. A woman had fallen on the tracks in front of it. Frozen sparks fanned out from the steel wheels and from those wheels that the sound came. He listened to it with pleasure for a long time. He went back many days until the sound died away.

He discovered that if he went to enough bars he could find hard brown streams of liquor that could be bitten off. On those days he went singing through the streets, smiling and nodding at the thousands of statues.

For many years he slept in one of the department stores, one that had a door blocked open. The bed he found was like stone but he discovered that after what seemed like an hour or two of sleep he sank into it, into a hollow that made sleep more comfortable. Once, when he was very tired, he slept in that bed for a very long time.

He awakened and sat up to see a woman who had been looking toward the bed when he had climbed in. Her expression had changed to one of incredulous surprise. He knew that if he had slept for ten subjective hours, she would have had a whole second to see him there. It would look to her as though he had appeared by magic. This pleased him. He ate and returned to the bed. He lay very still and watched her. Over the long hours her face slowly turned brick red. Then he tired of the game.

But it gave rise to other experiments. He found a fire escape and climbed it one day to find a woman sunbathing on the flat roof. He lay beside her and went to sleep, directly within her line of vision. When he awakened, her mouth was wide in a scream he could not hear. He did not know how many days passed before he thought of her again. He went up and found her, eyes bulging, towels left behind, frozen in the act of running toward the small penthouse.

The dark years came. The sun faded slowly over a period of many sleeps and he saw the cloud that crept across it. It was during those years that he ceased his wandering. He went only as far as was necessary to find food that could be obtained without the danger of being trapped. He slept, when he was weary, on a pile of rags in a protected corner of an alley. He talked a great deal to himself. He measured the time of sleep by the people who walked by the alley mouth. One step, a step and a half, sometimes two steps.

The world slowly darkened. Each time he awoke more lights would be on. For weeks they came on, for months.

He was constantly cold and yet he had discovered that many of the doors, once open, were closing, and he dared not sleep inside.

Once he awoke in the darkness and he remembered that he had dreamed. He had dreamed of a girl and people who moved as he moved, and a shining network of tubes and a place a long way off. He had to go to that place. He was feeble and he walked slowly. But he knew he would reach it. . . .

THE DISTRICT man was Lieutenant Mareno. He folded his hands on top of the desk with exaggerated patience. "Dineen," he said, "if it takes a year, you're going to give me a story I can get through my thick head. Now try it again."

Howard said angrily, "You could understand it if you'd just concede one point, lieutenant. I smashed the apparatus because I hated it, because it had killed Linda. Or rather Sam Banth killed her. But when the thing was working it made time go very quickly for the person inside it. Sam Banth was using it to decrease the reaction time of athletes, professional athletes. You've heard of Wally Christopher, I imagine."

"Who hasn't? Four eighty-three batting average."

"He couldn't hit until we treated him. We used a different method on him but it amounts to the same thing. Banth collects fifty percent of his gross. You grab him and he'll help prove what I'm trying to say. Now try to understand. From something Linda said I think Banth got her to sign over her stock in Champions, Incorporated, to him. He took us to that room to kill us by putting us in that apparatus and making time go very quickly for us. When we were dead he was going to leave with the apparatus, I'm sure. The police would find two people dead of thirst and starvation."

"I want to know how."

"Look, lieutenant. What if you were locked in this office for ten days?"

"I'd die, naturally."

"Then suppose I could fix you so that while you were living ten days, the rest of the world was living two or three minutes. It would only take you two or three minutes to die, wouldn't it?"

Mareno scratched his gray head. "I don't quite figure it."

"Then, dammit, how come Miss Tomlinson is dead of what your own medical examiner calls dehydration? And how come we both can prove she was in perfect health at nine o'clock this morning, twelve hours ago? Answer it some other way, lieutenant. I wouldn't be wearing this bandage if I hadn't been slugged by Banth, would I?"

"Look, Dineen. My job is to turn enough over to the prosecuting attorney so he can make a case. What the hell!"

"Banth killed her."

"Look. Could you rig up some kind of gadget and come into court, provided we catch Banth, and prove maybe with an animal how it works? The S.P.C.A. will crucify us, but I don't see any other way."

"I could do that."

"Okay. Now what happened to Banth? What did he do after you slugged him and took Miss Tomlinson's body out of that machinery?"

Howard looked away for a moment. He said easily, "I hit Banth and he fell. I took Miss Tomlinson's body out. I was examining her and then I found that she was dead. I looked around the room and I saw that Banth had escaped from me."

"I don't see where the hell he went," Mareno said. "He's an easy guy to spot. We'll pick him up sooner or later. What a hell of a day this has been for the department!"

"How so?"

"A guy is killed thirty feet from the place where the Tomlinson girl was killed. Nobody knows what killed him. Something hit him and broke him almost into two pieces. The whole town goes crazy all at once. We get calls that a cafeteria is serving disappearing food. Can you tie that?"

Howard Dineen wore an odd expression. "It sounds strange."

"And that ain't half of it, brother. Hysterical women phoning in about seeing ghosts in the daytime. They call in from all over the city and always it's the same ghost, an old nekkid guy with a bushy beard that appears suddenly and then disappears just as they yell. We combed a department store for him where three people seen him. No dice. Two bars or maybe it was three phone in that somebody is stealing liquor. Sergeant Rausch, a friend of mine, covers one case. The bartender shows him. He pours liquor into a shot glass. He pours out half the bottle before he can fill the glass. Rausch is quitting the force. Then we got maybe fifty, sixty cases of people banged up, nobody knowing what hits 'em. Busted arms, shoulders, legs, heads, backs. Two dead already and maybe two more going to be. A hell of a day. The witnesses say these people were walking along and all of a sudden they take a big dive onto the sidewalk or out onto the street."

The phone rang. Mareno picked it up. He listened, replied in monosyllables and then hung up. He wiped one big hand slowly down his face.

"I quit," he said weakly. "I resign."

"What now?"

"They got a call to go back to that same address. Where you were. There is an old naked guy there with a white bushy beard and hair halfway to his waist. He was on the steps and nobody knows how he got there. The ambulance boys say he died of old age and pneumonia. It isn't the ghost those women saw because they said the naked guy had a dark beard. I was sworn in by Valentine and he never told me there'd be days like this."

Howard stood up. "Would it be all right if I left now?"

"It will suit me fine. Don't plan on moving away or joining the army, though." Mareno looked up suddenly. "Say, would you know anything about that old guy—no, that's a silly question. We'll be in touch with you. When we locate Banth you'll have some work to do for us."

Howard Dineen walked out into the night city. The cool breeze that had come with the fading day chilled the perspiration on his forehead and upper lip. Around him was the sound of traffic, fragments of sentences, subterranean roar of the trains.

Above him the timeless stars moved in infinite orbits.

John D. MacDonald wrote quite a few stories for
the sports pulps in the late forties and early fifties, so
it should not come as a surprise to find a science
fiction story of his built around a "sport."
This story's excellence and terrific feel for small
town life was immediately recognized, and it was
reprinted in **Human?**, one of Judith Merril's
earliest and best anthologies.

THE BIG CONTEST

Worlds Beyond
December, 1950

THERE was a blueness in the sharp-edged shadow
cast by the Fire House, a blueness that hinted of dusk.
There had been a piece in the *Cardon Gazette* about the
man over in Chamber County who claimed to have seen
a flying saucer. Through the heat of the long Saturday
afternoon the front of the Fire House had been the focal
point for the saucer discussion. Men came and went all
afternoon and the talk at times grew as hot as the sun
against the pavement and storefronts across the way.

Hobe Traik had been in the same faded blue kitchen chair all afternoon, tipped back against the weathered wood, his belly resting comfortably against his beer-keg thighs, his store teeth clamped into the deep grooves of the pipe stem, a mist of sweat gleaming on his bald head. He had taken no part in the discussion, which was so unusual as to be remarked upon many times that Saturday. But each time Hobe merely smiled with enigmatic amusement.

Now the group was down to five, if you don't count the small boy. There are always small boys around fire houses. This one had a brown face, pale blue eyes, taffy hair and a pair of jeans so big for him the cuffs were rolled up. The five were Hobe Traik, Stu Ganser—the only other old timer in the group, a grizzled, indestructable man much given to belching—young Harry Darian from the bank, prissy Arthur LeBlanc trying hard, as usual, to be one of the boys, and Brad Sedwell, the cattle buyer.

Brad and Harry were hunkered down against the wall. Hobe Traik, Stu Ganser and Arthur LeBlanc were tipped back in the three kitchen chairs from the card room and bunk room over the Fire House.

Harry's argument with Brad Sedwell about the saucers being mass hypnosis had petered out as arguments will when dusk begins to spread layers of stillness over the town.

Hobe took his pipe out of his mouth and spat toward the road. It was a very respectable effort, carrying across the sidewalk and curb out onto the pavement. He cleared his throat. "Now I've heard a lot of fool talk today about these here saucers. Might be I'm a little tired of it. Me, I've been a-waitin' on them for just about forty years. Ever since Woolmutt left town. You remember Woolmutt, Stu?"

"Can't say as I do," Stu Ganser said, applying the usual terminal belch.

"That spitter."

"Oh! *That* Woolmutt."

"You're a damned old fool, Stu Ganser. There was only

the one Woolmutt in this town, ever. You're gettin' so darn old, that head of yours . . . . "

"What's a spitter got to do with saucers?" Arthur LeBlanc demanded in that voice of his, just a little bit lispy.

"Now you just settle back there," Hobe said, "and listen to it the way I want to tell it. It was 1911, the year we built this here Fire House so we wouldn't have to keep the pumper over in Hooly's barn. Good thing we got it built when we did. The next week that barn burned to the ground. I was a sprout then. Full of sass. Seems like every minute I wasn't courtin' them Loomis sisters, I was right here at the Fire House. Both of 'em finally said no to me. Mary Alice married Clarence French from over Bellville way. Had nine kids afore Clarence fell the hell off that silo, but that's neither here nor there.

"That was the year we had the spittin'. Crown Street wasn't paved then, of course, and in a dry spell it was just plain dust. Yella dust. Choke you to death when somebody stirred it up. Now I don't rightly remember just who it was started it. You could say we all started it one hot day when there wasn't a breath of wind. Somebody just up and spit and in that dust you could see where they hit and just how much roll they got. So somebody else, he spits a little further. First thing you know we got us a line drawed and rules made and we're takin' turns.

"You take a town like this in the summer forty years ago, there wasn't so much for people to do. Surprisin' how spittin' contests caught on that year. I've always been a right fair spitter myself, but there was a couple boys I just couldn't beat. Fred Tunnison was one. Fred got killed in the first war. Luke Amery was the other one. Luke later went over to Youngstown and got in the banking business. Built a big house and sired four kids off that junior leaguer he married and then jumped the hell out of his office window in 1930.

"Well, Fred would win one contest and the next one Luke would win. The way we had it all set up, each contestant got three spits. Took turns to give each man time to work up something to spit in between. Why, we had boys coming over from Lake Valley and far away as Dunstan to try against Fred and Luke. Sort of swept the county you might say.

"It must have been after the spittin' had been going on for a month that this Woolmutt fella started comin' around to watch. One of those fellas, he was, you don't even think once about. You don't see him come and you don't notice him leave. Little chunky fella with washed-out eyes, sort of a stupid look and a big mouth. He was workin' as hired man over to old Cable Fisher's place on the east side of Perry Woods.

"Now you know how these contests go. Some of the boys Luke and Fred out-spit went back and practiced up and the first thing you know we get ourselves a big Fourth of July contest all lined up. I kind of took charge of it, me havin' no urge to do any spittin' against Luke and Fred. Those boys could stand right at the near edge of that walk right there and let one go that would carry out as far as that white line down the middle of the road. Everybody that wanted to get in the contest had to put twenty-five cents in the hat for every time they tried a string of three spits. We roped off the street to keep traffic off it, and I made up some blocks of wood painted bright colors so we could set 'em out to mark the best spits.

"In those days Marty Loofer's Saloon was right around the corner on Chestnut and it being so handy to bring the buckets of beer around, we figured that nobody'd get too dry to spit, anyway. Well, the start-off time was two o'clock and I collected six dollars and a quarter in the hat. You got to remember, you young fellows, that six dollars was a good week's pay in this town in 1911. Those boys had something to spit for.

"Just as we were gettin' started, this Woolmutt fella comes up to me, shy like, and drops a quarter in the hat. I knew he'd been watching a lot, but I knew, too, how tight old Cable Fisher was with money, so I tried to talk Woolmutt out of entering. No sir, he wouldn't have a chance, I told him. He had a funny accent and he didn't talk much, but he sure was stubborn. So I kept his quarter and told him that because he was the last one to enter, he could spit last.

"With so much at stake, everybody was taking their time, believe me. Old Fred, he strutted up to the line and got himself balanced nice on the balls of his feet, his mouth working. There wasn't a breath of wind. Sure was a hot day. When he was all ready and everybody quieted down, Fred sort of hunched back and then shot his head up and out like a blacksnake hitting a horsefly. He got a good explosion and a nice arc on that first spit. It was one of the best he ever did. A big cheer went up, because Fred was a pretty popular fella around this town in those days. He swaggered back from the line trying to look meek, but you could see he was pretty proud of that effort. The next few boys did pretty well, as far as spittin's concerned, but the best of them was a good four foot eight inches back of the red block set out to mark where Fred hit. Then Luke came up. His style was a little different, but just as good as Fred's, I'd say. Luke made himself just as high on his toes as he could get, and he stuck his head up just as far as he could get it, balanced there and let fly. You should have heard the yell when he got a good inch beyond Fred's effort. Fred turned red and then white. You could see him setting his jaw for the next effort.

"One fella from out of town got within six inches of Fred, but the rest of them were almost pitiful. Woolmutt was the last one up to toe the mark. All those people standing around seemed to scare him. I was off to the side because it was part of my job to see that nobody fouled by stepping across the line. So from there I could see how Woolmutt worked himself up to it.

"First thing I see, he sticks his tongue out. Now I tell you, boys, that was the biggest tongue I ever did see on anybody. He sticks it straight out, flat like, and then he curls it up from the sides to make a sort of tube. That tube is a good four inches out beyond the end of his stubby little nose. I see him take a breath. Big chest on the little fella.

"He goes Whih-THOO! And something goes bang across the street. Now afterward there were some claimed they could see that line of flight, right from the tip of his tongue over to the hole in the plate glass in the front of Winkelhaur's Merchandise Mart. Wilbur Winkelhaur is a spectator, and when he sees what happens to his front window, he lets out a scream of mortal agony. Then the yell of the crowd drowns out Wilbur. Fred and Luke, they look badly shaken. Little Woolmutt is sort of dazed by all the commotion.

"Fred and Luke, they try to get me to rule Woolmutt out of the competition. First they say he isn't spittin' at all and that he's got a friend hid somewhere with a gun. Then Woolmutt has to prove that he is spitting. He does so. Next Fred and Luke say that the little fella has some sort of a thing in his mouth like a blow gun. They make his stick his tongue out. It sure is big. Fred even reaches out slow like and pinches the end of it. He yanks his hand back quick and wipes it on his shirt and says, 'Yep, it sure is a tongue.' Then they say he didn't hit the road.

"Fred and Luke don't do so well the next turn around. A lot of the others have dropped out. Woolmutt steps up and hits the road. Where he hits there is a long line in the dust and a big cloud of dust comes up. It ricochets up and smacks the front of Winkelhaur's again, this time just under the busted window.

"On the third try, Fred and Luke are weaker than ever. The heart is gone out of them. You can see it. Woolmutt takes a long time aiming. He hits that red block that marks Fred's best shot and knocks it clean over onto the walk on the other side of the road. I kept that block around for years. Soft pine. Had a half-inch dent in the side of it. Never did know where it disappeared to.

"Well, I'm here to tell you that the rest of that Fourth of July was one of the gol-damndest days I ever did see. How about it, Stu?"

Stu belched softly, reminiscently. "Sure was," he sighed.

"You see," said Hobe, "the crowd sort of took Woolmutt to its heart. He was a kind of likeable little guy. And we knew that in him we had the best spitter in the state, if not the world at large. I announced him the winner and he shoved the money in his pants and they carried him on their shoulders around to Loofer's. I guess the little guy wasn't used to drinking. They loaded him up, and I do mean that they loaded him up. The better element went home. Along about mid-afternoon, Woolmutt, sort of loosened up at every joint, led what I suppose you might call a triumphant procession through town.

"You could hear him coming a block away. First all you'd hear would be the bang, bang, bang, as he hit the wooden buildings. After each bang all those fellas following him would let out a yell, Fred and Luke yelling louder than anybody. When he got closer you could hear the whole works. 'Whih-THOO BANG YELL. Whih-THOO BANG YELL.' It was something terrible. I was with him when Mrs. Thomas's cat, big yella devil named Wheedlekins, made the mistake of runnin' across the road in front of Woolmutt. Little Woolmutt really threw up the dust around that cat. Wheedlekins run up a tree, panting and yelling, and made the mistake of leaving a little bit exposed around the edge of the top limb. Woolmutt nailed Wheedlekins again and that cat dropped out of the tree and raced across town like its tail was afire.

"Judge Proctor's bay team caught it next. You might say Woolmutt sort of encouraged those horses. It's said that the Judge got them stopped just short of the county line. The good citizens who wanted no part of all this locked their doors and they didn't get in line with the windows either. Woolmutt proved himself a gentleman, though, even when he was the most carried away with it all. You gentlemen know Mrs. Iverson. Well, she was about eighteen then, and the way she dressed there were some ready and willing to say she'd come to no good end. A handsome filly always looking as though she'd bust right out of her clothes.

"When they came around the corner of Market and Crown, there was Hazel fifty feet away, bent over tying her shoe. They all pleaded, but Woolmutt refused. He said it wasn't right and proper. And . . . . "

"I don't see what this has got to do with flying saucers," Brad Sedwell complained.

"You young folks are always too damn impatient," Hobe said. "You're hurrying me. Well, on that day Harry Sewell's son, John, was in town, taking a vacation from the hospital down east where he was doing his interning. Smart boy, John Sewell. Of course, he's no boy now. It surprised me to find him following around after Woolmutt and then I noticed that he wasn't yelling the way the others were. He just kept his eyes glued to Woolmutt as though he couldn't take 'em off.

"When the whole mob stopped back here in front of the Fire House, John got right up next to Woolmutt, staring at him hard. The first thing we knew, he grabbed one of Woolmutt's hands and looked at it close, front and back. Woolmutt tried to pull away. Then John got his thumb on Woolmutt's pulse. He looked deep into Woolmutt's eyes and I could see him going pale. Woolmutt yanked free, plunged through the crowd and ran out of town. Nobody ever saw him again. And John Sewell wouldn't say a word about what he'd seen—but he didn't seem too surprised when he found out that Woolmutt had left the county for good. That's how it ties in with them saucers, Brad."

Brad snorted. "Oh, sure. Woolmutt came in a flying saucer."

"Use the brains God gave squirrels, Brad," Hobe said angrily. "It stands to reason that whoever flies around in the saucers has been watching us for a long time, maybe hundreds of years. I say they're making a study of us mortals. You ever read Charles Fort's stuff? He says right out that we're nothing but property. The more I pondered on Woolmutt and his accent and the funny way he looked, the more I began to think that Woolmutt was a spy from someplace. Someplace off this earth. They made him look like a man and they stuck him here on us to make out his reports. But the little bugger got lonesome. You know how it is. Here he was among strangers, maybe for most of his life, getting lonesomer every day. They didn't do a good job of making him look like a man maybe because they didn't know enough about us forty years ago. But when he saw the spittin' he knew that it was something he could do, something he could get in on. Just like the time that drummer told Nancy Carrwell she had a good singing voice. She like to drove the whole town crazy for three years until she got over it.

"Now John Sewell was a trained doctor and he could see things about Woolmutt that we wouldn't notice. Woolmutt, with his spittin', attracted too much attention and he knew it when John started examining him. So Woolmutt had to go back where he come from. Now they've had spies here long enough so that they know about the fix this world's gettin' into and they're coming around in their saucers and keep us from killing each other off—the same way you cut up a chicken run when they start peckin' each other to death."

The street lights came on with startling suddenness, turning the blue dusk to night. Stu sighed and shuffled off into the darkness. Arthur LeBlanc stood up and laughed nervously and said, "Well, this has all been very interesting." His lisp seemed more pronounced. Hobe's closing comments had seemed to put some restraint on the group. Brad and Harry mumbled something about getting home and went off together.

Only the boy was left. "You better be gettin' on home to your Ma," Hobe suggested gently.

The boy sighed as though awakening from a dream. "Sure, mister. Sure. G'night, mister."

He went off up the street. He walked down Crown to the tracks and turned east. When he got beyond the street lights the countryside seemed brighter, as though there was a bit of the day left.

He cut across lots toward Perry's Woods. When he neared the tangle of impenetrable brush he took a small irridescent cube out of the pocket of the jeans and held it to his ear. He spoke, listened a few moments, and then spoke again, his tone firm and brisk.

He put the cube back in his pocket. A small tawny

rabbit, barely visible in the dusk, stood atop a knoll sixty yards away.

The rabbit suddenly tumbled over and over, jumped up and scurried away. The small boy flattened the long tongue out again, smiled almost sadly, and rose straight up, with increasing speed, toward the navy blue sky of night.

This story is a good example of the dominant theme of modern science fiction—that of alienation. Appropriately, it appeared in science fiction's leading journal of social and political commentary, **Galaxy.** "Susceptibility" captures the suspicion, fear, and reaction toward many aspects of modern life that characterized the science fiction of the fifties. It was reprinted in H. L. Gold's **The First Galaxy Reader of Science Fiction.**

SUSCEPTIBILITY

Galaxy Science Fiction
January, 1951

SEAN MALLOY stood unnoticed at the edge of the clearing and frowned as he watched the girl work. Exposure to the rays of the yellow-white sun, half again the size of Sol, had turned her to copper bronze, against which the mane of yellow hair was quite startling. He found that he was taking pleasure in watching the smooth play of muscles in her naked back as she swung the instrument against the tree. Each stroke bit out a chunk of the soft yellowish wood, veined with green. Exertion had put a sheen of perspiration on her shoulders.

The proper paleolingual word eluded him. Suddenly he remembered. Of course—it was an ax.

The sound of it, biting into the wood, resounded across the clearing, a sharp, metronomic sound. He heard the crackle of fibers and saw her step back from the tree. Sean Malloy glanced up then, and saw the great mass of branches and leaves sway toward him. He gave a gasp of alarm, and forgetting all the dignity of a Praecursor from the Colonial Adjustments Bureau, he ran at right angles to the line of fall. After fifty feet of surprising fleetness, he struck a hummock of grass and fell just at the moment the tree thundered to the ground, so close behind him that the end of a branch rapped him smartly across the shoulders. He crawled out from under the leaves and stood up. The tall woman was hurrying toward him, buttoning on a shirt of coarse fabric, quick concern in her eyes.

"You're not hurt?"

"It so happens that I'm not," he said acidly.

He saw her glance take in his uniform, the CAB seal, the tiny gold question mark of the Praecursor blazoned upon it. She no longer looked concerned.

"People who wait for trees to fall on them generally get hurt," she said indifferently.

"I am Sean Malloy, Praecursor. They told me, in the village, that I should talk to you. You *are* Deen Thomason?"

She nodded. She looked regretfully at the tree. "I suppose I can just as well finish it tomorrow. Come along, Malloy."

She shouldered the ax and headed across the clearing to the mouth of a narrow trail. Her stride was long. Once again Malloy found himself taking a rather surprising pleasure in watching her. He made a mental note to apply, on his return to the Bureau, for deep psychological analysis. Praecursors who became emotionally involved with colonial women suffered a loss of efficiency. It would be wise to have this susceptibility tracked down and eliminated. In the meantime, to take his attention away from the swing of her walk, he asked hastily, "What were you planning to do with the tree, Thomason?"

"Cut off the branches today, saw it tomorrow, then split it and carry the pieces back to my place."

"But why?" he asked, baffled.

SHE stopped so suddenly that he almost ran into her. She turned around and he saw a mixture of amusement and irony in her gray eyes.

"Our winter season is coming, Malloy," she said. "I burn the wood in order to keep warm."

She was almost as tall as he. He said, as though reasoning with a child, "Wouldn't it be much simpler to ask for a heat unit? There's a field station here, an unlimited power source. All you have to do is . . . . "

"Of course, Malloy. It just so happens that I'd rather do it this way."

"But . . . . "

She had turned again and was striding along the trail. He had to trot to catch up with her. They emerged into a second clearing. A crude wooden house sat at the base of a hill and he was forced to admit that the setting, with the small busy stream foaming through the rocky channel, was superb. Primitive, though.

He followed her to the door of the house. It was open.

"Where is your mate?" he asked, realizing too late that his choice of words had been a bit hasty. It was undiplomatic to point out the backwardness of this unfortunate social order without shrewd preparation.

She looked more amused than angered. "Sit down, Malloy. I have not yet mated, if that's what you Bureau people prefer to call it."

"You built this house yourself?"

"No. I selected the spot. All the others helped me. It was built in two days. The Bureau would have been horrified. Everyone working with their hands. Dancing and food that didn't come from the field station and a strong brew made from fruits. Very barbaric."

He sat at a bench beside a wooden table. She lifted

a trap door, went down steps and returned with a corked earthenware jug. She poured a cup of water and handed it to him. The day was warm, the water cool and sweet.

"Thank you," he said. She sat opposite him.

He smiled officially. "Well, shall we get to it, Thomason? It took me a long time to find you. And I didn't expect anyone like you to be . . . head of the planet."

"Let us be accurate, Malloy. This year it happened to be my turn to represent the village at general meeting, and also the turn of my village to supply the chairman for the meeting."

MALLOY gave her a pained look. "My dear young woman, my duty involves contacting the person in charge here. Are you or are you not in charge?"

"If you could say anyone is in charge, I suppose I am."

"Then you keep the records, I gather. Issue orders. Take care of administration."

"There are no records to keep, Malloy. I issued one order, I think. I set the day of the next meeting. And the villages administer themselves."

Malloy stood up, walked to the stone fireplace, turned abruptly. "Please, Thomason. A Praecursor named Zedder was sent here to Able XII seven Earth years ago, five and a half of your years. His job was to find out why the field station was almost unutilized, why there were no entertainment imports, why you were canceled off the tour schedules for lack of business. Zedder came here and put his ship on homing automatic with his resignation fastened to the flight panel. That was so unusual that Able XII was put on emergency priority. Our press of business is so great that this is the first time you have had Bureau contact since then.

"I came here expecting to find most of the population gone. At first I thought I was right. No one seems to live at the Centers the Bureau built for you people. Then I found you of Able XII living out here in these crude villages and shacks. It has taken me two full weeks to locate you, Thomason. I'm a busy man. A very busy man. The field station is in perfect working order. I've tested it. I projected a perfectly satisfactory little flier, synthesized foods at random from the list that checked perfectly, even used the tele-tubes from Center to Center. My job is to find out what's wrong here, Thomason."

"Does something have to be wrong?" she demanded.

"Don't try my patience, Thomason."

Her gray eyes narrowed a bit. "I can think of very few things I'm more indifferent to, Malloy, than your patience or lack of patience. This is my home. You have all the normal privileges of a guest. An autocratic attitude is not one of those privileges."

He sat down wearily. "I'm sorry. It's just that I'm upset. Where's Zedder?"

"I'm sure I haven't the faintest idea."

"Isn't there any central record of population? Any index?"

"We don't find that necessary, Malloy."

"I can't spare the time to hunt in every village for him. I've got four more emergency priority cases to cover in other parts of the Galaxy."

"Then why don't you just get back into whatever you came here in and go take care of them?"

HE LIFTED his chin. "When the Colonial Bureau sets up proper resident facilities on a planet and stocks the planet with colonists, and when said colonists fail to use the facilities provided, it is the duty of the Colonial Adjustments Bureau to send a Praecursor to make investigation and recommendation as to what sort of adjustment team should be sent to rectify said non-utilization of standard facilities."

She looked amused. "I assume you're quoting from some sort of absurd manual, Malloy. Does it actually use the word 'stock'? As with fish in a pond?"

"There is a case on record where one colonial planet suffered such an emotional degeneration that the colonists acquired a superstitious fear of Center facilities and moved off into the woods."

"And they were adjusted?" Deen Thomason asked mildly.

"Re-educated," Malloy amended.

"That sounds dreadful. Just report, Praecursor, that the inhabitants of Able XII prefer a so-called primitive life, and that the facilities of the Centers and the field station are used when emergencies arise."

"That will make no sense to the Bureau," he said hotly. "You people live out here in absolute squalor. All the Center homes are empty. Insects have gotten in. Of course they can do no damage, but they have spun webs on the projector dials. It's untidy, a criminal waste. You could move to a Center. Everything you could possibly desire would be no farther from your hand than the nearest dial. It is incomprehensible to me, Thomason, that you should prefer to walk back into the earliest history of your race. Every possible comfort was made available when this colonial planet was set up for . . . ."

She raised her hand. "Please, Malloy. Stand up a moment."

He stood up, puzzled. She walked around the table, smiled enigmatically at him and suddenly, clenching her fist, she struck him hard in the diaphragm. He had just enough warning so that he was able to tense his muscles against the blow. Even so, it almost took his breath.

"To strike a Praecursor is. . . ."

"Oh, stop being so stuffy! Why are you a Praecursor? Why are you reasonably lean and hard and fit? Why aren't you sitting plump and happy within arm's reach of a dial on your home planet?"

He stared at her. "Why, I . . . there have to be Praecursors!"

"That point is debatable. But I'm asking why you are one."

"I like problems and new places, I suppose," he said hesitantly. "And I have to keep fit because sometimes I run into . . . strenuous situations. But no one forced me to be a Praecursor."

"Exactly," she said.

"I hope you realize that you are not making sense, Thomason."

"Indeed? I thought I was making a great deal of

sense. Anyway, you can report that we are not completely lost. One of the Centers is occupied, you know."

"Is it? Good! Which one?"

"Number Six. I'd like to visit it with you. I have a reason, Malloy."

He pressed the stud on his time ring and the correct sun time of the Able XII twenty-hour day came into his mind. He knew that she was standing near enough to him so that she caught it, too, though less strongly. She chuckled, and it was a surprisingly warm sound.

"Why are you laughing?" he asked.

"That toy. See the sun pattern on the floor? From that I could have told you the time within a half hour."

"Not much of a degree of accuracy."

"AGAIN you've missed the point, Malloy. It's accurate enough."

"I can't argue with unreason. Come on. That flier I projected is beyond the clearing where I found you. I'll leave it with you when I go."

"Thank you. I'd have no use for it. And we should eat before we go."

"We'll eat at the Center."

"Thank you, no. I'll get us something here. First, though, I must bathe."

He looked around the room. "No cleansing unit here."

"There's a perfectly good one in the stream, Malloy." She went to the shelves near the fireplace, selected a tunic of softer fabric than her work clothes, and a heavy towel. "You can make yourself useful, Malloy. Build a small fire in the fireplace. But first come here a moment. That's my garden. See those spiky green things? Pull up about a dozen of them and wash them in the stream."

Before he could decide whether or not to refuse the request, she had gone, walking toward the stream with that long stride of hers, supple and somehow wild. He selected small sticks and tried with infuriating lack of success to start them burning by using a short hot focus of his pocket heat unit. Angry at failing in so simple a task, he walked out and yanked up a dozen of the growths she had indicated. Black moist soil clung to the bulbular white ends that came out of the ground.

He took them to the stream, below the wider part that formed a pool. Remembering the extreme variations in attitudes of modesty on the colonial planets, he did not wish to look directly at her. Praecursors were trained to adapt themselves readily to many odd folkways. But in spite of his intentions he found himself gawking at her as she stood by the pool, tall and tanned and lithe. She smiled down the slope at him as she toweled her shining hair and he made a comparison oddly damaging to the soft pallid women of home.

She belted the short aqua tunic around her slim waist and he followed her back to the house. As he watched her she put some dried moss under the sticks in the fireplace, scratched an object which he recognized as being one of the crude firemaking devices of earliest times. It was called, he remembered, a "match." The small fire blazed. She brought ovoid white objects from the cellar, cracked them into an earthenware dish, chopped the bulbous white growths with a crude knife and stirred them into the mixture. The dish was then suspended over the flame while she sawed off heavy slabs of coarse bread, spread them with a yellow substance.

MALLOY watched closely. This primitive substitute for the extremely simple procedure of operating the synthesizer would form an interesting portion of his report. The odor that filled the room, however, made his salivary glands surprisingly active. The mixture firmed and she took the dish from over the fire, divided the contents into two parts, placed one part between two heavy slabs of bread and put it on another dish, set it in front of him.

Malloy took a cautious bite and then a much larger one. The taste was harsher and more concentrated, the texture far coarser than any food he had ever tasted before.

Before he knew it, his share was gone. She washed the dishes in the stream and replaced them on the shelf.

"That was very interesting," he said.

"But nothing you'd care for day in and day out?"

"N-no," he said.

She smiled. "I'm ready, Malloy. Shall we go?"

They walked to the small flier. Malloy watched her closely. She had no awe of it, accepted it as something routine and unimpressive. He ducked under the low door, sat down beside her, lifted the flier off the ground, swung around the crest of a clump of trees.

"Let me see," he said, "six would be. . . ."

"Turn it a bit to your right, Malloy. That's enough."

Air whined by as he upped the speed. Cabin heat increased and the cooling unit came on. The ground streamed by far below, flattened by the height.

He said, in a fatherly tone, "This would be a long trip afoot, the way you people seem to travel."

"Several days, Malloy. Through country where silvery fish leap high in the lakes, where the trees hold wild honey. At dusk you come to a village. You are always made welcome. Cheese and bread and wine and dancing in the dusk, and the fireflies are like little lanterns."

"Oh," he said distantly.

"But your way is, of course, much quicker," she added.

"I see the Center," he said.

HE BROUGHT the flier around in a long swooping curve and dropped it lightly onto cleared land outside the gates. Even as he got out he saw people walking in the wide pastel streets of the Center. It was like a scene from home. They wore clothes of all shades, hues, fancies, whims. A completely anachronistic shack stood outside the gate, though. A tall young man with a full blond beard sat with his back against the door frame. He grinned and stood up as Malloy and Deen approached. He wore the crude garments of the villagers.

"Thomason, isn't it?" he asked.

"That's right. This is just an inspection trip."

"Go right ahead," he said.

He turned to a metallic plate set beside the rude door, depressed a switch. Malloy, slightly baffled, followed Deen through the gate. As he passed through he felt the momentary tingle of a space-twist fence temporarily reversed.

Then he straightened his shoulders. He walked beside Thomason. "You see how pleasant life can be in a Center?" he asked proudly.

A well-larded woman sat in the sun playing with two romping fuzzy creatures she had created out of the mental projector. Beyond her a man slept propped against a wall, half-empty bottles surrounding him.

"Very pleasant," Thomason said.

"They all have everything they want. Who would want to live out in the brush when everything is right here, within arm's reach? Exotic foods, toys, amusement."

"Who indeed?" Thomason stressed with gentle irony.

Malloy beamed at the colonists. They had the familiar triple chins of the home planet, the same shortness of breath, the same bland look that comes of satiety in all things. But he was puzzled by the way they stared at the two of them. Dulled eyes, with the glow of resentment almost submerged.

At the end of the street he stopped. "But the rest of the Center is empty!" he said.

"Yes. There's just this one street. We can't go any farther. The fence will stop us."

She turned and started back. He caught her in two quick strides, grasped her arm and pulled her around roughly. "Why have you people installed a twist fence around this street?"

"Because there's no need to put it around a bigger area."

"Why put it around any area?" he shouted into her face.

"You are rude," she said coldly. "And more stupid than I thought. We'll walk back slowly. Look at their faces, Malloy. Look long and well. You see, this is the penal colony for this planet."

The breath whoofed out of him. "Penal? But. . . . . Wait. Anybody who lives here can have every last thing they want."

"Exactly," she said.

Subdued, he walked beside her and he looked at their faces.

IT WAS dusk in the heart of the village. He heard the thin eager voices of children at play. Smoke from the cook fires lost itself in the grayness overhead where the first strange star patterns were beginning to appear. Deen sat with her back against a tree. Sean Malloy lay stretched out on the grass on his back, the concavity of the nape of his neck fitting comfortably over the warm convexity of her thigh.

An insect lit on the back of his hand and he slapped it. He squirmed a bit. He wasn't yet accustomed to the scratchiness of homespun clothes. He squinted up at the skies and thought of his ship speeding toward Bureau headquarters, the resignation affixed to the automatic controls. This was the third night back at her home.

"A crazy thing to do," he muttered.

She took her cool fingertips from his forehead abruptly. "Sorry you did it, Sean?" she asked a bit frigidly.

He captured her hand, kissed the palm. "Not the way it sounded. My ship will get back there. They'll give Able XII a double priority. A new Praecursor will be here in probably less than four years. He may send an adjustment team."

The children were being called in from play. A few hundred feet down the unpaved main street came the first sounds of music.

"I wouldn't worry about that, Sean," she said softly.

He sat up, faced her. "Why in Sol not?"

She smiled at him. "Because when he comes, he'll go looking for the person in charge, won't he?"

"Naturally."

It was decided a long time ago that what little centralized administration we need should be handled by those of us least likely to be hungry for that sort of power."

"I don't get the connection."

"Village representatives to the general meeting are

always unmarried girls, and are always those considered to be the most pleasing to the eye. And we are beginning to find that anyone who has become a Praecursor seems peculiarly . . . susceptible to this sort of existence."

HE WAS silent for a long time, and then he laughed. "Poor Zedder," he said.

"And poor Malloy," she added teasingly.

Suddenly he became suspicious. "Did you have orders to—to—"

"Seduce the Praecursor? How strangely short your memory is, my Sean! I seem to remember that the shoe was on the other foot." She stood up quickly and held out her hand. "Come. They will expect us to dance. I shall teach you. It will make you hungry for the wedding feast."

"How barbaric!" muttered the ex-Praecursor as he urgently uptilted her mouth.

"How primitive you're becoming!" she taunted, and writhed out of his arms.

He caught her finally, but only because she let him. He needed some woodchopping and farming, maybe some hunting and hiking, too, before he could outrun her legitimately. A couple of months and she would see who was the stronger.

The film **Close Encounters of the Third Kind** has engendered great interest in the transcendental qualities of science fiction. However, as John D. MacDonald shows in this clever story about the nature of maturity (one of two stories of his included in **The First Galaxy Reader of Science Fiction**), the theme is not a new one.

COMMON DENOMINATOR

Galaxy Science Fiction
July, 1951

WHEN Scout Group Forty flickered back across half the Galaxy with a complete culture study of a Class Seven civilization on three planets of Argus Ten, the Bureau of Stellar Defense had, of course, a priority claim on all data. Class Sevens were rare and of high potential danger, so all personnel of Group Forty were placed in tight quarantine during the thirty days required for a detailed analysis of the thousands of film spools.

News of the contact leaked out and professional alarmists predicted dire things on the news screens of the three home planets of Sol. A retired admiral of the Space Navy published an article in which he stated bitterly that the fleet had been weakened by twenty years of softness in high places.

On the thirty-first day, B.S.D. reported to System President Mize that the inhabitants of the three planets of Argus 10 constituted no threat, that there was no military necessity for alarm, that approval of a commerce treaty was recommended, that all data was being turned over to the Bureau of Stellar Trade and Economy for analysis, that personnel of Scout Group Forty was being given sixty days' leave before reassignment.

B.S.T.E. released film to all commercial networks at once, and visions of slavering oily monsters disappeared from the imagination of mankind. The Argonauts, as they came to be called, were pleasantly similar to mankind. It was additional proof that only in the rarest instance was the life-apex on any planet in the home Galaxy an abrupt divergence from the "human" form. The homogeneousness of planet elements throughout the Galaxy made homogeneousness of life-apex almost a truism. The bipedal, oxygen-breathing vertebrate with opposing thumb seems best suited for survival.

It was evident that, with training, the average Argonaut could pass almost unnoticed in the Solar System. The flesh tones were brightly pink, like that of a sunburned human. Cranial hair was uniformly taffy-yellow. They were heavier and more fleshy than humans. Their women had a pronounced Rubens look, a warm, moist, rosy, comfortable look.

EVERYONE remarked on the placidity and contentment of facial expressions, by human standards. The inevitable comparison was made. The Argonauts looked like a race of inn and beer-garden proprietors in the Bavarian Alps. With leather pants to slap, stein lids to click, feathers in Tyrolean hats and peasant skirts on their women, they would represent a culture and a way of life that had been missing from Earth for far too many generations.

Eight months after matters had been turned over to B.S.T.E., the First Trade Group returned to Earth with a bewildering variety of artifacts and devices, plus a round dozen Argonauts. The Argonauts had learned to speak Solian with an amusing guttural accent. They beamed on everything and everybody. They were great pets until the novelty wore off. Profitable trade was inaugurated, because the Argonaut devices all seemed designed to make life more pleasant. The scent-thesizer became very popular once it was adjusted to meet human tastes. Worn as a lapel button, it could create the odor of pine, broiled steak, spring flowers, Scotch whisky, musk—even skunk for the practical jokers who exist in all ages and eras.

Any home equipped with an Argonaut static-clean never became dusty. It used no power and had to be emptied only once a year.

Technicians altered the Argonaut mechanical game animal so that it looked like an Earth rabbit. The weapons which shot a harmless beam were altered to look like rifles. After one experience with the new game, hunters were almost breathless with excitement. The incredible agility of the mechanical animal, its ability to take cover, the fact that, once the beam felled it, you could use it over and over again—all this made for the promulgation of new non-lethal hunting.

LAMBERT, chief of the Bureau of Racial Maturity, waited patiently for his chance at the Argonaut data. The cramped offices in the temporary wing of the old System Security Building, the meager appropriation, the obsolete office equipment, the inadequate staff all testified not only to the Bureau's lack of priority, but also to a lack of knowledge of its existence on the part of many System officials. Lambert, crag-faced, sandy, slow-moving, was a historian, anthropologist and sociologist. He was realist enough to understand that if the Bureau of Racial Maturity happened to be more important in System Government, it would probably be headed by a man with fewer academic and more political qualifications.

And Lambert knew, beyond any doubt at all, that the

B.R.M. was more important to the race and the future of the race than any other branch of System Government.

Set up by President Tolles, an adult and enlightened administrator, the Bureau was now slowly being strangled by a constantly decreasing appropriation.

Lambert knew that mankind had come too far, too fast. Mankind had dropped out of a tree with all the primordial instincts to rend and tear and claw. Twenty thousand years later, and with only a few thousand years of dubiously recorded history, he had reached the stars. It was too quick.

Lambert knew that mankind must become mature in order to survive. The domination of instinct had to be watered down, and rapidly. Selective breeding might do it, but it was an answer impossible to enforce. He hoped that one day the records of an alien civilization would give him the answer. After a year of bureaucratic wriggling, feints and counter-feints, he had acquired the right of access to Scout Group Data.

As his patience dwindled he wrote increasingly firm letters to Central Files and Routing. In the end, when he finally located the data improperly stored in the closed files of the B.S.T.E., he took no more chances. He went in person with an assistant named Cooper and a commandeered electric hand-truck, and bullied a B.S.T.E. storage clerk into accepting a receipt for the Argonaut data. The clerk's cooperation was lessened by never having heard of the Bureau of Racial Maturity.

THE file contained the dictionary and grammar compiled by the Scout Group, plus all the films taken on the three planets of Argus 10, plus micro-films of twelve thousand books written in the language of the Argonauts. Their written language was ideographic, and thus presented more than usual difficulties. Lambert knew that translations had been made, but somewhere along the line they had disappeared.

Lambert set his whole staff to work on the language. He hired additional linguists out of his own thin enough pocket. He gave up all outside activities in order to hasten the progress of his own knowledge. His wife, respecting Lambert's high order of devotion to his work, kept their two half-grown children from interfering during those long evenings when he studied and translated at home.

Two evenings a week Lambert called on Vonk Poogla, the Argonaut assigned to Trade Coordination, and improved his conversational Argonian to the point where he could obtain additional historical information from the pink wide "man."

Of the twelve thousand books, the number of special interest to Lambert were only one hundred and ten. On those he based his master chart. An animated film of the chart was prepared at Lambert's own expense, and, when it was done, he requested an appointment with Simpkin, Secretary for Stellar Affairs, going through all the normal channels to obtain the interview. He asked an hour of Simpkin's time. It took two weeks.

Simpkin was a big florid man with iron-gray hair, skeptical eyes and that indefinable look of political opportunism.

He came around his big desk to shake Lambert's hand. "Ah . . . Lambert! Glad to see you, fella. I ought to get around to my Bureau Chiefs more often, but you know how hectic things are up here."

"I know, Mr. Secretary. I have something here of the utmost importance and—"

"Bureau of Racial Maturity, isn't it? I never did know exactly what you people do. Sort of progress records or something?"

"Of the utmost importance," Lambert repeated doggedly.

Simpkin smiled. "I hear that all day, but go ahead."

"I want to show you a chart. A historical chart of the Argonaut civilization." Lambert put the projector in position and plugged it in. He focused it on the wall screen.

"It was decided," Simpkin said firmly, "that the Argonauts are not a menace to us in any—"

"I know that, sir. Please look at the chart first and then, when you've seen it, I think you'll know what I mean."

"Go ahead," Simpkin agreed resignedly.

"I can be accused of adding apples and lemons in this presentation, sir. Note the blank chart. The base line is in years, adjusted to our calendar so as to give a comparison. Their recorded history covers twelve thousand of our years. That's better than four times ours. Now note the red line. That shows the percentage of their total population involved in wars. It peaked eight thousand years ago. Note how suddenly it drops after that. In five hundred years it sinks to the base line and does not appear again.

"Here comes the second line. Crimes of violence. It also peaks eight thousand years ago. It drops less quickly than the war line, and never does actually cut the base line. Some crime still exists there. But a very, very tiny percentage compared to ours on a population basis, or to their own past. The third line, the yellow line climbing abruptly, is the index of insanity. Again a peak during the same approximate period in their history. Again a drop almost to the base line."

SIMPKIN pursed his heavy lips. "Odd, isn't it?"

"Now this fourth line needs some explaining. I winnowed out death rates by age groups. Their life span is 1.3 times ours, so it had to be adjusted. I found a strange thing. I took the age group conforming to our 18 to 24 year group. That green line. Note that by the time we start getting decent figures, nine thousand years ago, it remains almost constant, and at a level conforming to our own experience. Now note what happens when the green line reaches a point eight thousand years ago. See how it begins to climb? Now steeper, almost vertical. It remains at a high level for almost a thousand years, way beyond the end of their history of war, and then descends slowly toward the base line, leveling out about two thousand years ago."

Lambert clicked off the projector.

"Is that all?" Simpkin asked.

"Isn't it enough? I'm concerned with the future of our own race. Somehow the Argonauts have found an answer to war, insanity, violence. We need that answer if we are to survive."

"Come now, Lambert," Simpkin said wearily.

"Don't you see it? Their history parallels ours. They had our same problems. They saw disaster ahead and did something about it. What did they do? I have to know that."

"How do you expect to?"

"I want travel orders to go there."

"I'm afraid that's quite impossible. There are no funds for that sort of jaunt, Lambert. And I think you are worrying over nothing."

"Shall I show you some of our own trends? Shall I show you murder turning from the most horrid crime into a relative commonplace? Shall I show you the slow inevitable increase in asylum space?"

"I know all that, man. But look at the Argonauts! Do you want that sort of stagnation? Do you want a race of fat, pink, sleepy—"

"Maybe they had a choice. A species of stagnation, or the end of their race. Faced with that choice, which would you pick, Mr. Secretary?"

"There are no funds."

"All I want is authority. I'll pay my own way."

And he did.

REAN was the home planet of the Argonauts, the third from their sun. When the trade ship flickered into three-dimensional existence, ten thousand miles above Rean, Lambert stretched the space-ache out of his long bones and muscles and smiled at Vonk Poogla.

"You could have saved me the trip, you know," Lambert said.

A grin creased the round pink visage. "Nuddink ventured, nuddink gained. Bezides, only my cousin can speak aboud this thing you vunder aboud. My cousin is werry important person. He is one picks me to go to your planet."

Vonk Poogla was transported with delight at being able to show the wonders of the ancient capital city to Lambert. It had been sacked and burned over eight thousand Earth years before, and now it was mellowed by eighty-three centuries of unbroken peace. It rested in the pastel twilight, and there were laughter and soft singing in the broad streets. Never had Lambert felt such a warm aura of security and . . . love. No other word but that ultimate one seemed right.

In the morning they went to the squat blue building where Vonk Soobuknoora, the important person, had his administrative headquarters. Lambert, knowing enough of Argonaut governmental structure to understand that Soobuknoora was titular head of the three-planet government, could not help but compare the lack of protocol with what he could expect were he to try to take Vonk Poogla for an interview with President Mize.

Soobuknoora was a smaller, older edition of Poogla, his pink face wrinkled, his greening hair retaining only a trace of the original yellow. Soobuknoora spoke no Solian and he was very pleased to find that Lambert spoke Argonian.

Soobuknoora watched the animated chart with considerable interest. After it was over, he seemed lost in thought.

"It is something so private with us, Man Lambert, that we seldom speak of it to each other," Soobuknoora said in Argonian. "It is not written. Maybe we have shame—a guilt sense. That is hard to say. I have decided to tell you what took place among us eight thousand years ago."

"I would be grateful."

"WE LIVE in contentment. Maybe it is good, maybe it is not so good. But we continue to live. Where did our trouble come from in the old days, when we were like your race? Back when we were brash and young and wickedly cruel? From the individuals, those driven ones who were motivated to succeed despite all obstacles. They made our paintings, wrote our music, killed each other, fomented our unrest, our wars. We live off the bewildering richness of our past."

He sighed. "It was a problem. To understand our solution, you must think of an analogy, Man Lambert.

Think of a factory where machines are made. We will call the acceptable machines stable, the unacceptable ones unstable. They are built with a flywheel which must turn at a certain speed. If it exceeds that speed, it is no good. But a machine that is stable can, at any time, become unstable. What is the solution?" He smiled at Lambert.

"I'm a bit confused," Lambert confessed. "You would have to go around inspecting the machines constantly for stability."

"And use a gauge? No. Too much trouble. An unstable machine can do damage. So we do this—we put a little governor on the machine. When the speed passes the safety mark, the machine breaks."

"But this is an analogy, Vonk Soobuknoora!" Lambert protested. "You can't put a governor on a man!"

"Man is born with a governor, Man Lambert. Look back in both our histories, when we were not much above the animal level. An unbalanced man would die. He could not compete for food. He could not organize the simple things of his life for survival. Man Lambert, did you ever have a fleeting impulse to kill yourself?"

Lambert smiled. "Of course. You could almost call that impulse a norm for intelligent species."

"Did it ever go far enough so that you considered a method, a weapon?"

Lambert nodded slowly. "It's hard to remember, but I think I did. Yes, once I did."

"And what would have happened," the Argonaut asked softly, "if there had been available to you in that moment a weapon completely painless, completely final?"

LAMBERT'S mouth went dry. "I would probably have used it. I was very young. Wait! I'm beginning to see what you mean, but—"

"The governor had to be built into the body," Soobuknoora interrupted, "and yet so designed that there would be no possibility of accidental activation. Suppose that on this day I start to think of how great and powerful I am in this position I have. I get an enormous desire to become even more powerful. I begin to reason emotionally. Soon I have a setback. I am depressed. I am out of balance, you could say. I have become dangerous to myself and to our culture.

"In a moment of depression, I take these two smallest fingers of each hand. I reach behind me and I press the two fingers, held firmly together, to a space in the middle of my back. A tiny capsule buried at the base of my brain is activated and I am dead within a thousandth part of a second. Vonk Poogla is the same. All of us are the same. The passing urge for self-destruction happens to be the common denominator of imbalance. We purged our race of the influence of the neurotic, the egocentric, the hypersensitive, merely by making self-destruction very, very easy."

"Then that death rate—?"

"At eighteen the operation is performed. It is very quick and very simple. We saw destruction ahead. We had to force it through. In the beginning the deaths were frightening, there were so many of them. The stable ones survived, bred, reproduced. A lesser but still great percentage of the next generation went—and so on, until now it is almost static."

In Argonian Lambert said hotly, "Oh, it sounds fine! But what about children? What sort of heartless race can plant the seed of death in its own children?"

NEVER before had he seen the faintest trace of anger on any Argonaut face. The single nostril widened and Soobuknoora might have raged if he had been from Earth. "There are other choices, Man Lambert. Our children have no expectation of being burned to cinder, blown to fragments. They are free of that fear. Which is the better love, Man Lambert?"

"I have two children. I couldn't bear to—"

"Wait!" Soobuknoora said. "Think one moment. Suppose you were to know that when they reached the age of eighteen, both your children were to be operated on by our methods. How would that affect your present relationship to them?"

Lambert was, above all, a realist. He remembered the

days of being "too busy" for the children, of passing off their serious questions with a joking or curt evasion, of playing with them as though they were young, pleasing, furry animals.

"I would do a better job as a parent," Lambert admitted. "I would try to give them enough emotional stability so that they would never—have that urge to kill themselves. But Ann is delicate, moody, unpredictable, artistic."

Poogla and Soobuknoora nodded in unison. "You would probably lose that one; maybe you would lose both," Soobuknoora agreed. "But it is better to lose more than half the children of a few generations to save the race."

Lambert thought some more. He said, "I shall go back and I shall speak of this plan and what it did for you. But I do not think my race will like it. I do not want to insult you or your people, but you have stagnated. You stand still in time."

Vonk Poogla laughed largely. "Not by a damn sight," he said gleefully. "Next year we stop giving the operation. We stop for good. It was just eight thousand years to permit us to catch our breath before going on more safely. And what is eight thousand years of marking time in the history of a race? Nothing, my friend. Nothing!"

When Lambert went back to Earth, he naturally quit his job.

This is simply one of the most powerful psychological
stories in American science fiction. Bleiler and
Dikty picked it up for **The Best Science Fiction
Stories: 1953.** It has a lovely hard-boiled feel about
it that expresses the multiple pulp influences
of the author.

GAME FOR BLONDES

Galaxy Science Fiction
October, 1952

MARTIN GREYNOR was very very drunk, not
gayly drunk, not freshly six-quick-ones drunk, but drunk
in varying degrees since December tenth at ten P.M. Two
big red 10s in his mind, always with him—zeroes like a
pair of headlights. Ruth beside him, sweet-scented, fur-
clad. And one of his fits of stupid, vicious, reckless anger.
December 10. 10 P.M. Hitting the slick black curves hard,
motor droning, forcing her to tell him he was going too
fast. Once she said it, he could slow down and that
would be a little victory.

"Too fast, Marty!" she said. They were the last words she ever spoke.

Fat headlights and the long whining skid, and the crash, and the jangle that went on forever. Ripped fur and blood and gone the sweet scent.

Now it was New Year's Eve. Ruth was gone. His job was gone, the car gone. Money was left, though, money a-plenty. Funny about drinking. The wobbling, falling down, sick stage lasts about twelve days, he discovered. Important discovery. Boon to science. Then you're armor-plated. Liquor drops into a pit, *clunk*. Walk steady, talk steady. But in come the illusions on little soft pink feet.

Ruth ahead of you, hurrying down a dark street. "Ruth! Wait!"

Hurriedly she puts on a wattled mask, turns and grimaces at you, rasps in a mocking gin-husky voice. "Ya wan' something, sweetie?"

SHE has slipped around the next corner. Run, now, and see her in the next block. Cake the wet December slush on the shrinking, stiffening leather of the shoes that came out of that store window.

"Marty, let's buy you a pair of those. I like those shoes."

Suit she liked. Now a bit dribbled, a shade rancid. Apartment the way they had left it that night. Never gone back. Beds not made, no doubt.

Walk through the night streets, looking for punishment. Looking for a way to release the load of guilt. Now the old places don't want you. "Sorry, Mr. Greynor. You've begun to stink." The little bars don't care.

"*HAP*-PEEE NEW YEAR!"

The bar mirrors are enchanted. Ruth stands behind you. She said, "Never run away from me, darling. You'd be too easy to find. Wanted—a red-headed man with one blue eye and one brown eye. See? You couldn't get away with it."

The face that looks back has been gaunted, because you stopped eating.

He bent low over the bar until his lips almost touched

the shot glass, then lifted it in a hard arc, tossing his head back. It burned its way down into the nothingness. The bartender slapped the change down. Martin Greynor fumbled with it, pushed a quarter over to the far edge. The bartender slipped it off the bar with a surly grunt and clinked it into a glass on the back bar.

Martin turned around and saw the three girls again. He wondered if it was again, or if he was seeing them for the first time. The mind performs such odd little hop, skip, jumps. He debated it solemnly, got nowhere.

They were at a table. They were all looking at him with an air of watchfulness. That could be imagined, too. Three lovelies like that are not going to make the weary ginmill rounds with you and keep watching you. You ain't that purty, Martin.

When in doubt, you write it down on top of your mind and underline it very firmly and hope that when the situation occurs again, you can find the place where you wrote it down.

He walked out steadily and stood on the sidewalk. He had the strong impression that Ruth was stretched flat on the roof, her head over the edge of the building, grinning down at him. He turned sharply and looked up. The Moon hung misty over Manhattan, debauched by neon.

NEXT block. Don't turn right. That will take you toward midtown, toward the higher prices, toward the places where they let you get three steps inside the door, then turn you firmly and walk you back out. Stay over here, buster.

They'd rolled him a few times that first week. Made a nuisance to go to the bank and get more cash each time. Now they'd stopped bothering. One of the times they'd left him sitting, spitting out a tooth. His tongue kept finding the hole.

Neon in the middle of the next block. Two couples sitting on the curb.

"Down by-ee the old mill streeeeeeem . . . ."

Spotted by the prowl car.

"Break it up! Move along there!"

HE looked back. Three female silhouettes, arm in arm, step in step, tick-tock-tick of the pretty stilt heels avoiding the gray smears of slush.

He ducked into the door under the neon. This was a dark one. Dancing was going on back there somewhere to the cat-fence yowl of a clarinet and pulse-thump of piano. He edged in at the bar. The bartender came over fast, with that trouble-look on his face. Martin shoved the five out fast.

"Rye straight," he said.

The bartender paused for a count of three, then turned back to the rye department.

Martin looked over and saw them come in. He hunted on top of his mind and found the heavily underlined place. He read it off. Three blondes. Three arrogant, damp-mouthed, hot-eyed, overdressed blondes—sugary in the gloom. Same ones.

It brought him up out of himself, hand clutching the rim of his soul, for a quick look over the edge. One lone blonde in this place would have pivoted heads in tennis-match style. Two would bring hot and heart-felt exhalations. Three, he saw, seemed to stun the joint. It put a crimp in the rumble of bar-talk. It ran furry fingers down male spines.

They were watching him. He stared back until he was certain. Okay. Fact confirmed. Three blondes following him from joint to joint. Watching him. Next step—watch real close, see if anybody walks through them.

They got a table along the wall. He watched. A hefty young man strutted over to their table, hiking up his pants, making with the bold smile. He bent over the table. They all gave him cold looks. One shook her shining head. He persisted.

The young man turned fast and hard and went high and rigid into the air. Martin saw him go up in that jet-leap of spasmed muscles, head thrown back, agony-masked face. He fell like something pushed out of a window. People gathered around him. They blocked Martin's view.

He looked at the blondes. They were watching him.

In an empty lot in the back of his mind, a rabbit bounded for cover, where there was no cover, and the dogs sat watching, tongues lolling. Cold started at a spot at the base of his spine. It crept nuzzling into his armpits.

He drank and scooped up his change and left.

He ran to the corner and stood, and the trembling went away. The slush was beginning to freeze. It crunched a bit under his shoes. That was another thing. You didn't have to eat, and you didn't get cold. Ergo, one should be beyond fear. Go around being afraid of blondes and people will begin to point at you.

He snickered. The sound was as rigid as the rind of freeze atop the sidewalk slush. We have nothing to fear but fear itself.

Problem for the class: You got a guy, see. He's dying of cancer or something, see. He's in agony and somebody comes into his room and stands by his bed and lifts a big club to hammer him one. Is the guy afraid? If so, why? If he is, it means that fear is something divorced from an objective and intellectual appraisal of the total situation. It means fear is spawned in the guts, down there where the animal lives, down where the rabbit blood is.

A PIECE of paper scuttered around the corner and embraced his leg. He bent over, picked it loose and sent it on its way.

"Hell of a big hurry, aren't you?" he said.

Tick, tack, tick, tack. By God, perfect marching. Ex-WACs? All blonde and all coming along. So what can blondes do to you? He stood his ground for a slow count of ten.

Tick, tack.

Fear rocketed into his throat and burst out his ears and he ran like hell.

A cruiser nailed him in the spotlight, tracking him like a floorshow, making him feel as though he were running, running, running in one spot. He stopped and leaned against a building, panting. The spot still held him. It nailed his eyes to the wall behind him. Big shoulders blocked it. Creak of leather and brass gleam.

"What you running for, chief?"

"It's . . . a cold night. Keeping warm."

The cuff slid him along the wall and the hand on his rancid suit yanked him back upright. "What you running for, I said?"

"Those three blondes coming. They're after me." He could hear them coming. The spot went away. He was blind. But he could hear them.

"After you, you creep?"

"Yes, I . . ."

"Johnny, we better dump the chief here off at the ward. Come on, Mr. Irresistible."

Tick, tack, tock, tick. Silence.

"What do you girls want?"

Brass buttons took a high, hard, stiff-legged, stiff-armed leap. Martin fell into slush and rolled. Inside the cruiser, the driver stiffened, his head going *bong* on the metal roof.

MARTIN ran, bleating. An empty field and no cover. The wise eyes of the hunting dogs. Wait until he comes around again, fellows.

He turned, skidding in the freezing slush, and ran into an alley, tangling his legs in a bunch of trash, sprawling, clawing his way up again, running into a wall, stinging his hands. He turned. Three female silhouettes in the alley mouth. High-waisted, long-legged, stilt-heeled, cream-headed.

He made little sounds in his throat and pawed his way along the wall. An alley like a shoe box with one end missing—the end they were at.

He sat down and covered his eyes. Count to ten and they'll go away. One-a-larry, two-a-larry, three-a-larry, four.

New spotlight. This was a different one. It came at him from a lot of little directions, like one of those trick showers with a dozen spray heads.

"Got um," a blonde voice said.

"Up to spec, no?"

They stood outside the radiance.

"Color and out," one said.

"Take um."

Something grew in front of him, a red happy-new-year balloon. So it was a gag, maybe. It lobbed through the air toward him, turning in iridescence. He caught it. It was red jelly with a cellophane skin. It kept trying to slide down between his fingers.

"Yah-hah!" one of the blondes said.

It broke in his hands, showered green needles up to his nose to sizzle in his brain fat.

The sky broke in half and he went over backward and down, heels up and over, sizzling.

MARTIN slid naked across a mirrored floor. He was bug-sized and it was the mirror on his mother's dressing table a million years ago. He stopped sliding and tried to sit up. The bracing hand skidded and he hit his head.

He tried more cautiously. He could sit up by carefully shifting his weight, but he couldn't stand. The surface was frictionless. Compared to it, glare ice was like sandpaper.

He lay down and looked up. Overhead was nothing. He thought about that for quite a while. Nothing. No thing. Nothing with a flaw in it. A little flaw. He peered at it. It was in the shape of a tiny naked man. He moved a leg. The tiny naked man moved a leg. Everything clicked into focus. A mirror under him and, at an incredible height above him, another.

Now, he thought, I'm a germ on a big microscope. His body felt odd. He managed to sit up again. He looked at himself. Clean. Impossibly, incredibly clean. His fingernails were snowy. His toenails were like white paper. His skin was clean and pink with a glow of health, but the old heart went thudding slowly and sickly along.

Silence. All he could hear was the roar of his blood in his ears. Like listening to a sea shell. There had been a big pink conch in his grandfather's house.

"Hear the sea, Marty?"

The mirror tilted and he slid into a hole that wasn't there before. He came out into a square blue room.

His three blondes were there, watching him. We don't get pink elephants. We don't get snakes and bugs. We get blondes.

He stood up, too aware of his nudity. They watched him calmly, ignoring it.

"Now, look," he said, "can't we be friends?"

They had changed. Their mouths were different—vivid green paint in a perfect rectangle. They looked at him with that calm pride of ownership. Nice doggy.

"Now, look," he began again, and stopped when he noticed their strange dresses. He looked closer. Ladies, please, you can't dress with a paint spray. But they had.

"This," he said, "is a nightmare by Petty, out of Varga."

The paint job was nicely shaded at the edges, but just a paint job. One of them stepped to him, grabbed him by the hair and tilted his head back. She looked into his eyes and made a little satisfied clucking sound. She turned and pointed to the corner.

"Yup now," she said.

"How does one go about yupping?" he asked vacantly.

She looked at one of the other blondes, who said slowly and precisely, "Hurry—up—now. Late."

There was a pile of clothes in the corner. He went over, glad for a chance of regaining pants, even in a dream world. The garments were recognizable, the material wasn't. A sartorial cartoon of the American male, mid-twentieth century. Every incongruity of the clothing exaggerated. Sleeve buttons like saucers. Shoulders padded out a foot on each side. No buttons, no snaps, no zippers. You just got inside them and they were on, somehow. The buttons on the suit were fakes. The suit was bright blue with a harsh red stripe.

Dressed, he felt like a straight man in a burlesque.

From a distance he heard a great shout. It sounded like "Yah-hah!" from ten thousand throats. He suddenly had the strong hunch that he was going on display.

The nearest blonde confirmed that hunch. She stepped over and clamped a metal circlet around his forehead.

Three golden chains dangled from his headpiece. Each blonde took one chain. The nearest one to one of the blue walls touched it. A slit appeared and folded back. They went through. The blondes began to strut. A midway strut. A stripper stomp.

"Here comes Martin," he said feebly.

HE was in the middle of a garden. The clipped turf underfoot was springy. Tailored terraces rose on three sides. A fat sun and a billion flowers and several thousand exceptionally handsome people wearing paint jobs and nothing else.

The center arena had some people in it, people fastened to chains as he was, each one held by three blondes. The spectators were all on the terraces. There was a picnic atmosphere.

They went into the middle of the arena. The other captives were being led in an endless circle.

"Yah-hah!" the multitude yelled. "Yah-hah-hah!"

They posed in the center and then began the circling. Martin stared at his fellow captives. Some were men and some were women. One wore animal skins; another wore armor. One was dressed like the pictures of George Washington. Some wore clothing he'd never seen before.

He was led around and around. More performers took their center ring bow. Something was bothering him, some silly small thing. He couldn't fit his mind over it. Too much was going on in this delirium.

Then he got it—all the captives had red hair.

He turned and looked at the scared woman who walked behind him. She had red hair, one blue eye and one brown eye. She wore gingham and a sunbonnet.

He sneaked looks at the others. One blue eye. One brown eye. Red hair.

Everyone stopped walking. There was a great and final, "Yah-hah." Three sets of blondes stood in the center ring without captives. Their heads were bowed.

His blondes trotted him over, took off the circlet and

flipped him back into the blue room. The slit was closed. He pinched his leg.

"Hell," he said softly.

The slit opened after what he imagined to be an hour had passed. One of his blondes came back. She had a man with her, a chesty citizen dressed in cerise paint.

"Talkit ya tempo," she said, pointing at the chesty man.

He beamed at Martin. "Blessings," he said.

"Blessings yourself."

"Indebted. Thanking very much."

"Your welcoming very much, bud."

"Knowing all?" the man asked with a wide arm sweep.

"Knowing nothing. Not a damned thing! What's this all about?"

The chesty man beamed some more. He scratched his paint job lightly. He frowned. "Hard to say. You past. I future. Is party. My party. My house. My garden. Having game. Sending ladies your tempo, lot of tempos. All same thing. Bringing only with red on hair, eye brown, eye blue. Hard to find. For game."

Martin goggled at him. "You mean a scavenger hunt through time?"

"Not knowing. Is only game. Some ladies failing. Too bad."

"What happens to them?"

The man grinned. "No present for them. Now, present for you. Returning. Any place in tempo yours. To place taken. To other place. Sooner, later. Your choice."

"Return me to any . . . moment in my life?"

"All tempo function. You say—how?—resonance."

"Send me to December 10th, eight P.M."

MARTIN GREYNOR was sitting on the edge of his bed. He had just yanked his shoelaces tight in the left shoe. The tipped laces were still in his hands. He let go of them. He heard a shower pouring. The sound stopped suddenly.

His throat was full of rusty wire. "Ruth?"

She opened the bathroom door. She was wrapped in a big yellow towel.

"What is it now, Marty? My goodness, you've been needling me all evening. You're in a perfectly foul humor. I'm hurrying just as fast as I can."

"Ruth, I . . ." He tried to smile. His lips felt split.

She came to him, quick with concern. "Marty! Are you all right, darling? You look so odd."

"Me? I've never been more all right." He pulled her down beside him.

"Hey, you! I'm soaking wet."

"Baby, do we have to drive way out there tonight? Do we?"

She stared at him. "Good Lord, it was *your* idea. I detest both of them. You know that."

"Let's stay home. Just the two of us. Bust open that brandy, maybe. Use up some of those birch logs."

"But we accepted and . . ."

He held her tightly. He would never let her go.

She whispered, "I like you better this way, instead of all snarly and grouchy." She giggled. "I think we could phone and tell them you have a fever, darling. It wouldn't *really* be a lie."

SHE made the call, winking at him as she gave worried noises about his symptoms. She hung up and said, "She was huffy and painfully sweet. Tonight the Greynors are at home. Darling, it would have been a crummy evening."

"A . . . disastrous evening."

"They play kid games all the time. That's what irks me. Remember in the summer? They had a scavenger hunt. If that isn't the height of silliness!"

He looked at the fire glow reflected in her hair.

"It isn't a bad game, baby."

"What do you mean?"

He shrugged. "Guess it depends on who's playing it and what the prize is."

"Labor Supply" appeared in the same issue of
Fantasy and Science Fiction as "Snulbug" by the
late Anthony Boucher and "Lot" by the late
Ward Moore. It dropped from sight immediately, and
was never reprinted. It is a pleasure to make this
charming tale of gnomes and psychology once again
available to a wide audience.

LABOR SUPPLY

The Magazine of Fantasy and
Science Fiction

May, 1953

"THEY do what?" Dr. Vrees said, conscious of
inanity.

His patient was a large young man. During the
thorough physical checkup prior to this psychiatric ques-
tioning, Dr. Vrees had decided, with all the dolor of a
spindly man, that this Robert Smith was a truly amazing
physical specimen. He was muscled like a stereotype
picture of a Viking, and with lean cow-hand hips. There
were six feet four inches of him, and every inch in a
perfect bloom of health.

Robert Smith seemed lost in some dismal private thought.

"They do what?" Dr. Vrees repeated.

"Huh? Oh, they go whoop, whoop, whoop. Sort of."

"In your dreams do these . . . uh . . . whoops convey any meaning?"

"I guess I understand them all right. Or *we* understand them, you might say, because I . . . we . . . keep working. And all the Ruths, too."

"All the Ruths," Dr. Vrees repeated mechanically. Just one Ruth was almost too much to contemplate. Dr. Vrees was highly aware of her, out there in the waiting room. Ruth Jones was as dark as Robert Smith was fair, and she was built on the same heroic scale. At least six feet tall, and proud of it, moving like a ship under a full head of sail. Just to look at her tall beauty, sensing the ripeness of her, made Dr. Vrees unhappily aware of his yen for tall women, a yen which was successfully canceled out by his refusal to look ridiculous in public.

Dr. Vrees was also aware that these new patients irritated him. His attitude, he knew, was unprofessional. If their only possession had been their physical beauty, he could have taken refuge in his own sense of intellectual superiority. But Vrees had gone through a series of standard tests and found that both of them were as bright as he was, which was very bright indeed. Smith was a highly successful young civil engineer. Both of them had inherited money. Their marriage was being delayed until this matter of the recurrent dreams could be straightened out. And that, in itself, was an indication of thoughtful emotional stability.

"Recurrent dreams are not unusual," Dr. Vrees said. "Most of them are the result of some physical disorder. The others, as evidences of emotional turmoil, are most often found in late childhood and early adolescence."

Robert Smith inspected the big knuckles on his right hand. "You can see what we're afraid of, Dr. Vrees. We're afraid that . . . somehow . . . Ruth and I react on each other the wrong way. There must be some strain there, or we wouldn't have these ridiculous dreams. We're very deeply in love."

"Neither of you has any physical ailment, Mr. Smith. I confess I've never examined a healthier pair. And your histories, too. Both from long-lived familes who seem free of hereditary ailments. And both from very large families, too."

Smith flushed. "We hope to have at least a dozen kids, Doctor."

"I'm sure you will," Vrees said hastily.

Smith went on, slowly. "We talked it over. Gosh, we've talked this dream stuff over a hundred times. I suppose you doctors are accustomed to dig down into people's pasts and find out the root cause of . . . emotional trouble. Both Ruth and I had the happiest childhoods imaginable. And then, six months ago, these dreams started. I had them first. I told Ruth about them. Like a joke, you know. And then she started to have them."

"That's unusual, Robert, but not improbable. She began to worry about you. Out of sympathy, she duplicates your dreams."

"There's something pretty nasty about these dreams," Robert said heavily.

Vrees made a few meaningless marks on his notebook. "Well, suppose you go out and send Ruth in and I'll question her for a while."

"Okay, doctor." Smith got up, obviously glad that the interview was over. He held the door open for Ruth, closed it when she had entered the dimly lighted office.

Vrees was glad when she stopped towering over him and the desk and sat down. She seemed composed.

"Just tell me about these dreams in your own words, Miss Jones. I'll interrupt with questions when any occur to me."

She twisted her gloves, untwisted them. "There doesn't seem to be any pattern to them, exactly. And they aren't all really alike. Just the place is alike every time. So very hot, you know. And have you ever looked in one of those mirrors where you can duplicate yourself, so you see a whole line, and they're all you?"

"Of course."

"That's the way it is. There are just hundreds and thousands of me, and of Robert too. And working so terribly hard. All naked and toiling. And crying, sometimes. There are corridors, and you have to walk down them all bent over. But the new corridors are better. You can stand up in those. We're making them."

"With what tools?"

"The tools are easy. Like gold pencils with two little clocks on one side. They cut the stone and the stone is all blue. Really blue. Cobalt, I guess. And the stones have to be put in baskets. Those baskets hang in the air and when you load them up they sink almost to the floor. When you pull the first one, all the others follow it like . . . animals. And we have to dump them down a dark place. You never hear them hit bottom."

"You say you are duplicated almost endlessly. Do you always see things from the viewpoint of . . . any specific duplication of yourself?"

"No. It is always different, but still *me*, you understand. Sometimes it changes a lot of times in the same dream."

"But you have to perform this labor?"

"Oh, yes. They won't let you stop. If you stop, they have a flicking, stinging thing that you can't even see them use. It hurts, terribly. I scream when they use it."

"Can you describe these . . . overseers?"

"This . . . sounds so terribly silly. They're . . . gnomes. You know. Little gnarly men with squatty legs and lumpy red faces and hats that come to peaks and they wear soft green. I used to love fairy tales, and the gnomes were my favorites. Now . . . I hate them. I hate them!"

"Please, Miss Jones. Don't let it excite you. We'll find a way out of this."

"Oh, I hope so."

"These little . . . ah . . . men, they speak to you?"

"They make a funny sound."

"Can you describe it?"

"Sort of whoop, whoop."

"I see," Vrees said. "Whoop, whoop." The girl gave

him a sharp look, and flushed, then began glove-twisting again.

Vrees said, "We mustn't overlook the possibility of some sort of . . . ah . . . sexual connotation here. I mean, if both of you are rigorously sublimating your normal instincts toward each other. . . ."

"In the dreams they herd us into a sleeping place. There's a feeding place, where we eat something wet and gray, and then there's a sleeping place. And in the sleeping place all those thousands of Roberts and the thousands of me, we all . . . ." She covered her eyes, sat with her head bowed.

Vrees swallowed hard. "I was discussing the question of sublimation."

She lifted her head in a regal way. "No. We aren't sublimating anything."

"Now, to go on to another point. You didn't start having these dreams until Robert began telling you about them, in detail."

"That is correct. But you see, I dreamed details which he hadn't dreamed yet. Then later, he'd dream those same details. Like a place where three new corridors branch off, not far from the feeding place."

"Ah, but you told him the new details and then he would dream them!"

"You mean, I influenced him by telling him? We wondered about that, too. So we started writing down new things we saw in the dreams, and not telling each other. Then we compared notes quite a while later. They matched, almost perfectly."

Vrees smiled. "Of course, my dear. You see, you two people are very close. Some day we will be able to pin down more closely this business of thought transference. There is a channel between your mind and Robert's. I think that is quite evident."

The girl nodded, dubiously.

Vrees went on. "There are many cases on record. I try to keep an open mind. Often you will find that identical twins have that faculty to a higher degree than the rest of us. There is the classic case of the twin sister who was on the *Lusitania,* and her sister in New York dreamed the entire disaster in precise detail and it was such a shock to her that she wrote it all down the moment she awakened. Later it was found to match the eye-witness reports with astounding accuracy. If I were you, Miss Jones, I should not worry too much about your both dreaming the same thing. Our purpose here is to find out why Robert started having these dreams in the first place. Once we find that reason, and eliminate it, I am positive that you will both stop having the dreams."

"We've worried so much about it."

"They do sound ominously realistic, I grant you. Frightening."

She straightened out her gloves. "I don't know if this means anything, Dr. Vrees, but you see, I've been having the dreams for five months. With Robert, it's nearly six. And . . . lately . . . well, maybe it isn't important."

"Please go on, my dear."

She lifted her chin and said, almost defiantly, "In the dreams, all of my . . . duplicates are quite obviously pregnant."

Vrees closed his mouth after an unprofessional interval. He said, "A vague theory begins to present itself. Robert states that he had a happy childhood, that he enjoyed being a member of such a large family. Eleven children, weren't there?"

"That's correct."

"Let us assume for a moment that, subconsciously, he did not like being a part of a large family at all, that he resented all the others for . . . diluting the love his parents could have given to him alone."

"But Robert isn't . . . ."

"Just a moment. Let me follow through on this. He sees a horrid dream world where your love for him is diluted in a similar fashion. I do not yet understand the symbolism of all of the duplications of him, and of your-self, but I feel that our method of approach is through psychoanalysis. I can give him two afternoons a week, a two hour session each time. I shall try to uncover this childhood feeling of jealousy toward his brothers and sisters. You see how pregnancy comes in, don't you? Each time he saw his mother heavy with child, he knew that there would be yet another dilution of the amount of love she had to give."

"Yes, but . . . ."

"Now I'll ask Robert to come in and the three of us will talk this over."

A MONTH later, the analyst's couch having failed, sodium pentathol having uncovered nothing but further details of the dreams, Vrees was beginning to speculate about bringing in a colleague who had had a certain amount of success with hypnosis.

One day at lunch at his professional club, Vrees happened to sit with Louisoln, the physicist, and Cramer, another psychoanalyst. Out of common courtesy, Vrees wanted to avoid shop talk in front of Louisoln, but Cramer, having heard a bit of the Smith-Jones case, was eager to hear the latest developments, if any. In spite of his good intentions, Vrees found himself discussing the "hypothetical" case with a confidence so precarious that he was certain Cramer could see through it.

"What is this . . . duplication?" Louisoln asked.

"Just a dream, Doctor," Vrees explained. "A patient of mine has a recurring dream in which he sees himself endlessly duplicated, laboring in a sort of bondage to a bunch of gnomes."

Louisoln chuckled. "Duplication of matter. A pretty solution to the labor problem, no? Of course, if matter could be duplicated, the demand for labor would not be high, except for the most menial sort of work. For example, duplication of matter would be no good, if one wished a ditch dug."

Vrees laughed, a bit flatly, "You sound, Dr. Louisoln, as though duplication of matter was a possibility. To me the idea is quite shocking."

Louisoln raised one matted gray eyebrow. "Shocking? My boy, you are living with it, each day. I shall not go into the quantum theory."

"Please don't," Cramer said, softening rudeness with a smile.

"But please, gentlemen, consider a phonograph record. Say the music, as such, is a subtance. Using an electrical theory of matter, it is a substance. And it can be duplicated endlessly, by merely reproducing the same circumstances, a needle in a wax groove imparting an electrical impulse. With your kinescope the shadows of two dimensional television stars are also endlessly duplicated. So why should it be at all shocking to you, gentlemen, to fit your minds around the idea that if the electrical charges in the basic building blocks of matter can be precisely duplicated, the matter itself will be duplicated? It would take vast energy, of course, to work the mass-energy formula backwards, but inconceivable? No. Not at all." He gave them a leonine glare and delved back into his cheese cake.

It was then that Vrees began to live in mild fantasy. Louisoln's matter-of-fact statements gave idiotic credence to the Smith-Jones recurrent dream.

That afternoon, while listening to a well-upholstered matron relate, in doze-producing detail, an account of how, at the age of eleven, her half-sister had shoved her out of a cherry tree, breaking her collarbone, Vrees found himself playing the childhood game of "supposing."

Suppose the legends of gnomes have a basis in fact. Suppose they are underworld or otherworld creatures, far more advanced than man. Aren't there tales of humans being taken as slaves by them? Supposing these gnomes need more labor. A bigger supply. It would upset mankind too much to have a rash of thousands of disappearances. And then, of course, there would be the problem of selection of healthy specimens, good breeding stock, possessed of sufficient intelligence. Now if they could merely select two specimens with all the requirements, create endless duplicates, set them to work, wouldn't it be possible that some extrasensory thread might connect the souls of those duplicated and their hard-laboring counterparts who were underworld or, perhaps, otherworld. It could well be otherworld. There had been a rash of things in the sky. And where, even in the bowels of the earth, could you find cobalt blue rock?

"What do you think, Doctor? I'm still waiting?"

"Perhaps I can detect something significant, Madame, in the way you rephrase the question."

"I see. I'll ask it this way. Do you think there's any significance in the fact that it was a cherry tree I was pushed out of?"

Vrees groaned inwardly. "We have not yet reached the stage where we can discuss symbolism, Madame. If you would please continue."

A FEW DAYS later Mr. Smith and Miss Jones sat in the doctor's office. They had come at once when myriad Doctors Vrees had appeared in their dreams.

And Dr. Vrees had been expecting their call.

Although it was now dusk, he didn't turn on the lights. Mr. Smith and Miss Jones held hands. Tightly. Vrees had talked until his voice was husky. The avoidance of madness, he had found, was like working your way around and around the outside of a tall building, with your fingernails scratching the cornice.

Everything had been said, including the impossibility of trying to tell anyone else in the world.

They sat in silence. At last Vrees said, "I guess they decided they needed me to assist in the . . . ah . . . multiple births."

"And take care of the children, afterward, perhaps," Miss Jones said dreamily.

Vrees flinched inwardly. He smiled at all children, patted their heads and gave them gum. He detested them.

"Then there's nothing we can do, is there?" Robert asked.

"Nothing," Vrees said. "Perhaps, in time, as that . . . uh . . . regimentation causes an emotional and intellectual deviation from . . . our norms, the contact will gradually be broken."

Robert stood up. He said, "I guess Ruth and I better go ahead with the wedding. Will you come, Doctor?"

Again he winced inwardly. "Ah . . . I've a pretty full schedule."

"Of course," Ruth said. "We should all get together now and then, though, to sort of . . . check up."

"I'm prescribing sedatives for myself," Vrees said. "I intend to stop dreaming."

He walked them to the door. He could not help considering them his enemies. They had gotten him into this horror. And besides, they towered over him.

But he had to make some gesture.

At the door he said softly, so softly that they both had to bend down a little to hear him. "That sound they make. You . . . uh . . . were right. It's definitely whoop, whoop."

He sat alone in the dark after they had gone. He was an honest and objective man. Yet it took him an hour to isolate that final reason for his sense of bitterness. He realized it at last. Somewhere 1,000 Drs. Vrees attended 10,000 Ruths. Yet, through an irony of selection, they were all as unattainable as the original Ruth was to the original Vrees. Anyway, they'd all be too busy with the children.

One would be hard pressed to put together a book
entitled **The Best SF From Cosmopolitan**, but if it were
done, then surely this lovely fantasy would be
the lead story. Judith Merril included it in
The Year's Best S-F: 10th Annual Edition, 1965.
You may want to think about it the next time
you are on a lonely road late at night.

THE LEGEND OF JOE LEE

Cosmopolitan
October, 1964

"TONIGHT," Sergeant Lazeer said, "we get him for
sure."

We were in a dank office in the Afaloosa County
Courthouse in the flat wetlands of south central Florida.
I had come over from Lauderdale on the half chance of
a human interest story that would tie in with the series
we were doing on the teen-age war against the square
world of the adult.

He called me over to the table where he had the

county map spread out. The two other troopers moved in beside me.

"It's a full moon night and he'll be out for sure," Lazeer said, "and what we're fixing to do is bottle him on just the right stretch, where he got no way off it, no old back country roads he knows like the shape of his own fist. And here we got it." He put brackets at either end of a string-straight road.

Trooper McCollum said softly. "That there, Mister, is a eighteen mile straight, and we cruised it slow, and you turn on off it you're in the deep ditch and the black mud and the 'gator water."

Lazeer said, "We stake out both ends, hide back good with lights out. We got radio contact, so when he comes whistling in either end, we got him bottled."

He looked up at me as though expecting an opinion, and I said, "I don't know a thing about road blocks, Sergeant, but it looks as if you could trap him."

"You ride with me, Mister, and we'll get you a story."

"There's one thing you haven't explained, Sergeant. You said you know who the boy is. Why don't you just pick him up at home?"

The other trooper Frank Gaiders said, "Because that fool kid ain't been home since he started this crazy business five-six months ago. His name is Joe Lee Cuddard, from over to Lasco City. His folks don't know where he is, and don't much care, him and that Farris girl he was running with, so we figure the pair of them is off in the piney woods someplace, holed up in some abandoned shack, coming out at night for kicks, making fools of us."

"Up till now, boy," Lazeer said. "Up till tonight. To-night is the end."

"But when you've met up with him on the highway," I asked, "you haven't been able to catch him?"

The three big, weathered men looked at each other with slow, sad amusement, and McCollum sighed, "I come the closest. The way these cars are beefed up as interceptors, they can do a dead honest hundred and twenty. I saw him across the flats, booming to where the two road forks come together up ahead, so I floored it and I was flat out when the roads joined, and not over fifty yards behind him. In two minutes he had me by a mile, and in four minutes it was near two, and then he was gone. That comes to a hundred and fifty, my guess."

I showed my astonishment. "What the hell does he drive?"

Lazeer opened the table drawer and fumbled around in it and pulled out a tattered copy of a hot-rodder magazine. He opened it to a page where readers had sent in pictures of their cars. It didn't look like anything I had ever seen. Most of it seemed to be bare frame, with a big chromed engine. There was a teardrop shaped passenger compartment mounted between the big rear wheels, bigger than the front wheels, and there was a tail-fin arrangement that swept up and out and then curved back so that the high rear ends of the fins almost met.

"That engine," Frank Gaiders said, "it's a '61 Pontiac, the big one he bought wrecked and fixed up, with blowers and special cams and every damn thing. Put the rest of it together himself. You can see in the letter there, he calls it a C.M. Special. C.M. is for Clarissa May, that Farris girl he took off with. I saw that thing just one time, oh, seven, eight months ago, right after he got it all finished. We got this magazine from his daddy. I saw it at the Amoco gas in Lasco City. You could near give it a ticket standing still. Strawberry flake paint it says in the letter. Damnedest thing, bright strawberry with little like gold flakes in it, then covered with maybe seventeen coats of lacquer all rubbed down so you look down into that paint like it was six inches deep. Headlights all the hell over the front of it and big taillights all over the back, and shiny pipes sticking out. Near two years he worked on it. Big racing flats like the drag strip kids use over to the airport."

I looked at the coarse screen picture of the boy standing beside the car, hands on his hips, looking very young, very ordinary, slightly self-conscious.

"It wouldn't spoil anything for you, would it," I asked, "if I went and talked to his people, just for background?"

" 'Long as you say nothing about what we're fixing to do," Lazeer said. "Just be back by eight thirty this evening."

Lasco City was a big brave name for a hamlet of about five hundred. They told me at the sundries store to take the west road and the Cuddard place was a half mile on the left, name on the mailbox. It was a shacky place, chickens in the dusty yard, fence sagging. Leo Cuddard was home from work and I found him out in back, unloading cinder block from an ancient pickup. He was stripped to the waist, a lean, sallow man who looked undernourished and exhausted. But the muscles in his spare back writhed and knotted when he lifted the blocks. He had pale hair and pale eyes and a narrow mouth. He would not look directly at me. He grunted and kept on working as I introduced myself and stated my business.

Finally he straightened and wiped his forehead with his narrow arm. When those pale eyes stared at me, for some reason it made me remember the grisly reputation Florida troops acquired in the Civil War. Tireless, deadly, merciless.

"THAT boy warn't no help to me, Mister, but he warn't no trouble neither. The onliest thing on his mind was that car. I didn't hold with it, but I didn't put down no foot. He fixed up that old shed there to work in, and he needed something, he went out and earned up the money to buy it. They was a crowd of them around most times, helpin' him, boys workin' and gals watchin'. Them tight-pants girls. Have radios on batteries set around so as they could twisty dance while them boys hammered that metal out. When I worked around and overheard 'em, I swear I couldn't make out more'n one word from seven. What he done was take that car to some national show, for prizes and such. But one day he just took off, like they do nowadays."

"Do you hear from him at all?"

He grinned. "I don't hear *from* him, but I sure God hear *about* him."

"How about brothers and sisters?"

"They's just one sister, older, up to Waycross, Georgia, married to an electrician, and me and his stepmother."

As if on cue, a girl came out onto the small back porch. She couldn't have been more than eighteen. Advanced pregnancy bulged the front of her cotton dress. Her voice was a shrill, penetrating whine. "Leo? Leo, honey, that can opener thing just now busted clean off the wall."

"Mind if I take a look at that shed?"

"You help yourself, Mister."

The shed was astonishingly neat. The boy had rigged up droplights. There was a pale blue pegboard wall hung with shining tools. On closer inspection I could see that rust was beginning to fleck the tools. On the workbench were technical journals and hot-rodder magazines. I looked at the improvised engine hoist, at the neat shelves of paint and lubricant.

The Farris place was nearer the center of the village. Some of them were having their evening meal. There were six adults as near as I could judge, and perhaps a dozen children from toddlers on up to tall, lanky boys. Clarissa May's mother came out onto the front porch to talk to me, explaining that her husband drove an interstate truck from the cooperative and he was away from the next few days. Mrs. Farris was grossly fat, but with delicate features, an indication of the beauty she must have once had. The rocking chair creaked under her weight and she fanned herself with a newspaper.

"I can tell you, it like to broke our hearts the way Clarissa May done us. If'n I told LeRoy once, I told him a thousand times, no good would ever come of her messin' with that Cuddard boy. His daddy is trashy. Ever so often they take him in for drunk and put him on the county road gang sixty or ninety days, and that Stubbins child he married, she's next door to feeble-witted. But children get to a certain size and know everything and turn their backs on you like an enemy. You write this up nice and in it put the message her momma and daddy want her home bad, and maybe she'll see it and come on in. You know what the Good Book says about sharper'n a serpent's tooth. I pray to the good Lord they had the sense to drive that fool car up to Georgia and get married up at least. Him nineteen and her seventeen. The young ones are going clean out of hand these times. One night racing through this county the way they do, showing off, that Cuddard boy is going to kill hisself and my child too."

"Was she hard to control in other ways, Mrs. Farris?"

"No, sir, she was neat and good and pretty and quiet, and she had the good marks. It was just about Joe Lee Cuddard she turned mulish. I think I would have let LeRoy whale that out of her if it hadn't been for her trouble.

"You're easier on a young one when there's no way of knowing how long she could be with you. Doc Mathis, he had us taking her over to the Miami clinic. Sometimes they kept her and sometimes they didn't, and she'd get behind in her school and then catch up fast. Many times we taken her over there. She's got the sick blood and it takes her poorly. She should be right here, where's help to care for her in the bad spells. It was October last year, we were over to the church bingo, LeRoy and me, and Clarissa May been resting up in her bed a few days, and that wild boy come in and taking her off in that snorty car, the little ones couldn't stop him. When I think of her out there . . . poorly and all . . . . "

AT a little after nine we were in position. I was with Sergeant Lazeer at the west end of that eighteen mile stretch of State Road 21. The patrol car was backed into a narrow dirt road, lights out. Gaiders and McCollum were similarly situated at the east end of the trap. We were smeared with insect repellent, and we had used spray on the backs of each other's shirts where the mosquitoes were biting through the thin fabric.

Lazeer had repeated his instructions over the radio, and we composed ourselves to wait. "Not much travel on this road this time of year," Lazeer said. "But some tourists come through at the wrong time, they could mess this up. We just got to hope that don't happen."

"Can you block the road with just one car at each end?"

"If he comes through from the other end, I move up quick and put it crosswise where he can't get past, and Frank has a place like that at the other end. Crosswise with the lights and the dome blinker on, but we both are going to stand clear because maybe he can stop it and maybe he can't. But whichever way he comes, we got to have the free car run close herd so he can't get time to turn around when he sees he's bottled."

Lazeer turned out to be a lot more talkative than I had anticipated. He had been in law enforcement for twenty years and had some violent stories. I sensed he was feeding them to me, waiting for me to suggest I write a book about him. From time to time we would get out of the car and move around a little.

"Sergeant, you're pretty sure you've picked the right time and place?"

"He runs on the nights the moon is big. Three or four nights out of the month. He doesn't run the main highways, just these back country roads—the long straight paved stretches where he can really wind that thing up. Lord God, he goes through towns like a rocket. From reports we got, he runs the whole night through, and this is one way he comes, one way or the other, maybe two, three times before moonset. We got to get him. He's got folks laughing at us."

I sat in the car half listening to Lazeer tell a tale of blood and horror. I could hear choruses of swamp toads mingling with the whine of insects close to my ears, looking for a biting place. A couple of times I had heard the bass throb of a 'gator.

Suddenly Lazeer stopped and I sensed his tenseness. He leaned forward, head cocked. And then, mingled with the wet country shrilling, and then overriding it, I heard the oncoming high-pitched snarl of high combustion.

"Hear it once and you don't forget it," Lazeer said, and unhooked the mike from the dash and got through to McCollum and Gaiders. "He's coming through this end, boys. Get yourself set."

He hung up and in the next instant the C.M. Special went by. It was a resonant howl that stirred echoes inside the inner ear. It was a tearing, bursting rush of wind that rattled fronds and turned leaves over. It was a dark shape in moonlight, slamming by, the howl diminishing as the wind of passage died.

Lazeer plunged the patrol car out onto the road in a screeching turn, and as we straightened out, gathering speed, he yelled to me, "Damn fool runs without lights when the moon is bright enough."

As had been planned, we ran without lights too, to keep Joe Lee from smelling the trap until it was too late. I tightened my seat belt and peered at the moonlit road. Lazeer had estimated we could make it to the far end in ten minutes or a little less. The world was like a photographic negative—white world and black trees and brush, and no shades of grey. As we came quickly up to speed, the heavy sedan began to feel strangely light. It toe-danced, tender and capricious, the wind roar louder than the engine sound. I kept wondering what would happen if Joe Lee stopped dead up there in darkness. I kept staring ahead for the murderous bulk of his vehicle.

Soon I could see the distant red wink of the other sedan, and then the bright cone where the headlights shone off the shoulder into the heavy brush. When my eyes adjusted to that brightness, I could no longer see the road. We came down on them with dreadful speed. Lazeer suddenly snapped our lights on, touched the siren. We were going to see Joe Lee trying to back and turn around on the narrow paved road, and we were going to block him and end the night games.

We saw nothing. Lazeer pumped the brakes. He cursed. We came to a stop ten feet from the side of the other patrol car. McCollum and Gaiders came out of the shadows. Lazeer and I undid our seat belts and got out of the car.

"We didn't see nothing and we didn't hear a thing," Frank Gaiders said.

Lazeer summed it up. "OK, then. I was running without lights too. Maybe the first glimpse he got of your flasher, he cramps it over onto the left shoulder, tucks it over as far as he dares. I could go by without seeing him. He backs around and goes back the way he came, laughing hisself sick. There's the second chance he tried that and took it too far, and he's wedged in a ditch. Then there's the third chance he lost it. He could have dropped a wheel off onto the shoulder and tripped hisself and gone flying three hundred feet into the swamp. So what we do, we go back there slow. I'll go first and keep my spotlight on the right, and you keep yours on the left. Look for that car and for places where he could have busted through."

At the speed Lazeer drove it took over a half hour to traverse the eighteen mile stretch. He pulled off at the road where we had waited. He seemed very depressed, yet at the same time amused.

THEY talked, then he drove me to the courthouse where my car was parked. He said. "We'll work out something tighter and I'll give you a call. You might as well be in at the end."

I drove sedately back to Lauderdale.

Several days later, just before noon on a bright Sunday, Lazeer phoned me at my apartment and said, "You want to be in on the finish of this thing, you better do some hustling and leave right now."

"You've got him?"

"In a manner of speaking." He sounded sad and wry. "He dumped that machine into a canal off Route 27 about twelve miles south of Okeelanta. The wrecker'll be winching it out anytime now. The diver says he and the gal are still in it. It's been on the radio news. Diver read the tag, and it's his. Last year's. He didn't trouble hisself getting a new one."

I wasted no time driving to the scene. I certainly had no trouble identifying it. There were at least a hundred cars pulled off on both sides of the highway. A traffic control officer tried to wave me on by, but when I showed him my press card and told him Lazeer had phoned me, he had me turn in and park beside a patrol car near the center of activity.

I spotted Lazeer on the canal bank and went over to him. A big man in face mask, swim fins and air tank was preparing to go down with the wrecker hook.

Lazeer greeted me and said, "It pulled loose the first time, so he's going to try to get it around the rear axle this time. It's in twenty feet of water, right side up, in the black mud."

"Did he lose control?"

"Hard to say. What happened early this morning a fellow was goofing around in a little airplane, flying low, parallel to the canal, the water like a mirror, and he seen something down in there so he came around and looked again, then he found a way to mark the spot, opposite those three trees away over there, so he came into his home field and phoned it in, and we had that diver down by nine this morning. I got here about ten."

"I guess this isn't the way you wanted it to end, Sergeant."

"It sure God isn't. It was a contest between him and me, and I wanted to get him my own way. But I guess it's a good thing he's off the night roads."

I looked around. The red and white wrecker was positioned and braced. Ambulance attendants were leaning against their vehicle, smoking and chatting. Sunday traffic slowed and was waved on by.

"I guess you could say his team showed up," Lazeer said.

ONLY then did I realize the strangeness of most of the waiting vehicles. The cars were from a half-dozen counties, according to the tag numbers. There were many big, gaudy, curious monsters not unlike the C.M. Special in basic layout, but quite different in design. They seemed like a visitation of Martian beasts. There were dirty fenderless sedans from the thirties with modern power plants under the hoods, and big rude racing numbers painted on the side doors. There were other cars which looked normal at first glance, but then seemed to squat oddly low, lines clean and sleek where the Detroit chrome had been taken off, the holes leaded up.

The cars and the kids were of another race. Groups of them formed, broke up and re-formed. Radios brought in a dozen stations. They drank Cokes and perched in dense flocks on open convertibles. They wandered from car to car. It had a strange carnival flavor, yet more ceremonial. From time to time somebody would start one of the car engines, rev it up to a bursting roar, and let it die away.

All the girls had long burnished hair and tidy blouses or sun tops and a stillness in their faces, a curious confidence of total acceptance which seemed at odds with the frivolous and provocative tightness of their short shorts, stretch pants, jeans. All the boys were lean, their hairdos carefully ornate, their shoulders high and square, and they moved with the lazy grace of young jungle cats. Some of the couples danced indolently, staring into each other's eyes with a frozen and formal intensity, never touching, bright hair swinging, girls' hips pumping in the stylized ceremonial twist.

Along the line I found a larger group. A boy was strumming slow chords on a guitar, a girl making sharp and erratic fill-in rhythm on a set of bongos. Another boy, in nasal and whining voice, seemed to improvise lyrics as he sang them. "C.M. Special, let it get out and *go.*/C.M. Special, let it way out and *go.*/Iron runs fast and the moon runs slow."

The circle watched and listened with a contained intensity.

Then I heard the winch whining. It seemed to grow louder as, one by one, the other sounds stopped. The kids began moving toward the wrecker. They formed a big silent semicircle. The taut woven cable, coming in very slowly, stretched down at an angle through the sun glitter on the black-brown water.

The snore of a passing truck covered the winch noise for a moment.

"Coming good now," a man said.

First you could see an underwater band of silver, close

to the drop-off near the bank. Then the first edges of the big sweeping fins broke the surface, then the broad rear bumper, then the rich curves of the strawberry paint. Where it wasn't clotted with wet weed or stained with mud, the paint glowed rich and new and brilliant. There was a slow sound from the kids, a sigh, a murmur, a shifting.

As it came up further, the dark water began to spurt from it, and as the water level inside dropped, I saw, through a smeared window, the two huddled masses, the slumped boy and girl, side by side, still belted in.

I wanted to see no more. Lazeer was busy, and I got into my car and backed out and went home and mixed a drink.

I started work on it at about three thirty that afternoon. It would be a feature for the following Sunday. I worked right on through until two in the morning. It was only two thousand words, but it was very tricky and I wanted to get it just right. I had to serve two masters. I had to give lip service to the editorial bias that this sort of thing was wrong, yet at the same time I wanted to capture, for my own sake, the flavor of legend. These kids were making a special world we could not share. They were putting all their skills and dreams and energies to work composing the artifacts of a subculture, power, beauty, speed, skill and rebellion. Our culture was giving them damned little, so they were fighting for a world of their own, with its own customs, legends and feats of valor, its own music, its own ethics and morality.

I took it in Monday morning and left it on Si Walther's desk, with the hope that if it were published intact, it might become a classic. I called it "The Little War of Joe Lee Cuddard."

I didn't hear from Si until just before noon. He came out and dropped it on my desk. "Sorry," he said.

"What's the matter with it?"

"Hell, it's a very nice bit. But we don't publish fiction. You should have checked it out better, Marty, like you usually do. The examiner says those kids have been in the bottom of that canal for maybe eight months. I had Sam check her out through the clinic. She was damn near terminal eight months ago. What probably happened, the boy went to see her and found her so bad off he got scared and decided to rush her to Miami. She was still in her pajamas, with a sweater over them. That way it's a human interest bit. I had Helen do it. It's page one this afternoon, boxed."

I took my worthless story, tore it in half and dropped it into the wastebasket. Sergeant Lazeer's bad guess about the identity of his moonlight road runner had made me look like an incompetent jackass. I vowed to check all facts, get all names right, and never again indulge in glowing, strawberry flake prose.

Three weeks later I got a phone call from Sergeant Lazeer.

He said, "I guess you figured out we got some boy coming in from out of county to fun us these moonlight nights."

"Yes, I did."

"I'm right sorry about you wasting that time and effort when we were thinking we were after Joe Lee Cuddard. We're having some bright moonlight about now, and it'll run full tomorrow night. You want to come over, we can show you some fun, because I got a plan that's dead sure. We tried it last night, but there was just one flaw, and he got away through a road we didn't know about. Tomorrow he won't get that chance to melt away."

I remembered the snarl of that engine, the glimpse of a dark shape, the great wind of passage. Suddenly the backs of my hands prickled. I remembered the emptiness of that stretch of road when we searched it. Could there have been that much pride and passion, labor and love and hope, that Clarissa May and Joe Lee could forever ride the night roads of their home county, balling through the silver moonlight? And what curious message had assembled all those kids from six counties so quickly?

"You there? You still there?"

"Sorry, I was trying to remember my schedule. I don't think I can make it."

"Well, we'll get him for sure this time."

"Best of luck. Sergeant."

"Six cars this time. Barricades. And a spotter plane. He hasn't got a chance if he comes into the net."

I guess I should have gone. Maybe hearing it again, glimpsing the dark shape, feeling the stir of the night wind, would have convinced me of its reality. They didn't get him, of course. But they came so close, so very close. But they left just enough room between a heavy barricade and a live oak tree, an almost impossibly narrow place to slam through. But thread it he did, and rocket back onto the hard top and plunge off, leaving the fading, dying contralto drone.

Sergeant Lazeer is grimly readying next month's trap. He says it is the final one. Thus far, all he has captured are the two little marks, a streak of paint on the rough edge of a timber sawhorse, another nudge of paint on the trunk of the oak. Strawberry red. Flecked with gold.

Chosen by Harry Harrison and Brian W. Aldiss
as one of the best science fiction stories of 1968,
"The Annex" is a powerful psychological study
worthy of the best produced by the so-called "New
Wave" of the late sixties. It is also the most recent sf
to come from John D. MacDonald's typewriter.
Compare it with the first story in this collection and
experience the evolution of a fine writer of
speculative fiction.

THE ANNEX

Playboy
May, 1968

DURING the last hour of the night, the charge nurse
looked in at the critical in Room 11, intensive-care section, coronary. She scowled and made an ugly, displeased
mouth and hastened to replace the dislodged I.V. needle
in the vein inside the elbow of the right arm, immo-
bilized by the straps, the board and the side rail of the
bed. She checked the glucose drip, made a small adjustment of the flow valve, checked oxygen supply, listened

to the ragged labor of the pulse and went off and found the pretty little special drinking coffee in the treatment room and joking with the red-headed intern.

After chewing her out with a cold expertise that welled tears into the blue eyes, she herded her back to her night watch over the patient.

"I wasn't gone three minutes, honest," she said.

"An hour before dawn they get restless," the charge nurse said. "As if they had someplace to go, some appointment to keep."

WHEN the first gray light of the morning made the shape of the window visible, he dressed quickly and went out. He guessed that they would not be expecting him to leave that room so soon after arriving.

There were shadows of night still remaining in the empty streets, so that even though he knew his way and walked swiftly, the city seemed strange to him. They were changing it so quickly these past few years. The eye becomes accustomed to the shape and bulk of structures, giving them only a marginal attention; yet when, so abruptly, they were gone, one had the feeling of having made a wrong turn somewhere. Then even the unchanged things began to look half strange.

He turned a dark corner and saw the hotel lights in the distance. A taxi came swiftly to the cross-town corner, made a wrenching, shuddering turn and sped up the empty avenue, and he caught a silhouette glimpse of the sailboat hats of nuns in the dark interior, two or three of them.

He had not been in the hotel for years. He saw at once that it was quite changed. That certain quaintness of the lobby that once set off the high style of the moneyed people and the women of the theater was now merely a shabbiness. He realized that he could have guessed it, because were it not changed, they would not be mixed up in this sort of thing. And his shabby assignment in an unknown room would have occurred in some other place, perhaps even in another city at another time.

There was no one behind the desk. He felt in his pocket

for the identification he would have to present and felt fear and irritation when he did not find it at once. Then, among coins, he fingered the shape of it and took it out and held it in his clasped hand. As he wondered whether to tap the desk bell, he saw movement out of the side of his eye and turned and saw a man walking toward him out of the lobby shadows.

"Mr. Davis?" the small man said; and as he came into the light, his face was elusively familiar. He searched memory and finally recalled the image of the same face, a bellhop uniform in dull red and gray, big brass circle of the master key ring looped around the scrawny neck. And the name came back.

"Do you remember me, Leo? From before?"

"Sure," the man said. He leaned against the desk and yawned. Davis knew the man did not remember him at all.

"You're the manager now?"

"So they keep telling me."

"Come up in the world, eh?"

"I guess so." He yawned again. "You got that thing?"

He felt unaccountably shy about revealing what they had given him. He said, "I keep telling them that they should use ordinary things. But they get fanciful. It just makes everything harder to explain when things go wrong. What kind of a sentimental nut would have a gold miniature of his own dog tag made? A grown man is supposed to get over being in a war."

"Look, I have to see it." Leo's tone was patient and bored, and Davis knew the man had no interest in what he thought and very little interest in why he had come here.

He held his hand out and the little wafer gleamed on his open palm. Leo took it, glanced at it and put it in his own pocket.

"They didn't tell me you'd keep it."

"The room you want is four-two-four-two."

"Are you supposed to keep it? Did they make that clear?"

"Forty-two forty-two. Four thousand, two hundred and forty-two, Mr. Davis, OK?"

"All right. I'll assume you're supposed to keep it, Leo. It's their problem, not mine. But you're supposed to turn over the key, I know *that*."

"I can't, buddy, because the only keys here are the keys to the main house here. You should know that and they should know that. Right? What we're talking about is the annex. Which is being torn down."

"Then there isn't anybody in it?"

"Did I say that, mister? Did anybody say that?"

"There's no reason to get ugly about it, Leo."

"Who's ugly? Listen, they got old foops in there living there since the year one, and lease agreements and all that stuff, so about the only thing they can do is work around them until they get sick of all the noise and mess and get out. There aren't many left now. I think maybe your party is the only one left on that floor, but I don't keep close track. I've got enough to do here without worrying about over there."

"So what do I do about a key? Am I supposed to go knock on the door, for God's sake?"

"Mrs. Dorn is over there. She's got a master key to the whole annex."

"Does she know about me?"

"Why should she? Just con her a little, Mr. Davis. Play it by ear. OK?"

"I don't have much choice, I guess."

"Has anybody lately? Come this way."

Leo led the way back through the lobby and through a huge empty kitchen, where night lights picked up the gleam and shape of stainless steel racks and tables. He pulled a door open and turned on a weak bulb at the head of a narrow flight of stairs.

"The regular way over there has been boarded up, so what you do is just follow the way a red pipe runs along the ceiling there, and when you come to stairs finally, go on up and you'll find her around someplace."

Three steps down, he turned to say his thanks in some massively sarcastic way; but as he turned, the door was slammed. There were distant lights in the vast reaches of the basement, just enough for him to make out the red pipe suspended by straps from the low ceiling overhead. There was a sweaty dampness in the basement. In some far corner, a laboring machine was making a slow and heavy chuffing sound. It made a vibration he could feel through the soles of his shoes as he walked. He noticed that the red pipe overhead was of some kind of plastic material, sufficiently flexible so that there was a perceptible expansion and contraction as the machine made its thick and rhythmic sound.

He estimated that he had walked more than a city block before he came to the stairs, where the red pipe disappeared into a wall. These were unexpectedly wide and elegant stairs, marble streaked with gray and green, ascending in a gentle curve. At the top of the stairs, he pushed a dark door open and found himself in an enormous lobby. It had the silence of a museum. Dropcloths covered the shapes of furniture. Plaster dust was gritty on the floor. Some huge beams had fallen and were propped at an angle, as in pictures of bombings.

"Mrs. Dorn!" he called. "Mrs. Dorn!" The sound did not seem to carry. It died at once into the silence.

Then he heard a click-tock of high heels and he could not tell where the sound was coming from. "Yes?" she said. "You, there! Up here!" Her voice was musical; the tone, impatient. He looked up and saw her standing at the broad ornate railing of a mezzanine floor, looking down at him, in silhouette against a window beyond her. "Yes? What do you want?"

"Can I speak to you a minute?"

"I'm very busy. Well . . . come on up."

She turned away. He looked around and saw the stairs and went up. There was a library and writing room at the top of the stairs. Several doors opened from the room. He tried them, one by one, and found they opened onto corridors. Then, close behind him, she chuckled and, as he turned, startled, she said, "It's really very confusing. I used to get hopelessly lost when I first came here."

She looked like someone he had known, somewhere,

perhaps a long time ago. She had a soft and pretty face, dark wings of careless hair, and she looked at him in a familiar and mocking way of old secrets shared. She wore a shift of some tweedy gray substance over a young, sturdy body with a vital heft of hip and weight of breast.

"I wonder, Mrs. Dorn, if you could . . . . "

"Just a moment, please. I missed this room somehow, and the crews will be arriving any minute, and it would be just my rotten luck if they started here, wouldn't it?" She began to walk slowly around the room, pausing from time to time, pausing to hold at arm's length a piece of soft yellow chalk in the measuring gesture of the artist. She nodded to herself from time to time and then would mark with the chalk a piece of/paneling, or a chair, or the frame of an old painting.

At last she sighed and turned toward him with a smile of enduring patience.

"Done, I guess. As well as I can do it, anyway. They don't really give a damn about saving anything. You have to watch them like hawks. They'll pretend they didn't see the mark and they'll smash stuff to powder and then look so *terribly* innocent. They hate old things, I guess. And hate the loveliest old things worst of all. They just want to come in and biff, bang, crunch and truck it away and get it over with and go on to the next job. My, how they resent me, and resent having to save things and handle them so gently and take them to our warehouse. You wouldn't believe it."

The mark she made each time was a D with a cross drawn through it, like a cancellation.

"What did you want?" she asked.

"They told me that you're the one to see. You can lend me the master key."

"Really? And exactly what room do you want to get into? And why?"

"Four-two-four . . . oh, Forty-two forty, It will take only a . . . very few minutes."

"On the forty-second floor. Now isn't that quaint! Isn't that the living end!"

"What's so funny, Mrs. Dorn? I don't think anything is particularly funny."

"I couldn't possibly explain it to you. I'll have to show you."

"You could let me take the key, couldn't you?"

"My dear man, so much has been torn down and thrown away and smashed, you could wander around up there for weeks trying to find a way to the right floor and the right wing. Even if I believed you, I'd have to go with you in any case."

She led the way back down and through the silence of the lobby and to a back corridor, and into a bird-cage elevator no more than five feet square. She reached and clanged the door shut, turned a worn brass handle and they began to creak slowly upward. He stared up through the ceiling of woven metal strips and saw the sway of the moving cables and, far overhead, a pale square of gray sky.

The animation and mocking amusement had gone out of her. She leaned sagging, looking downward, finger tips on the brass lever, and he sensed that he had no part in what she was thinking. He could look at her with that feeling of invasion one has in watching someone sleep. There was a small mole below the corner of her mouth, on the pale concavity below the soft weight of her underlip. Her lashes were long and dark. He saw the lift and fall of her slow breathing and was aware of a warmth and scent of her breath. There were two deep pockets in the gray shift. The master key would have to be in one or the other. So it could be done. There was always a way.

Suddenly he had the feeling he was being trapped in some curious way, was being led from his assignment into a plan devised for some other reason, a plan wherein his role was minor; and looking at the panel above her resting hand, he saw what had probably given him subtle warning. There were brass buttons for the floors, pressed so many hundred thousand times the incised digits were almost worn away; yet when the gray light struck them properly, he could make out the topmost numeral of the vertical row—21.

"So that's it," he said. "That's what's funny." He made his mouth stretch wide in the knowing grin. The girl looked at him, startled and puzzled. "There's no forty-second floor," he said.

Frowning, she turned and looked at the row of buttons and then back at him. "You're serious? Don't you know about the annex at all? You know how the transients are. Top floor. Top floor. It's all they can think about. But the people who stay have to have private lives, don't they? Not all cluttered up with salesmen and people coming to town for the theater and all that. You've never been in the business, have you? All the city hotels are just the same, you know. The elevators for the transients go only so high, just to such and such a number, and the quiet floors, where people live, are above that, always, and they have their private ways to get up to them."

She was so very patient that he felt ashamed of accusing her and felt irritated with himself for not having guessed, long ago, what she told him. There had always been enough clues. There were always people going through the hotel lobbies, looking neither to the right nor to the left, walking by the regular elevators to some special place and service awaiting them.

But when the elevator stopped and they got out, she reached back into it, pressed the lowest button, yanked her arm out quickly and slammed the latticework door. It began to creak downward, with a clicking of pulleys and rasp of cables. She looked up at him and wrinkled her nose in mischief and mockery, saying, "Don't look so worried. There'll be other ways down." He remembered that she had not told him the joke, and he was once again annoyed at her.

These were broad corridors, pale gray, with composition floors, lighted by misted glass panels set into the ceiling. He tried to walk beside her, but she kept quickening her pace, and he realized she wanted him to walk behind her, a person guided rather than a companion. Many times they reached an intersection where the corridors stretched for vast distances, and sometimes she would pause to orient herself and then turn confidently right or left.

He noticed that all the numbers had been taken off the doors. He could see the raw holes where they had been screwed through gray paint into the plywood.

She was fifteen feet ahead of him, the dark hair bouncing at the nape of her neck to her swift, buoyant stride. The coarse gray fabric pulled in alternating diagonal tensions against her rear, and somehow he knew that were she quite still and quite bare, were he to place his hands so that his fingertips were hooked around the shelf of hip socket, feeling the warm, smooth slide of membrane over bone, holding her from the rear, his hands placed as a player holds a basketball for the long set shot, then through some delicious coincidence of design, the pads of his thumbs would fit precisely into the two deep dimples spaced below her spine. He shook himself out of the erotic musing, remembering how often they had told him that assignments were mishandled too often for exactly this reason.

At the end of a corridor, she pulled a heavy fire door open and turned to give him a bawdy wink, to run her tonguetip across her lips, as though she had read his mind and his weakness; and he determined not to look at her as she climbed the stairs ahead of him, and looked instead at the steel treads set into the concrete. He lost track of the number of flights they climbed. It winded him; and when he helped her push another fire door open, he tried to conceal his laboring lungs and to seem as fresh as she.

These corridors were a pale yellow, like weak winter sunlight, and at last they came to a small elevator standing open. The fluorescence inside was harsh and there was a sharp minty odor, as though it had recently been scrubbed with some cheap, strong antiseptic. It accelerated upward with silent velocity that hollowed his belly and made his knees bend slightly. It opened automatically on a narrower, dingy, old-fashioned corridor. She reached into the elevator as before; and when the door hissed shut and she turned to speak, he said, "I know. There'll be other ways down."

"That isn't what I was going to say."

"I'm sorry. What were you going to say?"

"I can't say it now. You spoiled it."

Again he followed her. These corridors were set at odd angles. The room doors were shiny dark with old coats of varnish. The room numbers were not removed and they were of tarnished brass, fluted and curly and ornate. All the rooms were in the 4000 series, but they were not in any reasonable order, 4100 and something across from or next door to 4800 and something.

She stopped very abruptly, and as he came upon her, he heard what she had heard—the gritty sound of latch and bolt—and then, twenty feet ahead of them, an old couple, dressed for winter, came out of one of the rooms, complaining at each other, fussing, asking if he or she had forgotten this or that, dropping small packages and picking them up.

Just before the old couple turned and noticed them, Mrs. Dorn hooked her arm around his waist and forced him to a slow walk. He put his arm, interlocked, around her, and she reached up with her free hand, placed it against his cheek, chuckled in a furry way, turned her mouth up to the awkward kiss while walking, so that as they passed the couple, he heard tsk's and clucks of their disapproval. "Darling, darling," she murmured. "Dave, darling."

Behind them he heard the old man's voice, without making out the words. There was a harsh resonance to it and then it cracked into a high quaver and then went deep again.

He smiled inside himself, thinking it sounded exactly like Ricky trying to manage his fourteen-year-old voice as it alternately squeaked and rumbled. The fingertips of the arm that was around her waist touched the top of the pocket on the left side of the gray shift, and with sneaky and daring inspiration, he slid his hand down into the pocket, bending his knees inconspicuously to lower himself just enough, the palm of his hand against round, warm thigh under fabric, and with his finger tips he touched the cylinder of yellow chalk and then the thin edge of metal. With the metal held against the nail of his index finger by the pad of his middle finger, he drew it out of the deep pocket and worked it into the palm of his hand.

She stopped and turned and leaned against the corridor wall and, with her hands resting lightly on his shoulders, looked up at him, still mocking him, saying, "You're just not very bright, Dave, darling."

The old people were gone, around a distant corner of the old hallway. Suddenly, he realized that she had cleverly kept them from seeing his face, so that they would be unable to identify him later. And with a sense of disbelief, he realized she had called him by his name.

"You could have told me how much you knew about this," he said.

"It's better for you to guess, dear. Look at what you took."

He opened his palm and saw the miniature gold tag. Name, rank, serial number, blood type O, meaning zero, meaning blood type nothing. The shock was enormous. He was suddenly afraid he might cry like a child and shame himself in front of her. "How did you . . . How could Leo have . . . . "

"Leo? Don't be silly. I had it all along. There were always two, you know. Don't you remember that, even? No, keep it, dear. If I have to have it back, you can always give it to me. Without any fuss. Promise?"

"Sure, but if you could just tell me . . . . "

"I can show you, Dave. Come along."

She paused at the next turning and bit her lip and, standing beside her, he saw that the floor itself dipped down in a gentle curve and lifted again at another place in the distance, where it turned again. It was swaying slightly, the whole corridor, like the bridges primitive peoples wove across deep swift rivers. She told him to walk carefully and stay close to the corridor wall. She motioned to him to stop and they were, he saw, on either side of a double door. It was room 4242. If she knew the rest of it, she would know the right number. It had been so placed that half of it was on each door, so that each was labelled 42. Even though she knew, he did not want her to watch what had to be done, watch the task assigned to him; but before he could ask her to go away, to give him the key and go away, go back and wait for him around the corner, out of sight, she put a bright red key in the lock and the double doors opened inward.

Inward, but outward. They opened onto the nothing of a dizzy height, making a vent for a cold wind that came hasking down the hallway behind him and pushed him a long clumsy stride to stand on the very brink. Far, far, far below, the bug shapes of city cars and trucks moved very slowly, as when seen from an aircraft. He teetered, toes over the edge, and slowly fought back the sickness and the terror, knowing he could not let her see that he suddenly realized how cynically and savagely they had tricked him. He adjusted himself to the slight sway of the corridor and rode it easily, smiling and casual for her benefit, aware of how narrowly she was watching him.

Then came a deep and powerful thud, more vibration than sound. It came welling up from below and it danced the swaying corridor, nearly toppling him out. It came again and again and again. He learned to ride the new motion. The girl whimpered. He looked far down, almost directly down, and said, "It's nothing. Your friends have come to work. They've got some kind of a derrick thing down there and they're swinging one of those big cannon balls against the foundation."

He stepped back with care and reached and took her hand. Her hand was cold and hesitant. He led her past the open and windy space and back to where, once again, the structure was solid underfoot, trembling almost imperceptibly to each subsonic thud. She pulled her hand free and, after walking slowly, looking at the room numbers, chose one, and opened the door, motioning him to come in. The room was in semidarkness, gray light outlining the window. She closed the door and he heard her sigh.

Reaction made him feel weak and sick. He saw the shape of the bed and moved to it and sat on the edge of it.

She came to him and pushed at his shoulder and he lay back, grateful that she understood. He swung his legs on to the bed and she went to the foot and unlaced his shoes and took them off.

"We'd better not make very much noise," she whispered.

"Of course."

"Do you understand about the old people?"

"I know there's something I'm supposed to understand."

"That's enough for now."

She disappeared in the shadows and then he saw her again in silhouette in front of the gray of the window. He heard her sigh and he saw her, with slow and weary motion, tug the shift off over her head, toss it aside, pat her rumpled hair back into order, then bend and slip her shoes off. She stood near the corner of the window, half turned, standing quite still in silhouette, hips in relaxed and wary tilt, and he remembered one of the girls in that Degas print standing off at the side, standing in exactly the same position.

He knew she would turn and come to him but would not understand about what weakness had done to him. He did not want to confess that kind of weakness to her.

He said, "Even when they do very tricky things, that doesn't mean the rules are changed. We have to follow the rules, just as if everything were happening to someone else, to some people they want to keep, instead of to us. You did it their way, and you know there isn't really any other way down from here. This is all we have left."

"So if I knew all along?" she asked, prompting him.

"If you knew how it was going to be, then you had to know you were a part of it, too."

Not turning, still standing at the gray of the window, she said sadly, softly, "See? You keep understanding more and more of it. Sleep for a little while, darling. Then you'll know the rest of it."

AT a few minutes past six, Dr. Samuel Barringer opened the door of Room 11 in the intensive-care section. In the shadows of the room, he saw the young nurse standing in silhouette by the gray of the window, looking out, standing there with a look of wistful grace.

At the sound of the latch as he closed the door, she spun with a guilty start, greeted him in her gentle and formal morning voice and handed him the clip-board with the patient's chart and the notation she had made since his visit four hours earlier. He held it under the low light for a moment, handed it back to her, then reached through the orifice in the transparent side of the oxygen tent to gently place the pads of his first two fingers against the arterial throb in the slack throat. He stood in a half bow, his eyes closed, listening and measuring through his finger tips. He was a big blond bear of a man, simultaneously clumsy and deft, as bears can be.

The nurse stood, awaiting instructions. He told her he would be back in a few minutes, and he walked to the far end of the corridor, to the waiting-room beyond the nurses' station. Sylvia sat alone there, at the end of the couch by the lamp table, staring out the big window. The hospital tower was higher than the buildings to the west of it, and she could see the wide, slow river in the morning haze. Daylight muted the yellow glow of the lamp beside her.

She turned and saw him and suddenly her dark eyes looked enormous and her face was more pale. "Sam? Is—"

"They didn't call me back. I just came in and checked him, and I have a couple of others to check, and it's standard procedure, Sylvie. No perceptible change."

He walked past her to the big window and shoved his fists into his hip pockets and looked out at the new day.

After a little while, she said, "He's been trying to take it easier since that little coronary. He really has. But you know how Dave is. He said he was going to weed his practice down to about eight very rich and nervous old ladies with minor ailments. Sam?"

He turned and looked at her, at the lean, mature vitality of her face. "What, honey?"

"What's the prognosis, Sam?"

He shrugged his bear shoulders. "Too early to tell." He looked out the window and saw a freighter being nudged into the channel by the tugs. He wished he were on it and that everybody on board was sworn never to tell Dr. Barringer where they were going or how long they'd be gone.

"Sam, please! That was a big one. Oh, God, I know that was a big one! Remember me, Sam? Eighteen years we three have known one another. I'm a nurse . . . was a nurse. Remember? You don't have to pat me on the head, Sam."

It was easy to remember the Sylvie Dorn of 18 years ago, that chunky, flirtatious, lively girl, now a whip-slender matron, dark hair with the first touches of gray. Thirty-eight? Mother of Ricky, Susan, Timmy—god-mother to his own pair of demons. And Dave is—was—is forty-two.

"Sam?" she said again.

He turned from the window and went lumbering to the couch, thinking of all the times you make this decision and then decide how to wrap words around it to match the person you tell. But this one was close to the past and all the years, close to the heart.

He sat beside her and took her hands, and swallowed a rising thickness in his throat, blinked, swallowed again and said in a pebbly voice, "I'm sorry, Sylvie. Dave hasn't got enough heart muscle left to run a toy train. And there's not one damned thing we can do about it or for it."

She pulled her hands free and lunged against him, and he held her in his big arms and patted her as she strained at the first great hard spasmodic sob and got past it and in about two or three minutes pulled herself back to a control and a forlorn stability he knew she would be able to maintain.

She dabbed her eyes and blew her nose and said, "Today sometime?"

"Probably."

"Tell them you've given permission for me to stay in there with him, will you?"

"Of course. I'll be in every once in a while."

"And thank your dear gal for taking over our tribe, Sam. Sam? Do you think he'll know I'm . . . I'm there with him?"

First, he thought, you throw the stone and then you throw the lump of sugar. No point in telling her that death had occurred, that Dave, as Dave, was long gone and that the contemporary miracles of medical science were keeping some waning meat alive, in the laboratory sense of the word.

"From everything we can learn and everything we can guess, Sylvie, I feel certain that he'll be aware of you being there, holding his hand."

WHEN the first gray light of the morning made the shape of the window visible, he dressed quickly and went out. He guessed that they would not be expecting him to leave that room so soon after arriving.

There were shadows of night still remaining in the empty streets, so that even though he knew his way and walked swiftly, the city seemed strange to him.

Afterword

These stories were written long before the most partisan fans of *Star Wars* and *Close Encounters of the Third Kind* were born.

I don't believe that makes a great deal of difference, especially when the stories are set so far in the future that one is not rudely overtaken by a panting, galloping technology.

The story titled "Flaw" illustrates the danger of staying too close to the year in which the story was written. I wrote it in 1948, and predicted that a nuclear drive would be perfected for manned space vehicles in 1960. I predicted a circumnavigation of the moon and return to earth in 1961, and a manned circumnavigation of Mars in 1964.

Though from the vantage point of 1978, thirty years after I wrote the story, it would seem that my crystal ball had been fogged, let me remind you that the prevailing opinion in 1948 was that any trip to the moon and return was outrageous fantasy. The more outrageous concept in "Flaw" is, of course, the inverted explanation of the expanding universe.

Other times the stories strike a false and strident note when we have since learned facts which make the settings impossible. "Dance of a New World" takes place within a plantation culture on Venus. Since 1948 when this one was published, we have learned enough to know that Venus will not support the life forms we know, at least not without a great deal of expensive plumbing and carpentry.

But in this one I find some small and interesting prognostications. Such as the boredom of the space pilot who gives up his profession because he has tired of the on-board computers that have guidance tapes fed into them, relieving the pilot of the responsibilities of control. And there is a drink dispenser in a hotel room that automatically adds the cost of the drink to the room charges in the accounting office on the ground floor. There are people called "synthetics" who have been born of the fertilization of a laboratory ovum, involved in a legal battle to determine their right to inherit. New nutrition laws are causing riots in the Asian block of nations. The basic premise of the story, that one must find the colonists for far planets from among the rebels on the home planet is hardly startling. Ask any Australian.

Stories like "Susceptibility" are the most fun to write, and perhaps to read. One is not constantly weighing the writer's "facts" against the known physical facts of our known earth. When one accepts his premise there are no jarring notes. The story is set too far away in time and place to respond to compulsive correction.

For the writer, fantasy and science fiction are a special brand of therapy. One can hide a substantial soap box behind the rocket ships and the alien flora. Some of the earliest and strongest of the antiracist, antisexist, anticorruption, antiforce messages gleam brightly in unexpected places, from Poe to Lovecraft, from Wells to Kafka. But once the soap box becomes visible, the story stumbles and dies. Tracts are not entertainment, and the stories must entertain. That's what they are for.

I am often asked if I will ever write any more science fiction. Consequently I have given the possible subject matter of any such stories I might write in the future considerable thought.

Certainly I will not write about heroic mankind emigrating to the far corners of our galaxy and beyond. We have found our own planetary system uninhabitable. The merciless mathematics of Einstein and Fitzgerald lock us into our own planetary system forever. We are not going out to the stars. It is not only cruel to hold out such a hope for mankind, but even in entertainment fiction, it is counterproductive to the races of man. Better we should think of ourselves as a virulent infection eroding this green planet even while we use it to sustain our teeming life form. When at last it dies—when at last we kill this planet—we die with it. We do not escape the consequences of our own barbarous acts by sailing off into the future. What we do here, we must live with. We must control our numbers and guard our environment or we shall all die, sooner than we might care to guess.

Would I write about invaders from the far reaches of space? One must be able to sustain one's own belief in order to write believable fiction. I know that physical, corporal beings from any conceivable beyond are trapped in the same time and motion trap as we. The limitation of velocity to sublight speed makes visitations and colonizations farcical. *No,* Virginia, there are no little green men, no saucers, nobody at all to save us from ourselves.

Through all of recorded history we find accounts of lights in the sky, of mysterious happenings, inexplicable phenomena. I would prefer fiction that deals with the visitors from within. By our life form we can see and measure light waves within certain parameters. We can hear sounds within specific ranges. Our requirements for heat, oxygen, foodstuffs are equally defined within narrow limits. I would write of a planet we share with other life forms whose requirements are so unlike ours, our lives touch but rarely, briefly . . . and alarmingly. What if they become aware that we are—by our very numbers—in the process of destroying our mutual home world?

If I write any more science fiction it will be a fiction turned inward, exploring the fantasy, magic and terror of our own journeys into the micro and macro worlds around us.

We are but a half-step into the world of micro-electronics, the fantastic chip that is going to change the patterns of existence to a greater degree than any other discovery since the onset of the industrial age. We are creating and altering life forms in the laboratory. The ethical considerations here, and the weight of superstition, would make very solid stories indeed.

The physicists who are dealing with the smallest particles of matter have managed to actually change the time frame in which a bit of matter—or electrical energy—exists. Though it is on the smallest conceivable scale, it *is* a form of time travel.

I believe that the idea that excites me most is an extrapolation from the familiar miracles of the transmission of sound and image. All matter, we know, is composed of the small electrical energies of the molecular structure. The dullest pebble is a complexity in constant motion, a matrix of forces. We "read" a symphony, translate it into electrical impulses, transmit it, and reassemble it at thirty million simultaneous receiving stations, with booster stations along the way to enhance the image. We scan pictures, send them the same way.

A solid object can be broken down into its electrical components. It can be read, the way the complex carbon-hydrogen molecules of living tissue are being read. With the help of the chip, and its ability to handle complex data with astonishing speed, it should one day become possible to create matter from energy, to direct the energy into a predetermined pattern.

Then, assuming a perfecting of nuclear fusion, could man, by translating the patterns involved, recreate his green planet? Could he people a woodland with maidens and unicorns? Could he translate atomic wastes back into puppies and hummingbirds?

Who will control the men who do the translating?

Or will they become the new kings?

Those are the directions I would take—should I be tempted back into this fiction I still feel such pleasure in reading.

Bibliography

"All Our Yesterdays," "John Wade Farrell" — *Super Science Stories*, April 1949

"Amphiskios," JDM — *Thrilling Wonder Stories*, August 1949

"The Annex," JDM — *Playboy*, May 1968

Best SF, 1968, Ed. Harry Harrison Putnam, 1969 hc; Berkeley, 1969 pb

Playboy's Stories of the Sinister and Strange; Playboy Press, 1969

Seven; Fawcett Gold Medal, 1971

The Late Great Future; Ed. Gregory Fitzgerald & John Dillon; Fawcett, 1976

"Appointment for Tomorrow," JDM — *Super Science Stories*, November 1949; Greenberg, 1952 hc

Ballroom of the Skies (Novel), JDM — *Two Complete Science-Adventure Books;* Winter, 1953; Fawcett, 1968 pb

"The Big Contest," JDM — *Worlds Beyond*, December 1950

Human, Ed. Judith Merril; Postal Publications (Lion), 1954

Worlds to Come; Ed. Damon Knight; Harper & Row, 1967 hc; Fawcett Gold Medal, 1968 pb

"But Not To Dream," JDM — *Weird Tales*, May 1949

"By The Stars Forgot," JDM — *Super Science Stories*, May 1950

"A Child Is Crying," JDM — *Thrilling Wonder Stories*, December 1948

The Science Fiction Galaxy; Ed. Groff Conklin; Garden City (Permabooks), 1950

The Shape of Things; Ed. Da-

"The Great Stone Death," JDM — *Weird Tales*, January 1949

"Half-Past Eternity," JDM — *Super Science Stories*, July 1950

The Human Equation; Ed. William F. Nolan; Sherbourne Press, 1971

"Hand from the Void," JDM — *Super Science Stories*, January 1951

"The Hunted," JDM — *Super Science Stories*, July 1949

Beyond the End of Time; Ed. Frederik Pohl; Doubleday (Permabooks), 1952

"Immortality," JDM — *Startling Stories*, May 1949

"Incubation," JDM — *Future Tense;* Ed. Kendell Foster Crossen; Greenberg, 1952

"Journey for Seven," JDM — *Thrilling Wonder Stories*, April 1950

"Labor Supply," JDM — *Magazine of Fantasy & Science Fiction*, May 1953

"The Legend of Joe Lee," JDM — *Cosmopolitan*, October 1964

The Year's Best S-F: 10th Annual Edition; Ed. Judith Merril; Delacorte Press, 1965

"Like a Keepsake," JDM — *Thrilling Wonder Stories*, June 1949

"Mechanical Answer," JDM — *Astounding Science Fiction*, May 1948

The Robot and The Man; Gnome Press, 1953

"The Miniature," "Peter Reed" JDM — *Super Science Stories*, September 1949

The Big Book of Science Fiction; Ed. Groff Conklin; Crown, 1950

"Minion of Chaos," JDM — *Super Science Stories*, September 1949

"Ring Around the Redhead," JDM — *Startling Stories*, November 1948

Science Fiction Adventures in Dimensions; Ed. Groff Conklin; Vanguard Press, Inc., 1953

"The White Fruit of Banaldar," JDM — *Startling Stories*, September 1951

Wine of the Dreamers (Novel), JDM — Greenberg, 1951 hc

Pocket Books, 1953 pb (as *Planet of the Dreamers*); Fawcett Gold Medal, 1968

The Universe of Science Fiction

☐	CLONED LIVES—Sargent	14067-9	1.75
☐	THE EXILE WAITING—McIntyre	13781-3	1.50
☐	THE STOCHASTIC MAN—Silverberg	13570-5	1.50
☐	THE CITY: 2000 A.D. Urban Life Through Science Fiction— Clem, Greenburg & Olander	22892-4	1.95
☐	THE DAY OF THE TRIFFIDS—Wyndham	Q2720	1.50
☐	EARTH ABIDES—G. Stewart	23252-2	1.95
☐	THE JARGOON PARD—Norton	23615-3	1.75
☐	THE LATE GREAT FUTURE— Fitzgerald & Dillon	23040-6	1.75
☐	THE TIME MACHINE AND THE WAR OF THE WORLDS—Wells	30837-5	1.95

Buy them at your local bookstores or use this handy coupon for ordering: